FRACTURED FLAME

FIREBIRD UNCAGED BOOK 1

ERIN EMBLY

First edition January 2020

ISBN 978-1-7344570-0-1

Cover design by Ravenborn Covers

Published by Poppythorne Publications

www.erinembly.com

For Mom & Dad,
still my biggest cheerleaders
even though I'm a grown-ass lady

Special thanks to my amazing beta readers:
Nikki Dekeuster
Wendi Adams
Sam Rooney
Emma Butler
Patti Connelly
Karen Mead
Kellie Babineaux
Laurie Harris
Melissa Mayo
Cindy Glickman

CONTENTS

Chapter 1	1
Chapter 2	10
Chapter 3	26
Chapter 4	32
Chapter 5	38
Chapter 6	47
Chapter 7	54
Chapter 8	64
Chapter 9	79
Chapter 10	92
Chapter 11	105
Chapter 12	119
Chapter 13	134
Chapter 14	148
Chapter 15	160
Chapter 16	172
Chapter 17	185
Chapter 18	200
Chapter 19	208
Chapter 20	220
Chapter 21	240
Chapter 22	251
Afterword	261
Assassin Divined	265
Preview	267

I KNEW the murderer had found me as soon as I stepped out of my apartment into the cold. I could smell her.

The world was empty, roads covered in fresh snow and tree branches encased in ice that glittered under the afternoon sun. This morning's storm was over, but not many people in my nocturnal neighborhood would be out before dusk on a day like today. And certainly not many people who smelled like roses and herbs—the same combination of scents that had been burned into my mind as a mark of death to come.

Fucking finally, I thought as I worked hard to keep from running, my muscles twitching while I walked across the slick, uneven brick sidewalk on my way to work. I had been waiting for this moment for months. I'd given up my whole life—my reputation—in the hopes that this woman cared enough about hers to come after me. And until now, I'd been starting to worry that she never would.

Now she was as good as dead. Well, maybe not *now*, but she'd be dead as soon as I could get her a safe distance from my apartment. One of my roommates had her six-year-old son staying over today, and I didn't want to traumatize the kid by giving him a dead body to gawk at, even if it did belong to a monster. So I pulled my scarf tight around my face, wrapped both hands around my travel mug filled with steaming coffee, and took dainty steps past the deceptively cutesy old row houses lining every street in this area.

What used to be a charming neighborhood for rich old ladies to go antique shopping near the nation's capital was now something more like a red-light district, and the only rich old ladies who still lived here were also probably immortal and deadly. I'd been a small child living across the country when this place had last been fit for decent company, but I was pretty sure I liked it better this way. Antiques were boring as hell, and I was grateful to have somewhere to live now that I'd been outcast from decent society.

Once I was a couple blocks away from my apartment, I took a deep breath to make sure the murderer was following me. The sickeningly floral scent of her "evil-warding" potpourri coated my lungs, and it took every ounce of my willpower to emit a relaxed sigh instead of a gag.

I doubted that concoction of dead plants would really ward off a demon or a vampire—or even a were-kitten, for that matter—but it was still serious overkill for her to try to use it against me.

Maybe she wanted me to recognize it, so I would know it was her. That or she didn't know what I was. *I guess I should be flattered.* But if I were her, I would have done better research.

If I were her, I would have attacked me already. So what was she waiting for?

Then I realized—she was waiting for me to get to my desti-nation. Work. Or at least, the place I'd called work since I'd tanked my Guardian career last year by failing to take this bitch down.

I'd gone from pantsuits and pistols on Capitol Hill to push-up bras and shot glasses in a seedy strip club, and this psycho wanted everyone to know it. She wanted everyone to see just how badly I'd failed, and where it had gotten me. She wanted to take a fucking picture so everyone would remember the image of my eviscerated corpse on stage, naked, in heels, probably with some fairy glitter for good measure.

Well, the joke would be on her, either way. I actually liked my new job, fairy glitter and all, and she wasn't going to take this one away from me, too.

A squeak and a crash from behind me jerked me out of my thoughts, and I turned on my heel instantly to see . . . nothing.

The sidewalk was barren, the snow behind me pristine except for my footprints, and I could hear nothing except the wind and the occasional clump of melting snow falling from the rooftops.

But just as I was about to turn back around, I heard it again—a faint whine this time, followed by a softer crash, and then grunting—and it was coming from the alleyway I had just passed.

Setting my coffee down gently on a windowsill, I pressed myself to the side of the building next to me and inched my way back toward the alley. When I peered around the corner, my heart sank.

I would like to think it sank because I saw a little girl whose life was in danger, but truthfully, what hit me harder was the disappointment of seeing that the woman attacking her was not the same woman who had turned my life upside down. Sent by the same people, probably, because she was definitely the source of that smell. But the woman in my nightmares was blond, and pale, and tall, and thin—and this one was short and muscular, with graying dark hair.

The little girl let out another tiny squeak, and I bit down hard on my instinct to run in and save her. The woman was holding her against the wall of the alley, restraining her, it seemed, not trying to kill her—at least not yet. And I wanted to know why.

If I was her target, what could a little girl possibly have done to distract her from me?

Then I saw what was causing the crashing noises. While holding the girl's neck with one hand, the woman lifted her other hand and conjured a chunk of malleable, magical ice, which took shape around the girl's arm and pinned it to the wall with a crash. The woman whispered something I couldn't hear to the girl, who was looking more and more frantic every moment. An interrogation?

It wouldn't help me to watch this nonsense if I couldn't hear what they were saying, so I peeled off my fluffy gloves and slipped my fingers beneath the sleeves of my jacket, where I always kept two knives handy. Even as a bartender, you never knew when you would need to cut open a lemon or threaten a handsy customer on the fly.

My first knife struck the woman in her forearm—dangerously close to the little girl's neck. Damn, I was seriously out of practice. I'd been aiming for the nice, big target of her back.

Okay, no more throwing knives for you today, rusty bitch, I told myself as the woman hissed and my bloody blade clattered to the ground beneath her.

She turned her head towards me as she let loose an enormous mass of ice to fully trap the little girl, leaving only the girl's head free. And when I stepped into the alley for a close-combat fight, the girl looked right at me and screamed my name.

"Darcy! Run away—she'll kill you!"

What. The. Absolute . . . I'd never seen this girl in my life, so how did she know my name? And why did she care about my safety? The shock of it almost cost me my life as I stood there staring at her, taking in her dark hair, tanned skin, and bright green eyes—all completely unfamiliar to me—as steam began to rise from underneath her icy prison, like she was melting it with magic. Because in that moment, another chunk of ice came blasting at me.

I only just managed to dodge it, and not entirely. My right arm went numb around the elbow as I dodged out of the way, but I could live with that. At least I hadn't slipped on the icy pavement and fallen on my ass.

I thanked myself for all the hours I'd spent in the past few weeks magicking my boots to be extra-super-extra nonslip. It was the kind of thing I would never have wasted time on in my past life, and I was glad that at least in some ways, my recent idleness had proven useful.

Not useful enough, though. Now all I had were magical boots, one knife, and terrible aim. I was too weak with magic during the brightness of the day to even think about using it offensively, and while I could dodge her ice attacks for a while, I would get tired and make a mistake long before she would at this rate.

So I picked up the first thing I saw that looked like it could help me—the lid of an old-school metal trash can—and held it up in front of me just in time to block her next attack.

While ice piled up against it, I braced myself and hoped my strength hadn't devolved as badly as my aim in the past year. I ran forward before she finished her attack, slamming my trash-shield into her as hard as I could.

Judging by her screams as she fell and her awkward squirming as she tried and failed to get up, I'd reflected some of her ice attack back at her and pinned her to the ground with it.

When she realized what had happened, she looked up and actually snarled at me. Papery thin, mottled skin scrunched up to reveal yellowed teeth, and the sound coming from between her lips was like a possum if I'd taken away its favorite rotten apple.

Okay, wow. I expected this kind of hatred from the assassin I had a history with, but it was a little irksome to feel such spite from someone I'd never met before. Almost as irksome as the other stranger here knowing me by name.

Since Possum seemed good and truly trapped—apparently she could create ice but not destroy it—I turned to the girl she had left in a similar state.

And found her halfway free. Her preppy school uniform was drenched in melted ice, and I had the fleeting urge to wrap her in a blanket before I noticed her skin steaming. Her left arm and leg were still partially trapped in the ice and, as it melted, the skin underneath appeared almost plated in some kind of hard, shiny, black material. This was disappearing quickly to reveal regular skin, albeit maybe a bit glowy.

She looked at me and began fidgeting, impatient. Not happy to see me.

"Hi," I said.

Her eyes shifted away from me, towards her still-trapped limbs, then at the street, then back to me. Panicked. Confused.

"I know I'm super pretty and all, but you're a little young to be a stalker, hmm?"

"I-I just wanted to help, okay?" the girl finally said, her eyes cast down now.

"Okay. Lucky me, I never knew I had a fairy goddaughter."

"I'm not a fairy." Fierce, now. Angry. Little bit of red in her eyes. "And I'm not supposed to talk to you."

"Okay, demon goddaughter; who told you not to talk to me?"

Her face scrunched up, probably realizing she'd screwed up by saying as much as she had, and she looked away from me with a humph. She was almost free now, and I had half a mind to restrain her again and interrogate her myself. I'd save cute kids all day if I could, but not kids who were stalking me for gods knew what.

My decision was made for me when a small chunk of ice hit my shoulder hard, bounced off my jacket, and fell to my feet. A glance back at Possum told me she had spat it at me. And judging by the size and pointiness of it, she'd probably been aiming for my neck. For a kill. Luckily, I wasn't the only one with bad aim.

I had been intending to try to get some information out of her, but now . . . well, at least now I had something to do with my knife. Without hesitating, I stepped over to her and used my left hand to plunge my blade into her mouth, not stopping until it struck the icy pavement underneath her head. She was gone in an instant, blood seeping out into the slush around her like a halo of strawberry sno-cone.

I turned to see the little girl's reaction, but she was already running toward the street, her shiny little loafers melting patches of ice away from the ground as she went.

Okay, demon goddaughter, you win this time, I thought. I was willing to bet I'd see her again, and I hoped I wouldn't have to kill her when I did.

I bent back down to Possum's body, yanked out my knife, and wiped it in the snow that had piled up against the side of the dumpster nearby. Then, all of a sudden, I felt a bit lost.

This was my first unsanctioned kill. Not that I was worried I'd be prosecuted—it was self-defense, after all. I just didn't know what to do with the body. I was a civilian now; there was no backup coming, and no rule-book to follow.

Well, I supposed the civilian rule-book only had one rule, and that was "Call the cops."

Ugh. That was the last thing I needed in my life right now. Cops. Questions. Cameras. Not again. Not when I'd finally managed to escape public scrutiny.

So I'd just dispose of the body myself. It wasn't like whoever had sent an assassin after me would be pressing for an investigation to find out who had killed her. They would want this covered up even more than I did.

I swung my right arm into the brick wall to crack the chunk of ice off my elbow, then thanked the universe that I'd already killed the woman so she couldn't witness the yelp I let out when I did so. After rubbing my elbow for a moment through my jacket, I picked up the trash-can lid I'd used as a shield and rammed it into the ice blanket covering the woman's body.

It broke open like an eggshell, and I pulled away the broken chunks to reveal my prize, an ugly, murderous . . . mage? Probably a mage, by the way she'd been throwing that ice. Mages were pretty rare, though, and the assessment didn't line up at all when I saw what she was wearing underneath her coat.

A small pin on her sweater, in the shape of a straw broom. Like a mythical witch's broom, very ironically. I'd seen that logo before, and the political group associated with it were the last people in the world who would knowingly hire a mage assassin, or any being with magical capabilities. They called themselves the Sweepers, in the sense of sweeping out the trash. They basically wanted to outlaw all non-humans and turn the world back to the way they thought it had been twenty years ago, when all the magic had gone down behind closed doors.

If you had asked me a year ago, I would have said these people were total nutjobs. Now, after having experienced for myself just how dangerous vampires could be—even the ones who meant well—I thought they might be right in some cases. But any goodwill I might have felt for them went out the window considering what had just happened.

Not only had these people just tried to have me killed, they must be the ones who had sent the assassin a year ago to ruin my career. I couldn't remember much from that night, but I remembered the killer's face and the floral stink of her ward.

Roses and herbs, the perfect concoction to confuse a vampire just long enough to . . . *Enough*, I told myself. No point in dwelling on the past.

Regardless, the Sweepers wouldn't have wanted to do anything to risk drawing negative attention to themselves now —like using magic to go after me, a washed-up Guardian who was useful alive as a perfectly good scapegoat for one of their crimes. If I was right about what this group had done, they had major skeletons to hide. And if their connection to me ever got out, they would be done for.

So sending this woman now was a huge risk for them. And as I tossed her body into the dumpster and produced a small flame with my fingertip to set fire to the trash around her, I wondered what I had done to make killing me worth the risk.

Oh well, I thought, bending over to recover my knives. Once I'd secured them back under my sleeves, I straightened my scarf, picked up the coffee I'd left on the windowsill, and resumed my walk to the club. *I suppose I'll find out soon enough.*

2

THE CLUB WAS dark when I arrived, the first one as usual. I didn't have so much work to do that I needed to get here this early, but I liked the quiet. Living with roommates wasn't easy, especially when one of them had a kid, and I couldn't afford my own place anymore. Not without my Guardian salary.

At least I would always have my training, even without the salary. I turned on the white lights with a grimace and quickly moved through all the rooms one by one, clearing the space and securing the entrances. A good rule of thumb I'd learned was that if someone wanted you dead enough to send an assassin, they probably wanted you dead enough to send two.

But no shadows jumped out at me as I walked through the club—no murderers waiting in ambush. A small reprieve. I'd be on my guard again once the club opened, but for now I could relax.

I turned off the lights again and let out my breath. This darkness was another benefit of getting here early. No windows, and no one to bully me into keeping on the white lights. I let the shadows wash over me for a moment before turning on the stage lights, dim and colorful as they reflected off the chrome poles, just enough for me to see by and to spark up the magic inside me.

My individual relationship with magic was strongly tied to light and dark. Other people had other ways of sensing it, but I had been taught by a coven of mages who used the moon as their focus. A coven of mages dedicated to healing—light in the midst of darkness. That was the energy I had been taught to see and feel and manipulate, and it was why I had a tattoo of the moon on my ankle. Elusive, perception-distorting, hope-igniting . . . like fireflies in a child's backyard.

So while I wasn't strictly nocturnal—not like a vampire, who might actually burn up on a sunny day—I tended to feel more energized in the darker hours and spaces of the world. The blacker the night, the more magic would come from just a glimmer of light. The more power would be available at my fingertips. To feel that little tingle all around me in the dark, the hum of potential in every breath I drew—it was better than ten cups of coffee.

A bitch still needs her coffee, though, I thought as I walked over to the espresso machine. Yet another perk of the job.

The phone rang before I could get the machine going, and I cursed Baz under my breath. The owner of the club was literally ancient, a djinn with an irrational hatred of mobile phones. Even though that technology had been around long before I'd been born, it still felt new and scary to someone so old—and genies were known to get trapped in small objects, right?

Baz wasn't too keen on the antique landline, either, but someone had convinced him he couldn't run a business without it.

It all worked out for the dancers, because making customers check their phones at the door meant they couldn't slyly take free pictures. I just wished I didn't have to walk across the floor every time the damn thing rang.

I pressed the phone to my ear and stuck my finger through the curly cord that was probably older than my grandparents. "Hello. You've reached Bawdy Baz's Bits and Bats." Like every time I said it, I tried not to cringe. Baz cared deeply about his corny names, and messing them up was about the only thing he'd ever gotten mad at me for. "How can I help you?"

"Darcy? Is that you?" My roommate's voice came through sounding hoarse and frantic, unusual for her normally cheerful self.

"Nope, definitely not me," I said automatically. "What's wrong with your voice? You sound like you've been smoking, or screaming . . . Please tell me Noah didn't set our place on fire." Becca's son was a sweet kid, but he was still a kid, and all kids were disasters waiting to happen in my experience.

"No . . ." Becca coughed. "I'm just running . . . He needed me to help him with something, so I had to go into the city." She coughed again, and I frowned.

The combination of her frantic tone and slow, careful words made me think she was hiding something.

Becca was fae, so she couldn't lie. Not straight out, at least. She could tell half-truths and manipulate implications and connotations all day long, and she was damn good at it. But living with her for the past year had made it easy for me to recognize her tells, even over the phone.

"You went into DC to—"

"Yes," she cut me off, the sneaky thing, answering only the first part of a question I was now sure she didn't want to face. "Look, I'm just calling because I'm going to be late."

She sounded annoyed with me now, and it took me off guard. Becca normally had much more patience with me than most people, which was one of the many reasons I liked living with her.

"Okay, sorry . . ." I started.

She let out another cough before asking, "Can you get someone to cover my first set?"

"Sure. But it sounds like you should maybe just take the night off, Bex. Are your lungs even still inside your body? If you cough them up, I'll have to hunt them down, and it'd be way easier to just share my tips with you tonight."

She was quiet for a second, and I wished I could see her to gauge whether I'd pissed her off further or made her smile. Eventually, she said, "I'm fine, Dumbo. Just cover for me. I can't afford to lose this job. Not now."

Her voice seemed a little more relaxed, and it made me feel better to hear. Even so, she hung up the phone before I could tell her that no one would fire her tonight for anything—Baz had told me yesterday he'd be taking today off.

Luckily, Baz's absence meant I still had my phone on me when normally I would have dropped it in my locker first thing. I pulled it out and sent a quick text to Etty, our other room-mate, asking her to wrangle Becca into bed and give her some tea if she showed up at home.

Etty sent back an incomprehensible string of emojis, as usual, and I figured I'd done the best I could.

My instincts were telling me to go find Becca and take care of her myself, at least to get her settled. I still had enough time before my shift, too. But with more assassins possibly out to get me, the best thing I could do for anyone I cared about today was to stay the fuck away.

I went back over to the espresso machine and made myself a double shot. The drink sent a good amount of warm, fuzzy excitement through my bones as I started prepping the bar.

If I could catch another killer coming for me tonight, maybe I could keep them alive long enough to get some answers out of them. Otherwise, I might be tempted to march right into the Sweepers' HQ tomorrow and demand to know why they wanted me dead—and that wouldn't end well for anyone.

A COUPLE HOURS into my shift, no assassin had appeared, and I found myself wishing the night would get crazy enough that I could practice my knife-throwing without scaring the customers away.

"So, you like assholes?"

The words came out of my mouth almost compulsively as I polished my twentieth shot glass for the twentieth time, my mind grasping out for anything to distract me from obsessing over the woman I'd killed earlier.

The quiet guy sitting at my bar jerked a little at my question, like a teenager caught looking at porn. But when he turned his gaze to me from the bare ass gyrating in his direction on stage, I could tell he'd remembered where he was. A nearly empty strip club, in which the bartender had so little to do she could give him all the special attention in the world.

"Is that . . . an offer?" he asked. He looked even more terrified now.

Feeling like a child with a new toy on a rainy Sunday, I smiled brightly and held up my favorite bottle of rum. "Of course! It's called a Flaming Asshole, and it's my special tonight."

He let out a breath, though his face was still tense. Relieved, yet skeptical. I shrugged. I knew the drink was famous for tasting like—well, like ass. But I had tweaked the recipe and made it delicious, because that was pretty much the only talent I could still rely on to make me money these days. The only thing I was good at that I was still allowed to do.

"I promise it'll be tasty. Probably not as tasty as hers, but . . ."

That made him smile, and I savored his amusement far more than was probably healthy. He even gave me a nervous laugh. Not that this was an impressive feat, since I could always get the men in the club to laugh. Well, the human men, at least. The craziest, dirtiest, nuttiest shit could come out of my mouth and they would either think it was hilarious or just ignore me.

Not for the first time, I wondered why I hadn't figured this out sooner. My life had been hell when the odd dick joke had either brought on judgmental glares or sexual harassment. But then, my life had also been purposeful and meaningful and delightfully dangerous, and—*Stop*, I thought, jolting myself out of that useless spiral.

"I'm Darcy, by the way," I said, plastering the smile back on my face. "And you should be drinking *something*, or the ladies in here might think you're a cop."

No human would want to be suspected of coppery in a place like this. Not that anything illegal went down in here, as far as I knew. It was a strip club, not a brothel. But it was an inter-species strip club, which made it a target for haters of every nasty variety. And after all the unjust arrests and violence human cops had caused in places like this over the last twenty years, their particular brand of trigger-happy paranoia was unofficially very unwelcome.

"Alright. Give me your best shot," Mr. Asshole said after a moment of hesitation.

"It *is* a shot!" I replied with genuine excitement, surprised by the pun.

My face fell when I turned to grab a glass and spotted Becca's golden, glittery head of hair resting on the bar a few seats down. The shining strands magically stretched out over the wet surface, slowly shifting and floating towards me, drawn to my movement. I sighed, disappointed to see Etty hadn't managed to keep her from showing up.

"Becca," I called to the head buried under the ethereal mane.

She was normally so playful and energetic at work that it was disorienting to see her like this. It was a slow night, though, and some customers did love dramatics. Even after how awful she'd sounded on the phone, I expected her to pop up any moment with an exasperated sigh, whining in a baby voice about how no one wanted to play with her. But she only groaned softly.

"Bex—girl, are you okay?"

Her hands slid up to the surface of the bar, fingertips turning red as she struggled to push herself up. When her head finally lifted, I noticed a sheen of sweat on her face and neck. Her makeup was running, her teeth chattering.

Damn, she looked even worse than she'd sounded over the phone. What could she possibly be hoping to achieve showing up like this? It wasn't like she was working for wages; if she couldn't sell dances, she'd get nothing—especially on a slow night like tonight. And if Baz were here, he'd be more likely to fire her for trying to dance in this state than for staying home.

I sighed as my reluctant caregiver instincts kicked in, leaving Mr. Asshole to fend for himself while I moved to whip up a tonic for Becca.

Elderflower liqueur, dry Prosecco, and a spoonful of habanero-infused honey. I stirred it gently, leaving out the ice, and finished it with a sprig of charred thyme. It never hurt to make these things taste nice. Though I had to admit, the ingredients were more for my own fun than anything else. All that really mattered was the next step.

Gently, the backs of my fingers rested against the sides of the cool glass. My palms opened outward, casting invisible nets into the dark atmosphere and absorbing some of the tiny glimmers of magic that existed all around me. They crawled through my skin, through my blood, through my bone as I thought *feel-better* thoughts, and then into the tonic they sank.

The club's door opened just as I was finishing up, and the unexpected flash of bright neon lights outside made my heart jump. With my fingers still on the glass, I looked up to see a man walk in I hadn't seen here before. And I kept looking at him when he conspicuously kept his oversized coat on, coolly brushing past Mitch the bouncer when he offered to take it. *How many weapons could he be hiding under there?* I wondered, and my heart raced faster.

His eyes met mine for a moment as he made his way over to the stage, and I felt heat pulse through my veins. I bit my lip hard and looked down at Becca's tonic, taking my hands away from the glass as I mentally kicked myself. Yeah, the guy was sexy as hell—skin the color of summer, wide-set cheekbones, dark eyes, and hair that was just the right level of messy. But I saw attractive men all the time, so that probably wasn't why my dumb body suddenly wanted to throw down with him. Could it be because my paranoia had me thinking he was an assassin sent to kill me, and of course I was fucked up enough that *this* turned me on? I ran a hand over my face and groaned. This was a new low for me.

With a long breath in and out, I turned back to my roommate and slid the drink in front of her. Then I gave her head a little poke, and she slowly lifted it. "Here you go, Bex. Drink this, and then go home. Seriously. You need to rest, and if you keep dancing tonight you'll scare away your regulars."

As her lips wrapped around the straw, she stared at me with dull eyes and gave me a little salute.

"Aye aye, Captain?" a man called from the other side of the bar.

My head snapped back around to see Mr. Asshole looking at me with a cute, lopsided smile.

I must have seemed confused, because his head bobbed toward Becca and he continued, "Do you run this ship?"

"Only sometimes. The real man in charge is Baz. *Bawdy* Baz," I amended, hating myself for saying it. My corny boss would love this awkward guy with the pirate jokes at my bar. "But he's off for the night. Are you here to see him? Is that why you're sitting here, staring at my bottles of booze instead of the ladies?"

"I'm here with a friend." His eyes shifted over to the plush curtain hiding the private dance area, and I could tell by his tense jaw and clipped words how uncomfortable he felt. "This . . . isn't really my scene."

Ugh. The reluctant voyeurs were always the worst. Especially the humans. I could never tell whether it was the nakedness or the otherness of the women in the club that set them on edge. Either way, the implications were not nice.

"I'll try not to take offense at that if you try to have a little fun," I shot back at him. "For your friend's sake. Now turn around and watch the show while I make your drink."

As I gestured to the stage, I took the opportunity to make eye contact with Etty, who also danced here, across the floor. Maybe the emojis she'd sent me earlier had meant something along the lines of: "No Darcy, I will not keep Becca home no matter how sick she is."

I was a little bitter, yeah, but it wouldn't be the first time Etty had done something for no reason other than to piss me off.

She whispered something in the ear of my possible assassin, whose lap she'd been sitting in, and then promptly glided up to the bar.

Her velvety, dark-brown skin looked almost completely black in the dimmed light of the club, yet somehow it still glittered. And in her next-to-nothing thong and seven-inch heels, she seemed to embody an actual goddess as she walked toward me. Luckily, she had been roommates with me and Becca for long enough that I'd already done battle with the small feeling of envy that popped into my throat every time I looked at her. And I at least liked to think I'd won.

She veered toward Mr. Asshole, swaying her hips and reaching out to run her fingers through his sandy hair—probably thinking I wanted her to take him off my hands.

His eyes widened in panic, and he froze.

"Ey, hands off!" I snapped at Etty playfully. "This one's mine." Then I began pouring his drink, casting my eyes down as I said, "But I think Becca could use some lovin'."

Etty raised her eyebrows at me. "What? She seemed fine when she—"

Becca groaned and lifted her hot mess of a head up again, and Etty swore. She moved over to our shimmering, pale, sweaty blond roommate at the other end of the bar, immediately beginning to fuss over her, pushing her hair away from her face and rubbing her back. Judging by the jerkiness of Becca's movements as she reacted, my tonic was already starting to help.

Okay, so either Etty hadn't been paying attention earlier, or Becca had done a good job of hiding how sick she was. This whole thing was fucking weird, and the Guardian-trained part of me wanted to clear the club of everyone right now so we could get to the bottom of it.

But that would be ridiculous. I was no longer in a work environment where a colleague acting strange was cause for that much concern. Normal people acted nuts sometimes— even ones I knew and liked.

Forcing a smile, I put the final touch on Mr. Asshole's drink —a layer of overproof rum topping small pours of orange liqueur, banana liqueur, and cinnamon vodka. Then I produced a flame from my fingertip and lit it on fire, instructing him to please blow it out before enjoying. I briefly toyed with the idea of infusing a bit of lust into the beverage, just to mess with him, but something stopped me.

The way he was acting towards the half-naked women around him would normally annoy me—because how dare he not feel comfortable around my beautiful friends? But this man's discomfort felt different. He hadn't been looking at anyone here with disdain, or pity. It seemed more like anxiety to me. Like he knew he was the problem, and not us.

And I know exactly how that feels.

He downed my concoction in one shot, and after subtly licking his lips, he said, "That tastes a lot more like bananas foster than asshole." With a shrug, he added, "The orange is a nice touch."

I was about to thank him when his friend reappeared and slid in next to him, a wide grin plastered on his face.

"You missed out, buddy! When that one shifts, she's got at least five more tits on her!" He whistled and downed the Old Fashioned he'd left perspiring on my bar during his dance.

To his credit, Mr. Asshole froze up again with his mouth slightly agape, then closed it with determination and nodded slowly. As his friend dragged him out of his seat, he slipped a twenty from his pocket and nodded at me in what looked like both thanks and apology.

They made off to sit at the stage, and I chuckled to myself. Our resident werewolf, Laura, had become an expert in partially shifting to accentuate all the bits men loved, and I thought it was absolutely genius.

I looked back over to Becca and Etty, where things seemed to have taken a turn for the worse. Becca was crying softly into Etty's chest as Etty stood to shield her from the rest of the club. And Etty looked . . . frightened. I had to pause for a moment just to recognize it, because I'd never seen her even a little bit scared before. A woman with enough confidence to dance naked in front of complete strangers—and admittedly, enough power to decimate those strangers should they try anything funny—Etty was a woman with nothing to fear. Or so I'd thought.

"She's burning up," Etty said, locking eyes with me.

"Poor thing. She really should go home to rest."

"You don't understand."

"Don't understand what?" I asked.

"She's not sick." I gave Etty an incredulous look, and she continued, "She can't be sick. She's fae. It's not possible."

"But—"

"I can't go home yet," Becca piped up, interrupting me. Her red eyes peeked out from over Etty's arm, and one look at the panic in them set off even bigger alarm bells in my head. Becca never panicked. She'd always been the emotional rock in the club, the one who passed out hugs and reassurances when everyone else was stressed or anxious or wrecked.

When I'd only been working here for a week, she'd been the only one brave enough to confront me when I got carried away taking out all my frustration and self-loathing on some lemons I'd been brutally murdering instead of juicing. Now I wished I could return the favor, but I wasn't any good at comforting people without using magic.

"Ray is here. And I need to dance for him tonight. I need to tell him—" Becca hiccuped then, a louder sound than any I'd ever heard come out of her mouth, and she immediately put her hand over her lips and spun to hide her face from the rest of the club. Then the sobbing started again.

I raised my eyebrows at Etty, who shook her head with a small grimace. She seemed just as dumbfounded as I was.

"Sorry," Etty said softly, leaning across the bar so I could hear her. Her eyes shifted over to the stage, where my probable assassin was sitting. "I tried to cheer her up, told her the guy who just walked in was tipping well, and when she saw him . . ." Etty's eyes widened and she pursed her lips. Baffled.

"So that's Ray?" I asked, gesturing over to the bundled-up sexy beast.

"Honestly, I don't remember what he said his name was. But yeah, that's who she was talking about."

I tried to tune out Becca's snorting and moaning while I narrowed my eyes at the back of Ray's head. Maybe he wasn't an assassin sent to kill me. Maybe he was just a jerk who was making my roommate cry. That possibility sent cold through my veins instead of heat. No excitement, just anger.

The song that had been playing faded out as the dancer on stage picked up her cash, and our announcer—who was also Mitch the bouncer on a slow night like tonight—got on the mic to welcome "Bitten Kitten" to the stage. That was Kat, our token vampire. "Be careful, gents. She does bite," Mitch added, and I made a mental note to slap the bad jokes out of him next time he came to ask me for a drink.

Kat came slinking onto the stage in fishnets and a leather corset, twirling her signature 3-inch-long blood-red nails as she rolled her hips to the heavy drums in the music.

Becca lifted her head again and started whimpering. "I'm supposed to go on after Kat."

Etty turned to me. "Go tell Mitch I'm taking her place."

"No!" Becca almost yelled, then clapped a hand over her mouth again and stared frantically out at the crowd—where, luckily, no one had noticed her outburst. She stiffly removed her hand and whispered, "I need to dance."

I narrowed my eyes at her. "If it's just money you need—"

"It's not. It's him. I need to tell him."

She wasn't making any sense. Etty jerked her head at me, urging me to go talk to Mitch.

As I walked away, I thought I heard Becca tell Etty, "I love him . . ."

Just when I'd thought I'd seen everything . . .

Becca had never struck me as that type. She'd always seemed so independent to me. One of the ones who had become a dancer not because she loved it—like Etty and Kat—but because it was the best thing she could rely on to save up enough money for lawyers to win custody of her son from his dickwad of a father.

I wasn't surprised she could fall in love with a client. What surprised me was her desperation. She didn't seem like a woman in love right now. She seemed like a woman who'd let a jerk get under her skin. So what if she couldn't dance for him one night? If he couldn't let her rest when she needed it, he didn't deserve anything close to her love.

For a brief moment, I considered stomping over to tell him just that. But then I remembered this impulse was exactly why I was the bartender, and not one of the women pretending to be attracted to strange men for a living. I'd never been any good at bullshit. *And when the honest bitch comes out to play, the money goes away.*

So I went over to Mitch instead, like a good girl. I wasn't doing it for jerkoff Ray, but for Becca, who deserved the chance to fight her own battle when she came to her senses, and for Etty, and for every other dancer trying to make a living in this club tonight who would suffer if I made a scene. It made me feel even more useless than I'd felt a few minutes ago, but at least I wasn't obsessing over assassins anymore.

I made it to Mitch just as the song was finishing and Kat was making one last twirl around the pole with her claws slashing at the air.

"Got a lineup change," I said, snapping my fingers at him. "Etty instead of Bex."

"But . . ." Mitch trailed off, looking like I'd just asked him to do brain surgery.

"What? I can do it—give me the mic."

"No, she's already up there." Mitch said. "See?"

What I saw was a very pissed-off Etty marching toward me, her normally golden eyes a solid black. "She fucking bit me!"

I opened my mouth to respond, but Etty kept ranting.

"Psycho bitch bit me right on the tit! Look!"

I couldn't not look, seeing as she was so much taller than me that her afflicted tit was basically right in my face. At least it didn't look like Becca had broken the skin.

"I see it. Why did she bite you? Did you try to lure her away from the stage with a cupcake illusion?"

"What? No—"

"Because that would have been good thinking. She loves cupcakes more than it's possible to love any man."

The sight of fuming Etty trying not to laugh was almost enough to do me in. But then, as she was relieved of a little of her anger, I saw the fear creep back into her eyes.

She put her arm around me and pulled me a few feet away from Mitch, lowering her voice. "Something's really wrong with her, Darce. She downed her drink, said she felt better and then rushed onto the stage. I couldn't hold her. First she seems sick, and then suddenly she's crazy strong?"

True, that did sound worrying. For a moment I wondered if I might have slipped when infusing Becca's tonic and made it a lot stronger than I'd intended . . . but I'd never slipped like that before. Especially not on something so simple. "Any ideas what it could be?" I asked. "I know you're not exactly the same species, but you at least knew enough to tell me it couldn't be the flu."

"There are stories of fae going mad. But only very old fae. And I've never heard anything about attempts to reverse the process." Etty shrugged, frowning. "My kind tends to value sanity less than humans do."

From what I'd experienced having two fae as a roommates for the past year, that checked out. *But I value my little mortal life, so I won't say it.*

Instead, I offered, "That wouldn't explain the fever, the shaking, or the low energy. And I thought Becca was less than a century old."

Etty bit her lip. "I can ask my queen. But Becca belongs to a different court—a different kind. This may be something only they would know about."

"Then we'll ask them," I stated.

Etty didn't get a chance to tell me how dumb an idea that was because she was suddenly busy gaping at Becca's antics onstage. The music had picked up a few seconds ago, and our girl had climbed all the way to the top of the damn pole—the twenty-foot-tall pole that no one without wings ever climbed all the way to the top of—and now she'd started spinning on it, faster and faster, her back arched and her limbs twisted in a beautiful pretzel. It looked gorgeous, but . . . this was not in line with Becca's skill level. In fact, I had never seen her climb the pole at all before. She could rack up bruises easily and never did anything that might leave a mark, so as not to worry her son. She usually danced standing, or sitting, or with her back on the ground. *This* . . . it was like she'd been possessed.

Then she started screaming. And her back began to glow, right between her shoulders. Bright orange, like molten rock.

"No," Etty breathed, so soft I could barely hear it.

I wanted to ask her what she meant, but I was finding it hard to tear my eyes away from Becca, who looked like an angel glowing and spinning in the air.

"Wings . . ." Etty stepped forward, her arms outstretched, almost mesmerized.

She stopped when Becca burst into flames.

3

TIME SEEMED TO STOP, and it felt like forever before I could focus on anything besides Becca's charred corpse, still glowing, fused to the pole about ten feet in the air. Her face was nothing more than a black lump with holes where her eyes had liquefied, but I could still see the agony in her expression. Becca hadn't deserved to suffer so gruesomely, and it killed me to think I had let this horror happen.

I should have seen this coming. For four years, it had been my job to see this sort of thing coming. And even though mixing drinks was the only thing I could get anyone to pay me for *now*, in my soul I would always be a Guardian. Now, for the second time in so many years, I'd failed. And somehow it hurt worse this time.

The pain I was stewing in soon turned physical, and I jolted back to my senses to see Etty's sharp fingernails digging into the skin of my shoulder. I looked up at her face, which echoed the trance-like state I'd just come out of—and then back to my shoulder, where her fingertips were quietly absorbing small bits of my blood.

My momentary confusion dissipated when I remembered

this was how some fae fed from their mothers as children. Etty in this moment was no different than a child sucking on a pacifier, or a cat kneading a blanket with stretched-out paws. It was probably harmless, and it made me feel a little better to know she'd come to me for comfort. At least I could make one person feel safe.

But something told me I might need my shoulder tonight, and as much of my strength as I could muster, so I gently unhooked her claws and braced my heart against the grief that filled her face when I did. I'd never seen her so overcome before, by any emotion, and I was sure it had something to do with the fact that Becca had been fae. Whether or not Etty knew what had happened tonight or why, it wouldn't be crazy for her to worry she might be next.

I'd have to talk to her about it later, once she'd calmed down. Now, I had more immediate issues to deal with. Cops were already swarming my little club—because it was mine tonight, with Baz away. I supposed I should call him. How had the cops gotten here so fast, anyway? They weren't exactly known for speedy response times these days, unless . . .

Unless called by one of their own, I thought when I saw Mr. Asshole on his feet, furiously scribbling in a notebook as his "friend" barked orders.

I should have guessed. I had seen the guilt all over him; I'd just thought it was the regular type of guilt puritanical humans felt when surrounded by sex and magic. Well, no more drinks for that asshole. The nickname I'd given him suddenly seemed fitting.

His eyes met mine.

Bats.

He walked over to the bar, where I was sitting next to Etty, and I found myself looking up at him. That wouldn't do, so I stood up, and then I suppressed a curse when I was still almost a foot shorter than him. The lights in the club were brighter now that there was no dancing or drinking going on, and it annoyed me that this guy might be the only person in history who looked better in the brightness than in the dim reddish-purple light Baz had specifically designed to be flattering. I could see the warm tones in his sandy hair and light skin now, and the definition in his arms.

He extended his hand. Seriously? He wanted to shake hands—now? Somehow, I thought we were beyond that. But I took his hand anyway, willing to indulge him. It was better to give a little on things that didn't matter so I could feel better when I was a bitch about things that did.

"I'm Detective Crane," he said, looking me in the eyes. "My partner and I will be handling the investigation regarding what happened here tonight. I'm going to need to know how to contact . . . Bawdy Baz? If he's the owner. And a list of everyone working tonight. Can you do that?"

The nerve. "You mean you don't already know? You were here." I narrowed my eyes at him and lowered my voice, muttering, "Probably taking notes."

His fingers tightened around his notebook, and all the anxiety I'd seen in him at the bar melted away as he said, "The only one I was taking notes on is you." His jaw hardening, he leaned in towards me and lowered his voice. "Imagine my surprise when I let myself be dragged to a place like this, only to find the bartender looks *a lot* like the assassin who was all over the news last year. Darcy Pierce—you're that Darcy, right?"

"*Alleged* assassin," I corrected him. Honestly, after what Senator Simeon Drake had done to me, I wished I'd been the one to kill him. But it never would have happened. Back then, I'd been more his thrall than his bodyguard, too distracted by his charm to even do my job.

He'd made my mind so foggy I could barely remember what had happened that night, aside from his corpse and the woman who'd made it. Served him right in the end. And I would never trust another vampire again—never protect another monster like him.

"So you don't deny it's you?" the detective pried.

"Why would I? I didn't do it, and no one can prove otherwise. I have every right to be here, tonight or any other night. You're the one who never should have set foot through those doors," I shot back.

"I was off duty."

"Even if that's true, we both know a person like you is never really off duty." Which I knew because I was a person like that, too. Even now, a year after ruining my Guardian career by failing to guard my charge—and somehow letting everyone think I'd assassinated him instead.

It was also why, now, I could barely hear Detective Asshole Crane trying to tell me I would need to come in for questioning. I was razor focused on the line of people forming to leave the club after showing ID to Crane's friend.

Becca's man—Ray—was right at the front of that line.

They wouldn't know to stop him, because they wouldn't know how creepily obsessed with him Becca had been acting right before she died. Only Etty and I knew that. Somewhere, deep down, I also knew the sensible thing to do was give this information to the detective right in front of me whose job it was to care about it. But my gut told me he wouldn't be able to react in time. If Ray slipped out that door right now, none of us would ever see him again.

So, I sprinted. Nearly knocking over Crane in the process.

And almost as soon as I'd made my move, Ray made his. The cop taking names screeched as Ray shoved him through the door, and I got a strong, fresh whiff of burning flesh when I followed them.

I had no time to evaluate the damage done to the cop, Mr. Five Extra Tits, who was still writhing on the icy pavement of the dark, narrow alley outside the club. Instead, I gave silent thanks that as the bartender, I could wear my ugly, flat, magically grippy boots to work every day. It meant I could chase the bastard running frantically away from the club—and I had a good chance of not falling on my ass in the process.

Chilled air bit at my arms and neck as my feet pounded down, crushing the ice underneath. I had always been a fast runner, which had been one of my biggest strengths as a Guardian. But I didn't think I'd ever truly needed to be as fast as I was. In my experience, not many people were prepared to outrun someone determined to catch them. They never fully understood the implications when they took off, thinking they could turn a corner or hide behind a car, or simply get enough of a head start that no one would bother to close the distance.

But I always closed the distance.

As I slowly pounded my way closer to Ray, I could hear the ground sizzle with every one of his steps. Looking down, I realized his feet were actually melting the ice, just like the weird little girl I'd saved earlier. What were these people, demons for real? More fae with mysterious fevers? Fire mages? Bats, they could be anything.

He turned a corner with me right behind him reaching out, my fingertips searing as they brushed the edge of his coat and failed to grasp it.

But he stopped short, swiveling around and clutching at my arm before I could react.

Damn. This one had wanted me to close the distance, and now I might regret it.

My feet lifted off the ground and my face fell forward, a strong hit to the gut knocking the wind and the sense out of me all at once. Burning heat ran through my bones, starting where his hand still clutched my arm, and I was paralyzed. Moving through the air, at his whim.

Was he flipping me over, or was I flying? It didn't matter,

because in the next moment I crashed to the ground. Ice-cold agony hit my spine, and my head spun as I tried to make sense of the extreme temperatures fighting for control in my body—and the powerful wind still soaring past me.

When his hand released me, the cold took over.

And when I came to my senses, I wasn't in the alley anymore.

4

RAY WAS GONE. Utterly, inconceivably vanished.

And instead of the brick and mortar of the shops lining the street I'd just been on, black crystal cavern walls surrounded me on all sides. And heat, and light, and magic.

So much magic that my *scrye* swelled, the part of my consciousness I'd been taught to use to access magic exerting electric pressure against every cell in my body. I did my best to let it out, let it pass—but the reflective stone sent most of it right back at me.

I screamed, grinding my teeth together and squeezing my eyes shut, trying hard to at least imagine darkness inside me so I could regain control.

Wherever I'd been transported, it seemed like a place designed specifically to torture me.

Normally, there was a limit to how much light could exist in a dark space before it just became a bright space. But this space was both. Both the brightest and the darkest space I had ever been in. It probably had something to do with the cave's walls, both black and reflective. Obsidian? This must be some sort of volcanic cave. But where was the light source, and how could it be so strong?

I forced my squinted eyes a tiny bit open and reached my hands out to push myself off the ground. My palm sliced itself on something sharp, and I bit back a yelp. Strangely, the pressure on my scrye immediately released, and the light dimmed. I still felt the magic all around me, but it was almost like it had been attacking me a moment ago, and now we were coexisting.

Looking down, I saw my blood coating a jagged piece of the black glass that had fallen onto the ground. The dark liquid began to absorb into the glass, and a few seconds later it was like it had never been there. But my hand continued to bleed.

Great. *That's not ominous at all. A magical cave that's trying to eat me.*

Opening my eyes all the way, I decided to test the water. It didn't *feel* like I was a frog in a slowly heating pot, but then I supposed the point was that it never would. I tapped gently into my scrye to heal the slice on my hand, and the skin zipped up so fast I could barely even feel it, cells linking perfectly and dividing into new flesh to erase any evidence of the wound. Even the pain was gone, which was odd. Pain tended to linger after magical healing, because no one's nervous system was wired to understand the things I could do.

Still, these were all good signs. If the magic was doing what I wanted, it wasn't likely to fry me anytime soon.

Looking up, I saw a tunnel to my right. And if things hadn't been creepy enough before, they certainly were now that the wind had started to die down and a scratching, scuttling noise was growing to take its place—coming from the tunnel. At least it sounded like it was moving away from me.

But aside from the tunnel, I could see no way out. And I didn't know how I'd even gotten here, so I couldn't go back the way I'd come.

Ray was still nowhere in sight, and that at least was good

because he'd totally kicked my ass back on the street. I really had gotten rusty in the past year. Now I resented ever letting Becca convince me to stop trying to do Mitch's job when men needed to be thrown out of the club. She'd said we would all make more money if I was less scary, and she had been right. It hurt now to remember her innocence, which had been strong enough to rub off on even me.

A Guardian caught off her guard, I thought, feeling naked and weak.

But I still had to hope it was Ray who'd brought me here, whether intentionally or by accident. If not . . . then I was lost in every way imaginable.

It seemed I only had one choice.

Once again feeling grateful for my thick-soled boots, I put one foot in front of the other and made my way across the small cave.

The tunnel shone brighter than the cavern I'd just been in. That should be a good sign. Wherever the light source, I was moving toward it. And now that the magic in here had stopped attacking me, I could appreciate its beauty. The walls of the tunnel were obsidian, same as the cavern, but it didn't look like anything natural had created them. If this space had been created by volcanic activity long ago, I would have expected the obsidian to be lumpy, rough, and dull. Instead, it looked as if a jeweler had carved precise facets over every inch of the walls. The subtle light streaming through glittered as it glanced across every surface, the effect mimicking the vision of stars in the darkest night sky.

Even the creepy scuttling noises added to the breathtaking effect, sounding musically in tune with the movement of light over the reflective facets of black glass.

That was, until the noises started moving toward me.

Whatever it was, it sounded so close, yet still I couldn't see anything except stone and light and empty space. It paused for a moment, and then I could swear I heard it above me.

When I looked up, something small and black and hard dropped onto my face.

I opened my mouth instinctively to let out a scream, but it sounded garbled because tiny, sharp claws had fallen between my lips.

Not cool. *Better my mouth than my eyes*, I thought in an attempt to stave off panic. I bent over and shook, trying to spit the creature off, but it held tight and crawled further up towards my scalp.

Then it bit me. Maybe. I didn't even know if this thing had a mouth to bite me with, but I did know that it fucking hurt.

My hands flew to my face, pulling the thing off and hurling it at the wall. It crashed and then slid down with the sound of falling marbles. If those marbles could also chirp like a bird. But when I squinted to get a closer look at the fallen thing, it wasn't marbles or a bird. More like some kind of tiny rabbit, closer to the size of a rat.

But if a rabbit had pounced on my head and bitten me, it wasn't like any other kind of rabbit I'd ever known. My fingers gingerly crept through my hair, searching for the throbbing wound. And they came away wet with yet more of my blood.

Another thing trying to eat me? Or . . .

I looked closer at the rabbit, which was now picking itself up, shaking off its defeat like a dog would shake off water. And I could see no damage. In fact, it looked far too perfect for any living creature. It wasn't real. More like a little sculpture crafted by a skilled artist and then animated by magic. And the crafting material? Obsidian.

So, still the same thing trying to eat me, with a different mouth this time. I needed to get out of here, fast.

But the evil little bunny beat me to it, running off through the tunnel toward the light, and a moment later hundreds of identical shiny black rabbits had scurried down the walls to join it. I took a step forward and then stopped, wondering if it was really a good idea to follow this horde, even though it seemed to be my only way out.

Something squeaked by my feet then, and I looked down to see a few of the obsidian bunnies looking up at me expectantly. They *wanted* me to follow. I wasn't sure if that made things better or worse, but I didn't really have a better idea.

I ran, and I didn't stop until I found myself shrouded in the light at the end of the tunnel, my vision blasted as the walls disappeared and the bunnies dispersed and the world seemed vast and overwhelming again.

Overwhelming because this world was clearly not my world. The light wasn't golden like the sun's or silver like the moon's. And the sky wasn't any sort of comforting shade of blue. It was all . . . not exactly red, but whatever you would get if you could somehow mix red with black and white at the same time. Red, but ethereal. With smoke and clouds and silvery sheens of magic floating every which way before a snow-topped mountain in the distance.

And in the midst of it all, right in front of me, a row of bodies tied to stakes. No, not stakes. Spits. Vertical spits, as the invisible, magical fire all around them roasted them alive.

Sacrifices . . . Could this be the realm of a god? I really hoped not, because everything I'd been taught about magic growing up was based on the idea that gods were a thing of the past—and that we were all better off leaving them there.

But the bodies lined up in front of me looked like nothing I'd ever seen. Some were completely charred beyond recognition, like Becca had been at the club.

Becca.

I ran closer to the spits. Not all of the people on them had fully burned yet. Not all of them were dead. And the one all the way on the end had a shining blond head of hair.

It was definitely Becca. No . . . It was Becca's soul. After all the grueling work I'd done in my coven's hospital, keeping screaming souls inside their dying bodies long enough for other mages to heal them—I knew a soul when I saw one. That distinctive shimmer, that unique aura of helplessness . . .

When I got closer, the eyes on Becca's soul locked on mine, and her ghostlike mouth opened wide but no sound came out. Tiny flecks of her skin glowed molten and then floated away from her into the atmosphere. A slow process that would eventually land her exactly where she'd been at the club. Burned. Dead. Gone.

My hands reached out to untie her arms. If I could get her out of here . . .

But I couldn't, because as soon as I touched her, she disappeared. It all disappeared. The air was suddenly cool and empty, the magic and the smoke and the dead bodies gone. All but one. Becca the charred corpse was on the pole in front of me, my hands reaching out to her in a gesture that hadn't been futile a moment ago but certainly was now.

I'd somehow come back to reality and found my way back inside the club. Yet now, it was exactly where I didn't want to be. It was wrong. Becca was already gone here, but she was still alive in whatever fantasy realm I'd just been in. Even if it wasn't real—even if it couldn't be real—the hope inside me felt real. And all I wanted was to find my way back to a place where I could still save my friend.

5

STRONG HANDS RESTRAINED me before I could even think to stand up.

"Darcy Pierce, you are under arrest for fleeing an active crime scene." This wasn't Asshole Crane speaking, but his partner. The guy with the kink for extra tits.

His voice was louder, stronger—which didn't surprise me. He was a human cop who'd just gotten drunk in an interspecies strip club and was now arresting the bartender. Fucking brazen.

"I didn't flee. I was chasing the man you should be arresting. I—" I stopped.

There wasn't really anything I could say. They were technically right. I should have told them to chase Ray instead of chasing him myself.

I wasn't a Guardian anymore. It wasn't my job to chase anyone, and more than that, it apparently wasn't even allowed. I'd forgotten that, letting my feelings for Becca cloud my judgment, and now this drunken cop was clasping cold metal around my wrists as punishment.

Had I been so wrong to think I could just walk away from

that life? Making drinks for horny men instead of saving people's lives? I'd counted myself lucky to escape from Simeon's clutches after he'd basically brainwashed me and made me useless, but maybe it wasn't enough for me to refuse to protect monsters like him. Maybe there were more monsters in the world than I'd ever realized, and maybe I would have to start playing offense if I wanted to have any semblance of a life I didn't hate.

"Okay," I said, releasing the tension in my arms to show my compliance.

"Okay what?"

"Okay, arrest me. You're right. I did leave a crime scene without permission. I'm sorry. I was a Guardian for four years, and Becca was my friend. I acted on my instincts without thinking, and I know what it must have looked like. I just want to help."

He snorted. "You, help? Crane told me who you are, lady. The only way you'll help is by sticking a knife in my back."

Ugh. I was starting to think I'd been wrong in deciding last year that I could live with a ruined reputation. I could have fought harder to prove my innocence, but I'd chosen not to. My brain had been so scrambled at that point, it'd seemed better to be thought a betrayer than go back to the Guardians and admit I'd let a vampire cloud my judgment. But I knew it wasn't better to be evil than incompetent—that was just my bruised ego, scrambling my brain even more.

It would certainly make things more difficult for me now.

I was about to tell the extra-titty lover that even if I really was an assassin, I doubted any of his enemies would be able to afford my fee. But then Crane stepped in front of us and saved me from myself.

"Let her up, Dirk." He extended a hand down to me, then turned red when he realized I was cuffed and couldn't take it. "Sorry."

"That's okay," I said, wondering why he was being nice to me. "I can stand up without hands." And, with only a small brush against Dirk to get him out of my way, I did just that. Rusty or not, I still had strong legs.

A chunk of my hair fell into my face when I popped up, so I pulled some magic into my breath and blew it away, the dusty dark waves tickling my nose as they flew up and back, tucking neatly behind my ear.

Crane narrowed his eyes at me. "Ah, are you . . . ?" He looked at the bar for a moment, then back at me. "Did you . . . ?"

I had no idea what he was getting at, and apparently neither did Dirk, because he walked around me to smack Crane in the back and said, "Spit it out, man. What'd I tell you about questioning? You gotta ask full questions with your mouth. Not everyone's a mind reader."

Which one of them is a mind reader? I wondered. Gauging their lack of reaction to my clearly thought question, I realized it was probably neither of them. Someone else, then. I'd be on my guard.

"Did you do something to my drink?" Crane finally managed to ask, a tinge of hurt in his voice.

Wow, I thought. Either this was an act, or Detective Asshole was way too sensitive for his job.

"Nope, definitely not," I said. *I only thought about doing something to your drink.* "But it wouldn't have been illegal if I had," I pointed out, partly wishing I'd gone through with it.

If I had given him a touch of lust to drink, he'd be uniquely motivated to help me out of these cuffs.

"Then why . . ." He seemed unable to go on, and his face turned even redder.

"Words, man," Dirk piped up.

"Never mind," Crane mumbled, then quickly changed the subject. "So, are we bringing her in?"

"Yep," Dirk answered. "Said she'd come willingly. Bet she knows lots. Put her in a room with Miriam, we might even be able to put her away for life."

Huh. So Miriam must be the mind reader. And these two must be hoping to catch my "assassin" alter-ego in addition to Becca's killer. Great. "Are you guys even DoSC?"

Department of Supernatural Crime. They were the ones with jurisdiction over everything involving magic. Created twenty years ago when all the "supernatural" creatures had outed themselves, one after the other, like dominoes, after the first business-minded vampire had started selling immortality to the masses.

The Opening, we called it now, because it had been like opening floodgates on a new market so high in demand that it changed our entire society. Inhumanity was very lucrative, it turned out—despite the many humans who would always want to remain human, and despite their many prejudices.

That was all before my time, really. I was only a child when it happened, and I grew up as an orphan, like so many others, never knowing if my parents had left me to become vampires or if they'd been some new vampire's first breakfast.

They were human; that was all I knew. And twenty years later, even though my adoptive family had taught me to use magic, I was still human too.

The DoSC, though? Twenty years later, they were still a joke. While the government had struggled for years to allocate resources properly and get their act together to contain the chaos, private security companies had formed and grown and stepped up to the task. I'd worked for the biggest, best one up until last year.

As a Guardian, I'd done my job so well I'd barely needed to have any contact at all with the regular police, let alone the DoSC. They operated separately, still, because the general populace couldn't bear the idea of disbanding the regular cops, and the regular cops were about as effective as floppy fish against brown bears when it came to the "supernatural"—a term that had been under fire lately for its racist undertones. Vampires, shifters, and the rest were just as "natural" as humans, they argued. But no one had been able to coin a better term yet that would satisfy everyone and stick.

"Nah, we're part of a new program," Dirk said proudly. "Gonna clean up the city, and then everywhere else. For good."

Whatever he was talking about, it sounded like a disaster waiting to happen.

"Umm," Crane interrupted, "that's not exactly—" He paused to rub his eyes, then continued, "We've been working with some DoSC agents for the past couple months. Collaborating; trying to see how we can help each other be more effective. It's just an experiment. Anyway—"

"Well, don't tell her everything. She'll use anything you say to witch her way out of those cuffs and turn it against you."

Neither Crane nor I knew what to say to that, it seemed.

Witch? Yeah, right. Like that was a real thing.

I supposed it had been, at some point. Technically, the society of mages I'd grown up in were descendants of witches. Their ancestors had been taught to use magic by a god they'd worshiped—that was the difference between witches and mages. Both used magic, but witches by definition were servants of the gods.

Witches were a thing of the past because gods were a thing of the past. Gods needed worshippers to stay in power, and humanity had largely stopped worshipping long before the Opening.

This was why most humans still didn't know it was within their ability to command magic. It was entirely possible for anyone, godly benefactor or no—it just didn't come easy.

I had spent my childhood pouring long, grueling hours into study and practice, deciphering old, wordy tomes, mastering multiple forms of meditation, connecting my mind to my will and then controlling it. It was a skill, like any other, and I'd worked hard to be good at it.

I could do simple things without even trying, like imbuing drinks with feelings and moving my hair out of my face with no hands. But outside of healing, which my adoptive family had forced me to become an expert in, I'd never really tried anything big.

In all my years as a Guardian, I'd never relied on magic to make my blades fly straighter or my legs pump faster. That seemed like a sure way to get myself killed. As skilled as I was with magic, I'd been taught to always remember I could never rely on it. It wasn't as much a part of me as my nerves, my strategies, my muscles. I could wield it like a weapon, but it would always be a borrowed one. It would never truly be mine. And anything that wasn't truly mine could betray me.

So now, as I stared at these two men who were clearly both in over their heads—and who would truly need my help if they could ever get past trying to convict me of a crime I hadn't committed—I wanted badly to magic my way out of this situation entirely and go hunt Ray on my own. But that would require some serious, mind-altering shit if I didn't want it to land me behind bars somewhere down the line. And I wouldn't mess with the serious shit unless I had no other choice.

"Tell you what," I said slowly. "If a partnership with the DoSC is in the works and you're still working out the kinks, why not add me to the mix for this case?"

My reputation was questionable right now, yes, but at the end of the day I was still a former Guardian. And I knew there was no precedent of the DoSC ever turning down help from a former Guardian.

If I pressed the issue, I might even be able to get them in trouble for trying to keep me away. I wouldn't mention that unless I needed to, though.

Before either one of them could answer me, I continued, "Since it's just you two here doing the questioning, resources must be spread thin already. Doesn't look like you have anyone from the department here backing you up now—or am I wrong?"

That made them nervous, for sure. It was tough to tell with Crane, because he'd seemed nervous more often than not since I'd met him. But I knew I was in dangerous water when I saw the blood drain from Dirk's face as he gripped his bandaged shoulder, where Ray must have burned him earlier.

Shit. I hadn't meant that as a threat. Was he really still drunk, or was I really that menacing? Either way, the last thing I wanted was for him to think he had to attack me in self-defense.

Clearly, these guys had no idea what to expect from someone like me. I didn't know what to do to not scare them.

"Hey, I promise I'm really not a bad guy," I tried. "If you arrest me now, you'll just have to let me go in a few hours, because I guarantee you'll find no evidence to hold against me. But if you let me work this case with you, find the jerk who set my girl on fire, you'll get to spend some quality time with me. Now, I'm sure that will convince you I'm innocent—but if you're right and I'm not, that's the best chance you'll get of finding anything to hold me on. Think of what it could do for your careers . . ."

Crane was smiling when I broke my stare away from his partner. He might actually believe me on the case of my innocence. Or maybe my magic had somehow gone completely rogue tonight and I really *had* put lust in his drink just by contemplating it.

That would explain Becca's mysterious burst of strength right before she'd gotten on stage, too. I hoped that wasn't the case, because it had never happened before. And as much as I knew it was foolish to rely on my magic being . . . well, reliable

—it was unsettling to think I could have such a complete lack of control.

But if Crane was standing across from me burning with desire right now, that would be a little hilarious.

"I . . . think it could work," Crane said cautiously. "As long as we keep an eye on her, at least we'll know she's not causing trouble for anyone else," he added, probably for Dirk's benefit.

"That's because she'll be causing trouble for us instead. What could she possibly help us with? We know what we're doing."

"But I know Becca—um, knew her," I amended, choking on the words just a little before continuing. "I know her behavior tonight casts suspicion on the man who escaped, and I know the best way to find him again."

"What would that be?" Crane sounded genuinely curious to know.

"Becca's son."

"She had a son?" Dirk's face scrunched up as he flipped through his messy-looking notebook.

"See?" I smiled. "I'm already helping."

"Okay," Dirk snapped as he clapped his notebook shut. "Compromise."

"Hmm?" Crane asked, but Dirk was already pulling his phone out of his pocket.

He squinted at it and after a few taps, it was against his ear. "Miriam," he barked, "I need one of your squishies."

What in all the hells was that? Judging by Crane's hand over his eyes, it wasn't anything good.

"Maybe you can help us, maybe you can't," Dirk added, putting his phone away. "Maybe we can put you away for good, maybe not. Either way, we can't afford to babysit you. We've got our own leads to follow."

Do they? I wondered. Or was this a matter of pride?

"So after a quick stop at the station, we'll let you go. Talk to

Becca's son. Find the man you think is so suspicious. Do whatever you like. We'll have someone watching."

"Meaning . . . you're sending someone else with me?"

Crane let his hands fall away from his face and, with a slight groan, said, "Not exactly—"

"Come on," Dirk snapped, already making for the door. "You'll see."

6

HALF AN HOUR and plenty of bitching later, I was walking up the steps to my apartment with a pink, gelatinous blob latched on to the back of my neck.

It had turned out Miriam was more than just a woman from the DoSC who could read minds; she was also some kind of psychic Barbie swamp monster who regularly shed bits of herself and turned them into minion parasite spies. The one attached to me couldn't read my full mind—supposedly—but it gave Miriam a clear, constant line to my stream of consciousness. Unless I suddenly became very good at lying to myself, she would always know where I was and what I was doing.

That alone, I wouldn't mind so much. But really, a pink blob?

I'd had to let my hair out of its usual knot to hide the damn thing, since it looked more like alien cancer than a terrible fashion choice—though I wasn't sure which would have worried Etty more. Now my skin was crawling as unruly waves of my long hair brushed against my cheeks and shoulders like flying insects. I hated bugs. And I absolutely hated wearing my hair down.

When I reached my apartment, I aggressively pushed my hair behind my ears and took a deep breath, resisting the temptation to burst through the front door. If Noah was here, I didn't want to scare him.

The poor kid would already be in shock, trying to process the loss of his mother. And Etty, too . . . Becca had always been the link between us, the one who loved both of us and made us get along with each other because we both loved her. Without her, were Etty and I even really friends? I had no idea, and now I felt almost like I was walking into an apartment with two bombs, ready to explode. I had to tread carefully.

So I turned the knob slowly and pushed the door forward, surprised to find it dark inside. I hadn't been gone that long, and it still wasn't too late. Midnight, maybe? Past the kid's bedtime? I still didn't know much about Noah's routine. He usually kept to Becca's room when he was here, but he spent most days and nights with his father. A man who seemed nice enough, but who had cheated on Becca and then expected her to stay with him for the sake of their family. When she hadn't, he'd turned against her and lawyered up, arguing that she wasn't devoted enough to be Noah's mother, and then that her choice of work made her unfit to be anyone's mother. With her gone, it seemed he'd gotten what he'd wanted. Noah would be his now.

The thought made me sick. Maybe I would steal Noah for myself, give those cops a real reason to put me away. Or maybe I'd find that his father was somehow behind Becca's death. Yes, that would kill two birds with one stone. Avenge my friend and save her son from an atrocious upbringing. *Let's do that*, I thought. But realistically, the man wouldn't have needed to kill Becca to ensure custody of his son. He'd already been well on his way to winning that, if what Becca had told me was true.

No, Ray was still the most obvious suspect, and I was willing to bet he'd gotten close enough to Becca before sending her up in flames that Noah would be able to tell me something useful about him.

"Etty?" I whispered as I stepped forward into the dark, perfectly comfortable without the use of my eyes.

I knew from experience to pick my feet up high over the 8-inch platform heels Etty always left right by the entrance. I'd stubbed my toes on them far too many times and gotten into far too many screaming matches with Etty on the subject before Becca had convinced me to suck it up and look before I stepped.

Feeling her absence in the apartment already, I turned left as soon as my outstretched fingers brushed the back of the furry sofa in the living room, then made my way to the kitchen. There, by the stove, I finally flipped on a light.

When the sudden brightness washed over me, I felt it in the stinging and sudden heaviness in my eyelids. They wanted to close. I wanted to sleep. But even if I didn't have a monumental task ahead of me, midnight would still be too early for bed.

As much as I'd been trying to delay it, to push it down until I had the spare time to deal with it, my grief over Becca was catching up with me. Slowing me down. Making me irritable. But I knew if I didn't focus on saving her, it would only get worse. I needed coffee.

As I opened the tin and savored the rich scent that filled my nostrils, I worked to recall Becca's image in my mind. Not as she'd been at the club, dead and gone—but with life and pain still in her eyes, the way she'd looked tied to that stake in whatever strange realm I had accidentally followed Ray to.

I spooned some beans into the grinder and pressed the lid down, relishing in the jolt to my nerves caused by the sudden loud noise. Almost as good as the caffeine itself. But when it got quiet again and I tipped the grounds into the coffee machine, I heard what sounded like an Etty groan coming from the living room.

I poked my head out the kitchen doorway and saw Etty sparkling gently in the shadows, face down on the fluffy white couch, splayed out like she was the one who'd been murdered tonight. I sighed, then went back to the coffee machine and opened the cabinet above it, grabbing two mugs instead of the one I'd originally planned for.

Mine was a dusty blue color in the shape of an elephant—the handle its trunk—and hers was cheetah print. Becca had gotten them both for us as gifts, saying they reminded her of us. I'd been offended until she'd explained that elephants are friendly and smart, but they have great aim with their trunks and everyone knows not to fuck with them. Now I would cherish it forever.

Taking care not to spill, I padded from the kitchen to the couch with the two steaming mugs in my hands—mine with cream but no sugar, and hers with about a pound of sugar but no cream. I sat on the sage-green rug on the floor beside the couch, strategically placing Etty's mug of coffee right beneath her sleeping face. Then I sipped mine and waited.

In less than a minute, her eyes were open and coppery irises were glaring back at me, shining with sadness more than anything else. This might be the one time I could wake Etty up without her getting mad at me about it; right now, she was too distracted by other feelings.

She blinked, and in a fluid motion so quick it couldn't be human, she swept up her coffee and sat cross-legged on the couch, holding the cheetah-printed mug under her face and closing her eyes against the warm steam billowing up.

"Hey," I said.

Her eyes still closed, Etty ignored me and took a long drink of her coffee, then set the mug down on the short table in front of her. She turned to me and just sighed.

I nodded gently towards Becca's room and asked, "Is Noah asleep?"

"Hmm?" she said. Then, once my question had really registered in her brain, she added, "He's not here."

My face scrunched up with worry. "Is he with his father? I thought Becca said she would have him today."

"Yep," Etty replied. "She said that. Then this afternoon she told me Baz was babysitting for a while."

"What? Baz?"

"Yep."

"Bawdy Baz?" I repeated, incredulous. "The thousands-of-years-old genie who keeps nothing but tea and booze in his kitchen is babysitting our girl's six-year-old?"

"Yep," she said, closing her eyes again to take another drink.

"Why?"

Etty pursed her lips and opened her eyes, shifting them far to the left. "Umm . . . That's a good question." She raised her voice a little as her words quickened. "Becca was saying a lot this morning but I wasn't really awake, you know . . . so I . . . I don't remember."

I could see the grief fight for control of Etty's face again, her lips quivering just a little, her jaw setting, and her eyes shining with wetness.

"And now she's gone." Etty set her mug down once more and covered her face with her hands. "She's gone and I don't remember what she said." Her words came out muffled through her fingers, and then the sobs took over.

Fuck. I took a deep breath, trying not to panic. I had no idea how to deal with this kind of thing. Crying. Sadness. Well, I could deal with my own damn emotions—but comforting someone else?

Before coming to work at Baz's club, I'd never been in any environment where that particular skill had been expected of me. And even there, as the bartender, I didn't need to be great at it. I could just pour drinks and crack jokes, and there were always plenty of naked women all around me who were much better at the "There, there, honey; it's okay" than me.

Etty was one of them. And now she needed . . . me. I briefly considered asking for her mug back and infusing the coffee with some comfort, but it didn't seem appropriate. Becca was dead, and any feelings that came from that deserved to be dealt with the real way.

So I reached out awkwardly and touched my hand to Etty's shoulder. I'd just barely made contact with her shimmering dark skin when she jerked away from me. And for an instant, the claws came out, and the glitter on her skin looked more like thousands of barbs on a cactus as she bristled.

It was over almost as soon as it started, and she was back to her soft, sad, sparkly self, staring at me with round eyes.

"Sorry," she said. "I just—"

"It's okay, I get it." I forced a tiny smile onto my face. I didn't have time for her emotions now anyway. We weren't friends with Becca gone, and that was okay. It would have to be okay. But I hoped we could at least be allies. "Um, do you think you could do something for me? For Bex?"

She looked up at me with fierce eyes and wiped away her tears. "What?"

"Remember how you said you could ask your queen? About what may have happened to Becca? Before she . . . you know. It was probably Ray who hurt her, but just in case we're wrong about that . . . or even if we're right, your queen might be able to help us figure out how he did it."

Etty was just looking at me, her eyes hard, her fingers slowly tightening around her mug.

"And you said something, when you saw what happened. Something about wings? If it's a fae thing, anything you can do to help me understand—"

"Wings." Etty closed her eyes and breathed in. "I said that?"

"You did, I think. When Becca was dancing."

"I don't remember that," she said quickly. "I'll request an audience with my queen, though. No way am I going to work tomorrow."

"Thanks. I'm gonna go hunt down Noah—call me if you get anything, okay?"

"'Kay," she said.

Without another word, I grabbed my emergency bag from the closet by the front door and made my way down the stairs outside.

I needed to know anything Noah could tell me about Becca's relationship with Ray, and now I also needed to know what the hell Becca had been thinking leaving her kid with our wacky, irresponsible boss.

She wouldn't have done that unless she'd been desperate, and anything that could have made her feel desperate the morning of the day she died was something that could help me catch her killer now.

7

THE PATHWAY to the garage underneath my apartment complex gleamed with black ice. Not the kind of invisible ice that caused car accidents, though—this was actually black. Pigmented. Like glassy coal covering the pale cement that usually didn't have any ice on it at all.

Everything was kept well salted in all seasons nowadays, because people thought it would ward off evil just as well as it did ice. Right now, as I remembered being surrounded by obsidian that looked eerily similar to this pathway, I kind of wished I knew whether that was true. If it was, I might have less to be afraid of. But the list of things that could and would kill me far outweighed the list of things that might be repelled by salted walkways.

Evil is far from the only thing in this world worth fearing, I thought, remembering the words Simeon had drilled into my brain on our first day together, three years ago. I'd thought I'd learned everything I would need to know in my four years of Guardian training as a teen, but my first charge had turned out to be my best teacher. He had taught me that a person with reasonable motivations is far more dangerous than the most straightforward of evil creatures, every time.

And in the end, that had been true. Simeon had been killed because someone had looked at him and seen what they'd thought was evil. I'd always known that, even if I'd only found out today it was the Sweepers who had sent his killer. And Simeon himself had been a good man, if I was honest. But that didn't make him any less of a monster when it came to the impact he'd had on my life.

I'd been careful in passing judgment ever since his death. It was why I hadn't balked at working in Baz's club, despite hearing all my life that sex work was degenerate work and that anyone who would stoop so low must be evil.

I had gone in with an open mind and seen firsthand how untrue that was.

Now, I was trying to keep an open mind while playing "follow the glossy black road" to my car. But it wasn't looking good.

When I turned the corner into the garage, I saw that the black trail led straight to the passenger-side door of my ride, eliminating any doubts that this wasn't connected to me. Shadows moved behind the windows, accompanied by a cacophony of clacking noises. Like marbles. Then came a single squeak from one of the back tires.

I crept towards it to see the same obsidian mini-rabbit that had bitten me in the cave, or one just like it. It was facing me directly, cautiously backing away underneath my car. When I pulled a knife from my bag's outer pocket, it began chirping wildly, and suddenly the underside of my car was a sea of black, clacking, obsidian-crafted bunnies.

They scattered, dashing away from the car in different directions, and I stood shocked for a moment wondering how so many had even fit in my car—and how they had gotten in to begin with. Would I find a gaping hole in the floor? Would the

car even still run? And what the fuck had they been doing in
there?

Before I could let my mind run away with more useless
questions, I realized all these creatures were succeeding in
running away from me. That would leave me with a violated
vehicle and absolutely no answers.

Bracing myself for pain, I reached down and grabbed one
of the rodents as it tried to hop past my feet. Luckily, I
managed to pluck it up by its ears, preventing it from biting me
in the process. I brought it up to eye level and watched as it
squirmed and thrashed, trying to get its tiny claws on some
part of my body.

Gotcha, I thought. But my moment of victory was brief.
Almost as soon as I'd caught the little creature, its friends
changed course, hopping towards me instead of away. Before I
realized what was happening, they were crawling up my legs.
Thank fuck for leather boots and thick denim. And for the cold
weather that had prompted me to dress this way.

I shook my legs and kicked, stomping wherever I could
while fighting the urge to screech. It was embarrassing. I was a
trained killer, but I'd never needed to kill dozens of tiny creatures swarming me. Their claws tore through my jeans and
into my skin, jabbing deeply to pull themselves up. These
suckers were heavier than regular rabbits, made of dense
volcanic rock instead of the usual fluff and cuteness. But it
didn't seem like they were trying to hurt me. Just trying to get
to their friend. Well, then. What if I killed it?

I squinted. How would I go about killing a rabbit made of
rocks? I'd thrown one against a wall already, back in the cave,
and it hadn't done any damage. Maybe if I yanked its head off
with my bare hands . . . but it was so tiny and so dense that I
couldn't make out its neck, so how would I know which part
even counted as the head?

A few of the rocky rodents had reached my torso now, and

I used my free hand to pluck them off before their sharp claws could do much damage to the soft skin at my middle.

Then the warmth in my body seemed to drain out from behind me all at once. Like I was standing in a heated room and someone had opened a window. Except I was already technically outside; this wasn't a heated or enclosed garage.

Something roared behind me, like an avalanche of icicles crashing down on a mountainside. When I turned, I saw an enormous mass of snow and ice and mist swirling around itself, chaos seeking order as it formed into the shape of a creature— a creature that was roaring.

Its teeth shook with the vibration of the sound, sharp spikes of ice quivering with the anticipation of ripping me to shreds. I could feel the magic rolling off it, like heat from a campfire, dancing on the thin line between comfortable and dangerous. It could kill me in an instant, but I'd never been around magic like this before, and I felt something strong inside me wanting to play with it, test it, see if I could bend it to my will.

That can't be healthy, I thought as I watched the chaotic pieces of ice solidify in the form of a wolf. It snapped its jaws and snarled at me, and I quickly dropped the bunny in my hand to switch it out with another of my knives.

The rest of the rabbits stopped moving, their friend no longer needing rescuing. But the ones already on my legs didn't detach, and the others made no move to run away. They just stood there, frozen in time, undecided, like puppets waiting for their next command.

As far as I was concerned, they could do whatever they liked as long as they didn't start trying to kill me like this ice wolf was clearly about to do.

It leaned back on its haunches, gearing up to charge at me, and I took the opportunity to launch one of my blades at it. My aim was still off, but old habits die hard.

Instead of the wolf's left eye, the tip of my knife connected with its right. Still an eye, though, so I'd take it. Except the tip only stuck for a tiny moment before bouncing off, leaving little more than a scuff mark behind.

Okay, so this thing was much more solid than it looked. That was troubling. Unless I resorted to magic, my knives would be useless in this fight.

I'd never fought anything that wasn't made of flesh and blood before. Sure, plenty of magical creatures could only be killed by decapitation or removing specific organs, or with specific types of metal . . . but everything could be incapacitated or at least hurt by cutting it up. Until now.

First the bunnies and now a wolf. Live beings composed of inorganic materials. It was weird, it was dangerous, and it was something I hadn't been taught to deal with.

Time to improvise, then. I braced myself as the wolf rushed at me, its icy paws leaving craters in the pavement where they landed.

Stepping aside just before it reached me, I flipped the remaining knife in my hand so the end of the handle was facing outward, then smashed it into the wolf's face. I missed the jaw but connected somewhere between cheek and neck— and did barely any damage.

Sharp pain ran up my arm and a few small chips of ice fell to the ground, but that was all.

A blunt weapon would work, but I needed something much bigger—heavier—like a mace instead of the friendly end of my dagger. Too bad I didn't keep a mace in my car.

Oh. But it wasn't just *my* car . . . I let Etty use it whenever she needed to lug her pole to teaching gigs, and she'd had one just last night. The heavy, sturdy cylinders of metal would still be in the trunk. The thing was expensive as hell, and Etty would kill me if I damaged it . . . but this wolf would kill me faster.

The beast took a brief moment to shake off the shock of

my pathetic attack on its face, then turned and snapped at my arm with its frigid jaws. I dodged just in time, but it had already lifted its paw to swipe at me in the direction I was lunging.

Its claws connected with my thigh, the force knocking me to the ground. But even as I felt the stinging blows to my spine and the back of my head as I landed on the pavement, I recognized that I didn't feel much pain in my thigh.

Had this creature completely taken off one of my legs? Was I paralyzed? I hoped not, because I wouldn't be alive much longer if I couldn't pop back to my feet. Cold magic bathed my face as the wolf loomed over me, its breath icy and powerful, getting a taste of me before the kill.

Nope, nope, nope. I brought up the leg it hadn't touched, my knee curled as close to my body as I could manage, and I shoved the bottom of my foot against the beast's rock-hard belly with as much force as I could. With my runner's legs, that was a decent amount of force. And the wolf didn't budge.

But the tiny rabbits who were still hanging on my leg began to move, hopping from my torn-up shin to the wolf's belly. And then the wolf budged.

It roared, so loud I thought the sound might kill me quicker than the teeth that were inches from my throat. Then it reared its head and lifted its paws, falling on its side and twisting to try to paw at its belly, where the bunnies had latched on and begun to glow orange, like molten lava, slowly melting the magical ice.

I sat up and chanced a look at my leg, the one the wolf had swiped, and I saw why I hadn't felt the pain of that attack. The rabbits on this leg had shifted their body parts around to form some kind of armor around my thigh. Obsidian armor. I looked from them to the glowing rodents on the wolf's belly and thought, *Volcanic rock, indeed.*

Scrambling up to my feet, I shoved my hand in my jacket

pocket and clutched at the car keys that thankfully had not fallen out in the fight. I raced to my car, stumbling a little as I rushed, not wanting to waste a single moment in case the wolf got back on its feet.

Smashing the unlock button, I hefted the partially frozen trunk open and groped for the cloth wrapped around Etty's pole. After unzipping it and cursing Etty for keeping it so tidily put away, I snatched the largest piece, about four feet of chrome-coated steel, and practically threw myself back at the wolf.

When I reached it, it was already starting to get back to its feet. Having gotten over the initial panic of molten bunnies on its belly, it was methodically picking them off with its claws, using different claws each time as they melted away.

Without halting my stride, I hefted the pole over my shoulder and brought it down directly between the wolf's ears. I didn't crush its head completely, but at least I made a respectable dent. If the thing had real brains in there, it would be dead. Shaking my armored leg, I tried to shoo the rest of the rabbits off.

"Go on! Get hot and help melt this thing!" Frustratingly slowly, the little creatures detached from each other and from my thigh. I winced as their claws unhooked from my skin, and I shook my leg again to help them hop off faster.

Then I braced myself and swung the pole again. And again, and again. Each swing crushed a bit more ice, until the wolf was no longer whimpering and the pole was sliding off remains that were slick as they melted from the heat of the rabbits.

I only stopped when I realized the heat was starting to melt the pole, too. A molten lump of metal was sizzling and turning black at the end as I pounded it into the pile of slush that used to be the wolf. Dropping it, I hunched over and sighed, then allowed myself to take a deep breath as I stretched my shoulders up and back.

When I shook out my muscles and looked around, the bunnies were black again and already hopping off—back towards my car.

"Hey, wait!" I didn't expect them to actually listen, but it seemed like they did. Or one of them did, at least. It stopped hopping and turned around, twitching its nose and . . . looking at me? Could obsidian see? This was ridiculous. "Um . . ." I said. "Why did you help me? And what are you doing in my car?"

I was sure I was crazy for even tentatively thinking this thing might be able to answer me—and it cemented my craziness when it turned back around and finished hopping away, into the shadows underneath my open trunk. If it did have eyes, I was sure it would be rolling them.

The black ice melted away into nothing at an obviously magical pace, leaving me confused as shit, wondering whether any of these creatures had anything to do with Becca's death.

But if so, why had they helped me now? And if not, why were they messing around with me at all?

I didn't have much time to be confused before horror started creeping back in as the wolf-turned-slush-pile transformed into something that definitely was neither wolf nor slush. The water that had seeped into the pavement from the melted ice retraced its path, gathering into a shape that seemed . . . human. And when it solidified, I could see exactly how much burning and bludgeoning we had done to it.

The face was unrecognizable, the skull not even round anymore. The whole thing was basically a mixture of bloody pulp and charred, melted flesh.

How? How could it have been a shifter? It was made of ice.

Suddenly I felt sick. I had killed people before, of course. But never without knowing it. And never inflicting this degree of damage. Damn . . . I would have stopped pummeling it if I had known.

Before I could stop myself, I dropped to my knees and clutched the gory remains in my hands, closing my eyes and tapping into my scrye. I could almost smell the chemicals of the clinic I'd been raised in, hear my aunts and uncles demanding that I grab hold of this poor boy's soul and keep it inside his mangled body.

It was already gone. I knew it was already gone. But I'd been forced to try in so many cases where the soul was already gone—it was a habit drilled into me. One I'd thought I'd succeeded in rooting out.

I hated this. I'd always hated it. It was why I'd left the clinic to become a Guardian in the first place, why I'd tried so hard to keep my healing skills secret. But Simeon had convinced me to use them for him, from time to time. Someone who could stop wounds from bleeding was too useful given vampires' notorious problems with self-control. And now that I'd been slipping away from my Guardian life, it made sense my old habits would try to come crawling back.

It took a few deep breaths before I could pry my hands away from the charred corpse. Blood and burnt flesh coated them, and I wiped as much as I could on the cement.

Swallowing against the nausea, I touched the shiny pink blob on my neck, even though I knew Miriam was listening—watching—no matter what I did. *It was self-defense, I swear*, I pleaded with her. The mind-reader would believe me, of course, but even her corroboration would only go so far once the cops got a look at this body. This certainly would not help my "I'm not a monstrous assassin" case.

But there was nothing I could do about it now, except delay the inevitable. Miriam would be sending the cops here soon to clean up my mess. And I wasn't planning on still being here when they arrived.

The cops would have a much better chance of figuring out who this wolf was once they got him to the morgue and pulled dental records.

I could already guess he was another gift to me from the Sweepers, since he and Possum had both come at me with ice magic. For a shifter to use magic unrelated to his beast, and for both of them to have command of the same type of magic, and enough power to use it offensively without faltering . . . if they were mages, they weren't like any mages I had ever known.

Maybe witches were a thing again. But where there were witches, by definition, there must be a god giving them power. And whoever this ice-loving god was, I still hadn't seen anything to directly connect them or the Sweepers to Becca's death. The timing of their attacks was suspicious, yes, but it could be unrelated.

Ray, on the other hand, I knew was involved. Even if it meant I would likely have to keep fending off ice-witch assassins, I had to prioritize Becca, so I had to prioritize finding Ray —and my best lead there was still Noah.

With too much adrenaline and not nearly enough pain, I folded myself into the driver's seat of my car.

No obsidian bunnies in sight, although I knew they must be hiding under the seats. After a brief look around to confirm they had done no visible damage, I put them out of my mind and sped out of the garage.

Time to pay Baz a visit.

8

"Go suck an ogre's tit!" I shouted through the windows of my car, so loud I wouldn't have been surprised if the driver behind me could hear me even though it seemed like he'd fallen over dead on top of his horn.

What, did he expect me to use magic just to park my damn car? Seeing as I hadn't even busted it out against the enormous wolf made of icicles, that wasn't fucking likely.

It wasn't my fault this spot was unnecessarily small. Or that this street was unnecessarily narrow. Or that driving in this city was unnecessarily nightmarish. I let out a small, primal yell as I realized my frustration was getting out of control.

Every moment that went by without me closer to saving Becca felt like a brand-new failure.

Every new bewildering occurrence, every question I couldn't answer, every stupid parking mishap that kept me from getting to Noah—all of it fell in the category of things I could have handled much better a year ago, before I had run away.

I could forgive myself for the running, given the state of my mind at the time. Letting myself become weak, though?

Complacent? Trying to heal a dead person like I was a fucking teenager again? I couldn't forgive myself for that. But I knew my rage would have to wait.

I took a deep breath, pushing the emotions away, feeling the pounding in my head ease just a little bit. And after exactly thirteen switches between Drive and Reverse, the honking finally ceased and an unnecessarily wide truck flew past me, nearly taking off my mirror.

Just a little bit more . . . *Got it.* It was tight, but it was parked. Now I just needed to hope one of the cars around me would leave before I needed to leave, otherwise I might really have to magic my way out.

I squinted into the side mirror, waiting for a break in the lights to open my door and get out. When it came, I practically leapt out of my seat—and my boots landed in a pile of grimy slush.

I cursed Baz under my breath as I yanked my feet out of the suctioning slush. He usually had his parking spot open for visitors, but today it was filled with a pile of old furniture. I had almost forgotten he'd said he was taking time off to redo his home, but getting rid of all his belongings and turning his parking spot into a mountain of trash just seemed . . . unnecessary.

Shaking off my boots as I went, I trudged up the stone pathway to the entrance of his town home.

The exterior was unpainted brick, standing out against all the cutesy colors of his neighbors' homes. Baz loved cutesy colors, but at his age, he also valued longevity more than most people. Whenever he did anything, he made sure it would stand up against time. This was also why he had no plants in his small front yard.

Other homes were decorated with expertly plotted minia-ture gardens and bare young trees that would flower in the spring. But Baz's decorations were all inorganic. A stone fountain with a mermaid spitting water, metal sculptures of owls and tigers and fish, and a whole bunch of other ridiculous nonsense.

At this thought, a small part of my brain inched closer to the theory that there was someone immortal like Baz controlling the weird inorganic animals that kept coming after me—were the rabbits built that way simply to last longer? And would the shifter's life have been prolonged by the ice it had been encased in? Yep, another tick in the box to tell me there were probably gods involved. And witches.

I sucked in my breath. Normally, dealing with Baz was a small annoyance at worst or great entertainment at best. But tonight, I had the patience for neither. I had a lot of questions to answer, and . . . well, I didn't feel like I had a lot of time.

Somewhere, deep down in the irrational part of my heart, I was still clinging to the vision of Becca I'd seen still alive. Burning. Silently begging me to save her.

I knew that couldn't have been real. Truly, I did. But it was affecting me the same way a bad nightmare would. When things feel real, they're tough to shake.

So I couldn't help but be in a hurry now. Even though my brain knew I should probably get some rest and approach this with more thought, more care—my heart couldn't forget that image of Becca, and every minute that went by felt like another minute she would have to burn.

If I'd thought there was any chance I could sneak in and talk to Noah without Baz knowing, I would have done it in a heartbeat. But slipping past Baz would be an impossible feat, so I clenched my fist and lightly tapped my knuckles against the frosted glass on his door.

And waited . . . for more than three seconds. That was strange.

Baz had superhuman hearing and could teleport himself anywhere instantaneously (as a marid, the type of djinn that supposedly grants wishes when rubbed the right way, he was really only *kind of* corporeal in the first place—and then, only when and where he wanted to be). I usually didn't need to knock at all, even though I did it lightly as a gesture of normalcy. And I certainly never had to wait.

Could he be somewhere else? I wondered as I stepped over the rails around his tiny porch and lifted myself up to try to peer in his window. I almost fell off when the door finally opened, and Baz actually clucked at me. Was he imitating a chicken or a disapproving mother? I honestly couldn't tell.

"I have a doorbell, you know."

I twisted my face at him and dropped to the ground, brushing myself off where my black jacket had rubbed against the bricks.

"No, I didn't know," I said. "Why would someone like you need a doorbell?"

"I didn't say I needed it, just that I have one." Then he broke into a huge smile, showing me perfectly white teeth. Anyone could tell which parts of Baz's appearance he cared about most just by looking at him, since he could change anything about himself with nothing more than a thought. And his teeth were at the top of the list.

I'm sure part of it was that he was proud of how solid they were; from what I'd heard, only very old or very skilled djinn could maintain fully solidified forms in the first place. But mostly, it was because he almost never stopped smiling. When you know you'll never die naturally, every day you live becomes a choice. And you don't get to be as old as Baz with a negative outlook on life. I wasn't sure how much he had to try every day to keep up his attitude, but regardless, I'd never seen him less jolly than Santa is supposed to be.

"Now, come on in," he said through his smile. "I don't know why you're here, but I don't want the neighbors to think I have *too* many lady friends." Then he winked, indicating that of course, he didn't really think there was such a thing as too many lady friends. He turned his back to me and walked inside, continuing to say, "When I bought the club, I promised myself I would keep business at work, but you know I could never turn you away, little birdie."

Still with that nickname, really? I thought. He had started calling me that when we'd first met, and I still had no idea why.

"Is that your way of telling me I look like a snack?" I asked as I walked in behind him, taking in the emptiness that somehow still seemed decorated. Without furniture, the gaudy chandeliers and gilded mirrors and hanging beads stood out even more than usual. "Do marid eat little birds alive?"

"Of course we don't." He stopped walking down the hallway and turned to me, and his smile seemed even wider now. He loved it when I teased him. "But you *are* human, little bird," he explained. "You'll always be a snack to someone." Then he turned back around and marched deeper into the depths of his home, beckoning me to follow.

And follow I did, wishing that one day I would meet a magical being who didn't equate humans with food.

He led me into the kitchen—twisting the knife?—and poured me a glass of tea from his kettle. It wasn't on the stove, but it started steaming and screaming almost as soon as he picked it up, and when he handed me the glass it was hot to the touch. It seemed I wasn't the only one who regularly magicked my drinks.

"Thanks, Baz," I said, gripping the handle carefully to avoid burning myself. "I'm kind of in a hurry, though—"

"Nah-ah-ah, birdie . . ." he cut me off, lifting his eyebrows expectantly.

"Ah, sorry—Bawdy Baz . . ."

"Good girl," he said, then turned into another room without furniture, though it did have a plush golden rug spread on the floor. Baz sat cross-legged and patted the rug next to him.

"I—" I started, before he narrowed his eyes at me and patted the rug again, a bit harder this time.

Fine, then. I sat next to him as quickly as I could, all the while complaining, "I really don't have time to sit and drink tea right now."

"Oh, come on. I know your kind doesn't live long, but it's not as if you'll fall over and die if you stop moving for a moment." He took a sip of his tea.

"That's a bit insensitive, given the circumstances, BB."

"BB?" He looked up at me, decidedly less jolly than he'd been a minute ago.

"Bawdy Baz is a mouthful. And like I said, I'm in a hurry. I need to talk to Noah. Is he asleep?"

"The fairy girl's boy? Is he supposed to be asleep? Ah . . ."

"Ah, what?" I snapped. This should not be as complicated as he was making it seem.

"I wasn't supposed to tell anyone he was here. How did you know?" The jolliness in his eyes continued to fade, and it was a little unsettling.

"Etty told me—"

"And—yes, that's right—I'm not supposed to let anyone talk to him," he cut me off again. "Sorry, birdie, looks like you came all the way here for nothing. Isn't the boy a little young for you, anyway? There are plenty more appropriately grown fish in the sea."

"Oh, bats." I stood, fighting the competing urges to be sick and punch Baz in the face. I was starting to really question Becca's decision to leave Noah with this man. He wasn't himself today, and I was smart enough to be scared by that. "I'm going to go find him. I promise you, Becca would have wanted me to talk to him right now."

He stood up with me, his eyes getting a little brighter as he did. "What do you mean 'would have'?"

I stopped and gaped at him. "No one told you?"

He didn't answer. Just stared at me without blinking, his eyes becoming brighter and redder by the second.

"No one called? Came by to ask you questions?" After my pit-stop at home and having to defend myself against the psychotic ice wolf, I hadn't expected to be the first one here. Especially since the cops had made it very clear they'd intended to talk to Baz.

What, had they gone home for a good night's sleep before starting their investigation? Sure, they hadn't seen what I'd seen in the cave, and they didn't have the same irrational fire under their butts to save a girl who was already dead . . . but they had to assume whoever had done this to her could be intending to do it to someone else . . . right?

I felt movement at the back of my neck just then, and reached around my head to find the blob of jelly . . . undulating? I shivered. Never in my life had I thought I would need to describe something attached to me as "undulating." I supposed that now, the cops would know very soon what I had seen in that cave.

At this point, the fire in Baz's eyes had dimmed slightly and he was looking at me with a grimace of gleeful disgust. "Please tell me you didn't go to work with that thing on you." Then he stepped forward, reaching out to lift my hair for a better look. "I pay you enough to go see a doctor, right?"

"No I didn't, and yes you do." I smacked his hand away. "Anyway, it's fine. It's just . . . a temporary pet. Baz . . ."

He opened his mouth to admonish me, but I continued before he could say anything.

"Just Baz. Now is not the time to be bawdy. Sit down again, please. There's something I need to tell you."

"Let me guess. You're pregnant?"

"What? No—"

"In trouble with the law again, then? Or maybe you've finally found religion?"

"Becca's dead," I blurted out before he could take any more wild guesses.

Baz's face went blank. Completely slack, like he'd shut it off and retreated into himself, leaving the facade unmanned. Even though I knew what he was and had always been aware his physical, tangible appearance was indeed a facade, this was unnerving. I'd never seen him drop any part of his act before.

It only lasted an instant before the life returned to his eyes. Not the fire, though—that seemed to have been fully extinguished by the news.

"Are you talking about the fairy girl who left her boy with me this morning?"

"Yes. Noah. Why did she leave him with you? Did she say?"

"No," he said, then closed his eyes for a moment. "I mean, yes. She said, but she lied."

"You can tell when people are lying?" I asked, even though I probably didn't want to know the answer. But then I realized he had to be wrong. Becca couldn't have been lying, because she was incapable of it as a fae. Wouldn't Baz know that? "Never mind," I said. "Can you tell me what she said anyway?"

"Hmm . . . I think she said she needed to hide him from his father for just a few days, and would I please watch him because she couldn't think of anywhere safer where his father wouldn't be likely to come looking for him."

"And you thought that was a lie?" It didn't sound like a lie at all. In fact, it sounded like exactly the most likely reason Becca could have for leaving her son with someone like Baz. But if she was trying to hide him from her ex, it meant there would have been a development in his case against her—a bad one. And if she had told Baz some sort of half-truth . . . what could she be hiding that was even worse than that?

"She was hiding the boy from someone, but not his father." With a glance at the skeptical expression on my face, he added, "That girl was never hard to read. I almost didn't hire her because she was so bad at lying. But a man with tits in his face is the easiest creature on the planet to lie to, so I figured she'd probably still do just fine."

I shook my head, trying to imagine how the world must look through Baz's eyes. It was like we were all the same to him, simple creatures, and he couldn't be bothered to distinguish fae from human from bird from the tiny ants under our feet. Of course Becca couldn't lie, but if she was the one fae in the world who was also bad at glamour and deception, I sure as hell hadn't noticed.

"She did do fine. More than fine," I assured him. Then, feeling spiteful that he seemed to not even know who she was, I added, "Until she spontaneously combusted in the middle of her dance routine a few hours ago."

"She died at my club? Why didn't you tell me sooner?"

"I'm sorry, I didn't realize that would be the most important detail to you. My friend, your employee, and Noah's mother has been gruesomely murdered—but I'm so sorry I didn't take a picture of the pole she died on so you could assess the damage." I stood up, nearly spilling my tea as I set the glass down a little too forcefully. "I'm going to find Noah."

"She was on a pole?" Baz screeched. Then he coughed as he scrambled up to follow me out of the room. "Never mind, I get it. You know it's not easy for me to keep track of your mortal priorities; I meant no offense."

I didn't acknowledge him, just stopped when I reached the first door in my path and opened it. Linen closet. I closed it and kept going. One of these doors would lead to Noah. I didn't need Baz's help.

"Okay, okay, I get it. You want to talk to the boy. I'll take you to him," Baz's voice rang out from behind me, the pitch a bit higher than usual.

Yep, it definitely put him on edge to have a human on a rampage in his home. Good to know. But this only solidified the decision that had been floating through my mind during our conversation—I wasn't going to leave this house without Noah. I didn't think Becca would want him here now, not with Baz acting this way.

When I spun around to face him, Baz jumped back a little. Then he put his big smile back on as he beckoned me off down the hall.

We turned two corners before he opened a door that led to a stairway, going down. Hmm. I hadn't known Baz had a basement. I shouldn't have been surprised, though. The town homes in this area were so narrow and packed close together that they probably all had basements, just in the interest of maximizing space.

The thing that made it odd was that most people I knew who lived in these types of homes had sectioned them off and built new entrances to each of the levels. Most people could only afford to live in a town home's basement, or first story, or second story, but certainly not all of the above. Baz wasn't most people, though.

"The boy is remarkable, you know," Baz said softly as he hobbled his way down the steps. "His father is not human."

"Isn't the father fae?" I had never asked Becca, just sort of assumed. Fae tended to mate exclusively with other fae. They were one of the few races who had been intermingling less and less as the years went by, instead of more. Back when magic and all its creatures had been secret to the world, the fae had thrived. They had perfected the art of manipulating humans, watching and analyzing and mimicking and poking and prodding, making a game of every exchange and always finding ways to come out on top. But these sorts of shenanigans only really worked when the humans were unsuspecting.

Once the world had become aware of the existence of other magical creatures, it became more and more difficult for anything to hide. The fae had nothing to gain by coming out into the open, but they were forced to do it anyway.

Human disbelief had been a powerful thing twenty years ago, but now that it was gone, the world would never be the same. The fae had been having a difficult time adjusting. While they used to fraternize and breed with all manner of other species before the Opening, now they tended to seek comfort in their own kind.

So I wasn't surprised to hear Noah's father was not human, but I was surprised that Baz would bring it up.

"No," Baz said. "Not fae."

Huh. "What, then?"

"Ah, that I can't say."

Can't, or won't? I wondered.

When I reached the foot of the stairs, I felt like I had wandered into someone else's home. More specifically, someone else's grandmother's home.

Noah was sitting on the floor, his chin propped up by pudgy arms that were braced on his knees as unruly wisps of white-blond hair fell over his eyes. In front of him was some kind of board game covered in marbles, which he didn't look away from even as I called his name.

Behind him, next to a cozy fire flickering in the brick fireplace, sat an old woman in a rocking chair who looked like she was sewing something.

What the batty hell was this? I really hoped it wasn't someone Baz had brought here just for the occasion of taking care of his employee's child.

"Oh, hello, dear," the old woman croaked cheerfully when she saw Baz, and I was instantly transported to one of my many idyllic childhood fantasies in which I'd grown up surrounded by a real family instead of a coven of mages who only cared about me as long as I was willing to train or heal.

I'd never had a grandmother to knit me sweaters or bake me cookies, and it was one of the few things I'd wanted so much, once upon a time, that the idea of it made my chest tighten and my cheeks heat up even now.

The old woman's eyes turned to me, full of protective suspicion that simultaneously made me like her and reminded me I was the one who needed to be protective right now. "Who's your friend?" she asked.

"That's what I was wondering," I snapped at Baz, trying to get a handle on my emotions. "Did Becca know you had someone else watching her son?"

Baz looked very much the part of an unsuspecting man caught between the competing wills of two women. Bewildered.

"Calm down, ladies. There's room in my heart for you both," he said when he caught his wits. "Darcy, this is my aunt, Salma. She's been helping me redecorate. And Auntie, this is Darcy, the woman who keeps my club from burning down when I'm not there."

"Poor choice of words for tonight, Baz," I reminded him, then nodded at Salma. "Did you say aunt? Meaning she's the sister of the woman who popped you out of her womb however many thousands of years ago?"

"I'm his father's sister, not his mother's," Salma answered, a small smile on her face. "But yes, that's the long and short of it. I'm not in this part of the world often, but I love to see my Bassam when I can. He never has enough socks, and never the right curtains." She tutted a little and then dipped her head back down to her sewing.

This couldn't be real. How did my crazy old genie boss

somehow have a family more normal—more human—than mine?

I raised my eyebrows in silence, and the look on Baz's face told me exactly what would happen if I ever dared call him Bassam. It was bad enough I had dropped the "bawdy" for tonight, but probably a good thing I hadn't said it in front of his aunt. I swallowed, the implications of the word "aunt" hitting me fully. How old this woman must be. Older than Baz, by potentially . . . a lot. She could be as old as the world itself. Then again, Baz had never told me exactly when he'd been born, so he could have been as old as the world itself, too. I'd somehow never let that put me on edge before, and now, with Salma acting all grandmotherly, the broken part inside of me seemed to find it oddly comforting.

At this point, Noah finally looked up from his game. He turned to Salma and smiled as the pieces on the board briefly lit up in flame and disappeared before resetting themselves to their starting positions. "Auntie, I won!"

I gaped. Father not human, indeed. And apparently, Noah was enjoying his temporary grandmother figure as much as I would have at his age.

"Noah," I said softly.

He looked at me with bright eyes—brighter than I'd ever seen them before. "Hi Darcy," he said, then looked back down to his game. "Can you tell my mom I don't want to go home yet? I'm having fun with Auntie!"

His words stabbed at my heart. And suddenly, I couldn't tell him that he'd never be able to go home again. Not really. My head swirled with justifications . . . *Won't it be better to wait until he starts missing his mom to tell him the truth? That way he won't feel guilty for not missing her.* I knew that was bat shit. But my stupid heart was still clinging to the stupid hope that Becca might not be gone forever, after all . . . so the bat shit won and

I put off what a more rational person would have known as inevitable.

I walked up to Noah and knelt down, wanting to touch him but somehow feeling like I shouldn't.

Twisting my hands together in my lap, I said, "Actually, your mom sent me here to ask if you wanted to stay with Auntie and Uncle for a couple more days." After meeting Salma and seeing the way she had Baz eating out of the palm of her hand, I felt much more comfortable leaving the kid here than I had a few minutes ago.

"Really?" Noah asked.

"Yep. She misses you so much, but she wants you to have fun. And she has something very important to do that you wouldn't like much."

"Oh." Noah reached out and moved a piece on the board, then looked up at me. "Well, can you tell her she should come play with us when she's done?"

Heart. Stabbed. Again. "Sure," I whispered as my chest swelled with anxiety.

"Do you want to stay and play with us now?" Noah asked, oblivious to my pain.

Oddly, I did want to stay, even though I usually avoided games. Simeon had loved to play games, in secret, when it was just me and him away from all the advisors and reporters and constituents. I'd always enjoyed it, but I would never know if that was real or just another part of his effect on me. It felt safest to assume the worst.

"Um . . . I can't play right now, Noah. But is it okay if I ask you some questions that might help your mom get done faster?"

"Okay." He put his hands in his lap and twisted his body to face me.

"Do you remember meeting a man named Ray?"

"Nope."

"Well . . . do you remember meeting any new friends of your mom's recently?"

Noah looked to the side for a moment as he chewed on his tongue. "I thought her only friends were you and Etty." He gave me a tiny shrug. "Sometimes she talks to my friends' parents at school. When she picks me up."

"Oh! That's good." I nodded in encouragement. "Any friend in particular whose parents she talks to a lot?"

"There's a new girl at school, Carina Sanchez. She's really pretty but she really likes snakes. It's kinda gross." He scrunched his face up and stuck his tongue out.

"And your mom likes to talk to her parents?"

"Just her dad. I don't think she has a mom. That's probably why she likes snakes so much. I know girls don't usually like snakes."

Oh, sweet innocent child. You have so much to learn. "Thanks, kid."

He narrowed his eyes at me, and for a brief moment I thought I could see fire swirling in their depths. But then it was gone, and all I could see were those chubby cheeks and that hilarious pout as he protested, "Hey, I'm not a kid!"

"I know, I know. A kid is a goat and you're a fairy."

". . . and I'm a fairy," he finished at the same time as the words came out of my mouth. It was something we'd started saying, at his insistence, after Becca had taken him to his first petting zoo and he'd been shocked to learn we'd been calling him the same thing as a baby goat.

I stood, then reached out and brushed my fingers through his soft hair. "Gotta go," I said to the room as I turned and bolted back up the stairs.

Noah was safe here for now, and I had an evil single dad to take down.

9

WHEN I BURST out of Baz's front door, the darkness of the empty street reminded me that school wouldn't be in session for another six hours or so.

And sure, I could always break in and hunt down a file with "Carina Sanchez" on it to find out where she lived. But there was no guarantee the school's records would be accurate; and in fact, if Ray had plotted to get close to Becca—if he was really someone capable of making a fae woman burst into flames and burn forever after in a magical realm full of weird obsidian rabbits—I was willing to bet the school's file on his daughter was not at all accurate.

My next few hours would be better spent researching.

I managed to get into my car without stepping in any slush this time, then managed to drive home without smashing anyone else's car to pieces.

The living room was empty when I got in. No Etty on the couch, and she had even taken both our coffee mugs into the kitchen and rinsed them out.

I plopped down into the furry sofa, propping up my legs on the coffee table and picking up my tablet. It would have been nice to have a more powerful computer, but I'd never had one that wasn't Guardian property, and I hadn't been able to justify the cost of a new one when I'd left. The tablet let me research cocktail ingredients and keep up to date on world news, and until now that had been more than enough.

Taking a deep breath, I opened the browser and typed "volcano bunnies" in the search box.

To rub salt in the wound of how pathetic my life had become, the first thing that came up was a video of a "volcano" cocktail being lit on fire by sexy women wearing bunny ears.

Yes, that looked really cool. But I wasn't going to help Becca by getting anyone drunk. Not this time.

I deleted my search terms and started over.

Think, Darcy. I was probably looking for a god. A fire god associated with volcanoes.

Vulcan was the obvious choice, but I'd never heard anything of him associated with rabbits. Plus, ancient Rome was crazy far away, both spatially and temporally. And because most gods had fallen from power before the Opening due to declining human belief, whoever I was dealing with had probably originated closer to home; they would be more likely to have believers keeping them in power in this place and time.

Okay. North America, then. Volcanoes.

"Where are the volcanoes in North America?" I asked my tablet.

It showed me a map with a bunch of red dots in Alaska, a bunch of red dots around the Pacific Northwest, and a bunch of red dots in Mexico. All pretty much equally far away from DC.

So I was dealing with either an Inuit god, a Native American god, or an Aztec god. Another quick search turned up nothing obvious for the first two, but there were multiple Aztec volcano gods. Xiutecuhtli, lord of volcanoes, was the first result to come up. But something made my eyes scan down the screen before I clicked, and I thought I recognized another name. Popocatépetl. Why did it look familiar?

I tapped to filter through the rest of my browser's open tabs, then went back to the map of volcanoes in North America. One of the biggest active ones that showed up in Mexico was named Popocatépetl. And there was a picture of a rabbit on its info page . . . "volcano rabbit, also known as *teporingo*." It was one of the few animals that lived in the area, and it looked just as small as the obsidian rabbits that had been stalking me.

Of course, I'd searched for "bunny" instead of "rabbit" at the start, or I would have found this immediately.

When I clicked through to read about Popo the god, I saw that he was part of a pair. His volcano was positioned next to a dormant one representing his sleeping lover, Iztaccíhuatl. Popo and Izta. And in the pictures, Izta looked remarkably like the mountain I had seen behind the burning sacrifices—behind Becca on the stake, pleading for my help. I would never forget the way she looked against that backdrop, the uneven, worn-down peaks of the low mountain, covered in snow, making everything about Becca look smoother and brighter. Izta's peace offsetting Becca's anguish.

This was it. The obsidian cave I'd run out of had to be inside Popo.

Even better, the fact that the god was attached to a real-life volcano of the same name made him more likely to be active in the world today. The other gods would be out of sight and out of mind now, even if they'd been more powerful in ancient times, but Popo's volcano would be a constant reminder to everyone who lived near it or visited it, and belief would stay alive much easier.

Then there was the story. Well, it looked like there were multiple stories from multiple sources. But the simplest one— the one that stuck in my mind and was likeliest to stick in the minds of others—was that Popo and Izta hadn't started out as gods at all.

They had been human lovers, wanting to marry. Izta's father would only allow it if Popo first went to war, and if he failed to return alive, Izta would have to marry someone else. Izta had so little faith in Popo's skill in battle that she killed herself to avoid having to be with another man. But he survived, and came home to find himself a dead fiancée.

And if I knew men . . . that shit would have traumatized Popo. The one person who was supposed to believe in him had thought so little of him she'd had no hope to even keep herself alive. Could this wound have fueled a grudge through all these years, leaving him to amass power and then . . . travel the world hunting women to burn that reminded him of Izta?

Nope, that didn't add up. Becca was the furthest you could get from an Aztec maiden. And moreover, the other victims I had seen burning next to her weren't even all female.

I squeezed my eyes shut and rubbed them, feeling the sting of exhaustion and frustration hit at the same time. When I laid my hands down and looked up, the glare of the rising sun pierced through the kitchen window across the room and washed over my face.

Time to get ready for school. The gods and their probably insane motives could wait. Or, hopefully, when I cornered Ray at his daughter's school and forced him to talk, he could fill in some of the blanks.

I yawned and got up, running my fingernails along my oily scalp to soothe an itch as I walked to the bathroom. Ugh. I really needed to wash my hair, now that I would be forced to wear it down in public. Especially if I was going to look professional enough to pull off what I had planned at the school.

Hope you don't mind, blobby, I thought as I gave Miriam's glob on my neck a teasingly affectionate poke. Then, using every single tidbit of Etty's sexy lessons I could recall, I popped out my butt and thrust my chest towards the mirror, slowly unbuttoning my top in a manner that would have gotten me all the bills in the room at Baz's club. Here, my only audience was Miriam, and I was willing to bet this would annoy her enough to give me some privacy for my shower.

The blob shivered a bit and I chuckled, savoring the peace as I stepped into the tub and let the hot water refresh me.

When I emerged, Detective Crane was sitting in my living room. Playing with the unfinished puzzle Becca and Noah had left in the middle of the coffee table.

"Don't touch that!" I shouted, then ran over to slap his hands away and stopped short when he backed away on his own.

His head snapped up and he froze, the whites of his eyes looking huge as the rest of his face darkened.

And then I realized I was in a towel, my hair still dripping wet, boobs ready to pop out if I so much as twisted in the wrong direction, bunny-claw wounds on my thigh on full display. Not that I cared about anyone seeing me like this . . . but it looked like he sure as hell cared.

I couldn't tell whether it was extreme fear or extreme excitement or extreme confusion, or some mixture of them all, but whatever it was, it was making him extremely uncomfortable. It only lasted a brief moment, though, before he coughed and squinted his eyes and choked out, "I'm sorry."

"You should be." I dropped to my knees by the puzzle and scanned it over, quickly picking out a couple pieces he had moved and replacing them. "This is Becca's."

The unfinished hummingbird stared back at me blankly, even though it had no eyes yet. It was just a blur of quick-moving wings and a purposefully sleek beak against vibrant foliage, with a jagged hole where its head should be. They always saved the most crucial part of the puzzle for last.

Because in that moment when the last piece completed an animal's gaze, it was like bringing them to life in one step.

Becca had grown up in the wilderness, only beginning her life as a part of human society less than twenty years ago, after the fae courts had been forced to shift their people around, change their tactics. She'd said she liked living in our world, but I knew she would never lose her love for nature. Breathing life into animals and plants. This puzzle was one of the ways she had been teaching Noah to do the same.

"It's for Noah to finish," I said softly, almost to myself.

"Of course," Crane said. When I looked up, he was staring down at me, specifically my wounded leg, which I had splayed out at an odd angle to keep from getting blood on the carpet. "What happened?" he asked.

For a moment, I just gaped. How could he not know what had happened? Then the blob on my neck squirmed a little, and I realized Miriam must not have told them about the creature who'd attacked me in my garage. But if anything, that was the one thing that had happened since yesterday that she absolutely should have told the police—I'd left a dead body there, after all, and it hadn't been there when I'd returned from Baz's. Had Miriam sent someone else to clean it up?

I made a bright-red, bolded mental note to pay Miriam a visit at some point, since she obviously knew something I didn't if she would keep this from the detectives.

Crane was still staring at me, and I was just staring back like a crazy person. I made a show of snapping out of it and said, "Ah, it's nothing. I fell on some sharp rocks when I was chasing Ray last night. Almost forgot about it. I'd better go put some ointment on . . . and clothes."

I stood up, trying to ignore the suspicion in his eyes as they followed me. Luckily, he didn't press the issue. But before I could walk away, he said, "Well, I just came to look at Becca's room, if that's okay. Can you show it to me? I promise I'll try not to touch anything you don't want me to."

Becca's room . . . it hadn't even occurred to me to search it. Because I hadn't yet accepted in my bones that she was truly dead. "How did you even get in here?" I asked, not ready to address the issue.

"The door was unlocked. And Miriam told me it would be okay to let myself in."

I almost snorted trying to hold in my laughter. "Miriam did?"

"Yeah, I'm in the habit of trusting her because, you know, she knows what we're all thinking. But I guess she doesn't always have the purest intentions."

"She must not like you very much, if she's telling you to walk in on someone who could so easily kill you."

"She must have known you wouldn't," he shot back, with a pointed look at the squishy pink growth on my neck.

Okay, I officially hated this now. *Touché, Miriam. No more peep shows for you.* "I need to get dressed. Sit down and don't touch anything, please." Without waiting for a response, I turned my back on his taunting smile and shut myself in my room.

I had to dig all the way to the back of my closet to find something that would be appropriate for the task ahead of me. I had gotten rid of all my pant suits when I had left my old job —or, more accurately, Etty and Becca had gotten rid of them for me when I'd first moved in with them.

Most of what was left was a mix of worn-in denim, loose T-shirts, and sexy bartending tops. But I did still have a dress one of my aunts had given me before I'd left for Guardian school.

She had bought it for me under false pretenses; that was, she'd thought I would be applying to college as a pre-med student, and this was supposed to be my interview dress. It was emerald green with gray details, a structured fit, and long sleeves.

With some long socks, clean boots, and my nicest jacket, I could make it work for this weather. And it exuded just the right amount of respectable without screaming business. Probably why my roommates had let me keep it.

It took some grunting and shifting to squeeze into, as I had undoubtedly put on some muscle since my high school days, but once it was on it didn't feel too tight.

Grumbling once again at Miriam's blob, I dug out the smoothing hair cream I hadn't used in ages and ran it through the dark, loose, damp curls that were already forming as my hair dried. I picked my fingers through it while drying it the rest of the way, like Becca had shown me months ago, and the result was . . . actually decent. The blob was covered, and the overall effect was shiny and wavy and—bats, I looked way more put together than I felt.

Becca would want me to at least put on some mascara to complete the effect, but she would just have to settle for me saving the time and using it to try to save her life. Or avenge her death. Whichever it ended up being.

After throwing my smallest gun into my biggest purse, I returned to the living room and was blasted by the smell of fresh coffee.

I narrowed my eyes as Crane peeked out from the kitchen, looking anxious.

It was disorienting, seeing him in my home like this. He was disorienting. With his height and stature and job title, he should have the same sort of confidence I had. He *looked* like the kind of person who could walk into any room and knock away anyone who tried to stop him. So why didn't he act like it?

"Hang on," he yelled across the room at me, then disappeared behind the wall.

I didn't hang on. And when I turned the corner into the kitchen, he was holding my elephant mug out at me, filled with coffee that looked like it had been made just the way I liked it.

"I told you not to touch anything," I said, but I took the coffee all the same.

"Right, but Miriam called again and convinced me you didn't mean it."

Miriam, as usual, had been right. After a quick glance to make sure Crane was drinking out of the visitor's mug (a ladybug—Noah's pick), I closed my eyes and took a sip.

It was delicious, and I wanted badly to stop myself from saying so. But Miriam would still know, and somehow the idea of trying to hide it was more embarrassing than just admitting I was grateful. So I said, "Thank you," and then swiveled around, walking towards Becca's room. "Come on, Detective Asshole."

"Hey," he said as he hurried to follow me. "Hang on a sec."

With the caffeine flooding my system and heightening my reflexes, I turned so quickly that he nearly ran into me. All burly six feet of him.

"What?" I asked as he got his bearings.

"You should also take this." He handed me a protein bar, with no further explanation, and I wondered whether Miriam had told him I'd forgotten to eat or if he could tell just by looking at me that I probably would.

"Thanks," I said tersely as I grabbed the bar.

Before I could turn around again, he reached out and briefly touched his hand to my shoulder, stopping me in my tracks. "And I . . ." he said. "Can we maybe start over? You can call me Adrian—that's my first name—and from now on I promise I won't do anything just because Miriam says it's okay."

I narrowed my eyes at him. "Is this a tactic to get me to

trust you so I'll tell you all my secrets about being a scary assassin and then you can arrest me?"

"What? No, I know you're not a—" He paused and shook his head. "Look, I'm actually pretty decent at my job, and I could tell from your reaction after your friend died that you were never an assassin."

"Oh."

"And if we're going to work together, we should be on better terms," he continued. "It's bad enough trying to get things done with someone like Dirk as my partner, I don't need you fighting me every step of the way on top of it."

"I wasn't—"

"You were," he said.

"Okay." I sighed and turned my back to him again, certain that Miriam had also told him coffee would make me more agreeable. I didn't know if I trusted him more or less now that I knew he had some social skills, but I didn't want to waste time debating it now.

I felt him behind me as I touched my fingertips to Becca's door, and although it felt like a violation of roommate trust, I pushed it open.

Sunlight streamed in from the windows behind her bed. As usual, her curtains were wide open. Unlike me and Etty, Becca had always been a creature of the daylight. And at least so far, Noah was the same.

Even though he didn't stay here often, Becca had gone to the trouble of making the queen-sized bed with two sets of pillows and blankets—flowers for her and stars for him. He could rarely stay awake for the darkness needed, but that kid loved to look at the stars and dream of other planets, faraway galaxies.

Coughing as an excuse to cover my pained face with my hand, I stepped out of the way and let Crane—*Adrian* in the room.

Then, as he stepped in past me, I coughed for real. And when I took a deep breath afterward, I smelled it. Gas.

That made no sense at all. There were no gas lines in the bedroom, obviously. We had just come from the kitchen, and it had smelled fine.

Adrian turned to me and scrunched his nose. "Do you smell—"

"Yes," I said as I rushed in. Chilling moisture came up through my stockings from the carpet. Adrian was still wearing his shoes, but I hadn't put mine on yet. I dropped to a squat and pressed my palm to the ground, then brought my hand to my nose. "It's in the carpet," I said. "It's like someone was planning to torch Becca in her sleep, but then decided he wanted witnesses."

"Or . . ." Adrian said, the word drawn out like he was putting off saying the rest.

I looked up to see him standing by Becca's trash can, a crumpled slip of paper in his hands that looked like a receipt. A long one. "Or what?"

"Or *she* was planning to torch someone else, and spilled in here by accident." He handed me the paper and I stood to read it.

A fuck-ton of money spent to buy a fuck-ton of kerosene, and matches, and salt. "Why the salt?" I asked.

"Maybe she was trying to burn some kind of demon? Trap it first, then kill?" He moved over to the corner of the room, behind Becca's dresser. "Look, though. She definitely stored it here."

I looked and, sure enough, there were marks in the carpet where multiple heavy containers seemed to have been sitting.

"Becca is . . . the least violent person I've ever met in my life. She would never hurt anyone unless it was to protect her son. And even then, fire would be her very last resort. She's a creature of the forest, trees. Fire has always terrified her."

"Becca *is?*" he asked.

"Yes, I remember—my friend just died. You don't have to be a dick about it," I said quickly. I had zero interest in letting the police think I was even crazier than they already thought.

It was starting to scare me how much my subconscious wouldn't let me think of Becca as dead. I was usually the one in the room screaming out cold, hard truths, no matter how tough they were to swallow. This felt like I was losing control of my mind.

"I have to run," I said, needing to get out of here. "Text me if you find anything else. And don't take anything."

"Sorry—" he started, but I was already in the other room.

No time to change my stockings, and I only had one decent pair with no rips anyway. So I slipped on the clean boots I rarely wore because they were too flimsy to protect my feet from falling knives and broken glass, and I hoped they were at least thick enough to hide the smell of my gas-soaked feet. Plus two of my smallest daggers, of course—though I wouldn't be upset if they didn't fit, since I had six more hidden in my jacket.

I had bought this jacket specifically for hiding knives, for when I wanted to be deadly without looking the part. It was still leather, sure, but with a perfect suede finish that made me look like I'd never rolled around in an alley covered in someone else's blood. It made me look soft. The power of zippers and inner lining.

Before I walked out the door, I noticed Etty had left her phone on the table by the entrance, under the whiteboard we used to leave notes for each other. And she had left me a message:

No phones in court. If you need me, clap three times and say <u>elephant bitch</u>.

There were hearts drawn around it. Smiling, I picked up her phone. No sense leaving it here alone. If I did need to summon her, then at least I could hand it to her. I slipped it into my jacket's pocket as I hurried out the door and down the stairs to the garage. Which was pristine.

I paused for a moment before walking to my car, a little shaken by how innocent this place looked, the perfectly normal white-gray ice on the pavement sparkling in the morning light. No blood soaked into the cement where I knew it should have been, from what I'd seen of the remains of the shifter I'd bludgeoned to a pulp just hours ago.

I made a snap decision when my hand grasped the car keys, and I dropped them back into my purse. It would be better to take the metro anyway, so I didn't have to wrinkle my dress sitting down.

I turned around, taking shallow breaths and wondering just who the fuck had cleaned this up if Miriam hadn't told the cops about it. And for the first time, I felt like I might really be in over my head. Questions were piling up faster than I could chase down answers.

The cave, the bunnies, the gods, the Sweepers' ice witches, Miriam, Becca plotting to commit arson of all things—and I was still just trying to track down Ray. I had never faced such a challenge without Guardian resources, which would have included a whole team on something like this.

Maybe it had been a bad decision to keep so much from Adrian, who was just in my apartment without his useless partner, trying to help me. But it was too late for that, for now. I could work on trusting him more next time.

More than anything, I had to keep moving forward. And my plans for Ray were long overdue.

Snowflakes swirled in the air as I walked up the school steps.

Noah would love this, I thought, and then I wondered if Baz or Salma had thought to bring him in today. I hoped not. Running into him could put a snag in my plan.

When I opened the door, it screeched, the sound echoing into the empty hallway.

No matter how old I got, being in a school's hallway while classes were in session would probably always put me on edge. The knowledge that so much was happening behind so many closed doors, and the implied forbidden nature of being outside of them all, skipping class . . . Of course, it didn't help that in Guardian school, we'd been subjected to magical torture for doing just that.

Psychics roaming through our minds to pick out our worst memories and fears, then intensifying them. Fae hijacking our nervous systems to make it feel like our bodies were turning into intricate, bloody pretzels. And of course, vampires letting our blood while making us want it, which was enjoyable during the act but horrifying enough to whip anyone into shape after the fact.

Yeah, many of my classmates had dropped out with trauma they'd probably be dealing with their whole lives. But that was the point. If they couldn't handle it, they couldn't be allowed to graduate. The organization was only successful because of the stellar success rate of their graduated Guardians—I was a rare case.

And as I walked past the green lockers, smoothing the wrinkles out of my dress and patting the melted snowflakes out of my hair, I tried to will myself back to the Guardian I'd been before failing. Confident. Calm. Calming. My presence shouldn't put people on edge; it should make them feel safe.

I stopped in front of the administrative office door, taking a deep breath.

I let it out as I turned the knob, my eyes alert and the smallest smile I could manage behind my cheeks.

Holy bats, I thought immediately, trying not to let the shock show on my face. It felt like I had stepped right back into the Guardian Academy. The office looked more like the lounge at a country club than a place of work, and it smelled like a library—but an expensive library. A university's library. Chairs were plush, desks were grand, and books filled the walls that somehow looked old and shiny all at once.

Of course, I should have known this would be an expensive school, with what I knew about Noah's father. And the Guardian Academy had been much like this. But that was a professional school directly run on the profit made by its graduates, who were all adults; this was glorified babysitting for six-year-olds.

"Hello, ma'am, can I help you?" the woman at the desk closest to the entrance asked. She looked a little younger than me, maybe early twenties or late teens, and was wearing a plaid sweater with a button-down shirt underneath. Every single button was buttoned, all the way up to her neck. It had been a while since I'd seen a woman dressed like that. Suddenly I realized how odd it was that I felt more separated from regular society as a bartender at a strip club than I had as someone who killed people for a living. At least with the killing, I hadn't flashed my cleavage on the regular.

I looked Buttons in the eyes and gave her a small smile, reaching into my pocket. "Yes, hello. I'm here on official business."

Quickly, but relaxed, I slipped my old Guardian badge out of my pocket and flashed it at her, holding it open for a good few seconds while maintaining eye contact.

Long enough so she would feel awkward about asking me to show it to her again, but short enough that she was unlikely to notice the name and the date of expiration as she felt compelled to keep looking back to my friendly-as-fuck face out of politeness.

"I need to see Carina Sanchez," I said, diverting her attention before slowly putting my badge away. "Her father is a client and we have reason to believe he and his family may be in danger."

That was true enough. He was in danger from me.

"Oh, of course. One moment . . ." She tapped her short, lilac-colored fingernails onto her keyboard, and her butt was out of her chair before her eyes left the screen. "106," she mouthed to herself, then turned to me with a smile as she stood upright. "I'll take you to her now."

I narrowed my eyes and twisted my neck to watch her as she walked past me into the hallway, disbelieving. She wasn't even going to call Ray for permission to release his daughter?

Shit. I hadn't expected them to actually let me anywhere near Carina. I'd just been planning on the threatening phone call to lure Ray to meet me somewhere.

I supposed that in a school like this, emergency Guardian pickups must be commonplace. Simeon was the only politician I'd worked for, and he hadn't had any children, but I knew many of them did. And they were probably all used to being shuffled around on the regular for their safety.

My heart twisted a bit at the reminder of just how trusted Guardians were, on such a large scale. How powerful my Guardian badge really was. How much it meant. How much I'd lost. Maybe the fact that I was using it to kidnap a small child now just proved how much I'd never deserved it.

Buttons beckoned to me from the hallway, looking a bit wobbly in her long pencil skirt and heels that were clearly meant for sitting at a desk—nowhere near as stable as the ones the dancers wore at the club. I cleared my throat and followed her, walking stiffly as my mind raced trying to decide what I was going to do with Carina once I had her. I had only been planning to threaten her as a bluff, but that would be much harder to do if I actually had her as a hostage. If she was right there with me, it would be obvious I didn't mean to harm her.

Buttons stopped at a classroom and motioned for me to wait in the hall while she went inside. When she came back out with a familiar-looking little girl trailing behind her, I realized that maybe I wouldn't have to bluff my threats after all. The girl's green eyes lit up when she saw me, and after just a tiny moment of shock, she ran over and threw her arms around me.

"Darcy!" she said with her face pressed against my dress. "My hero! We were about to have a math quiz, but now I don't have to take it!"

Ah, my demon goddaughter. I knew we'd meet again.

I patted her hair and smiled at Buttons, who was watching the display with just a hint of disapproval. "Thank you," I said. "I'll be sure to let her father know how helpful you were." Then I looked down at Carina, who was still attached to my dress.

"Come on!" she said, and without another word she

grabbed my hand and marched down the hallway, leading me out of the school.

A FEW MINUTES LATER, I was watching the demon child swing back and forth at the playground outside of the school, snowflakes melting and then sizzling on her skin as they fell, while I squinted at her trying to decide whether or not she was plotting my death. She had texted Ray before we'd even gotten outside, telling him to meet us here, and I half expected him to show up guns blazing.

Instead, I was greeted by a warm hand on my arm, a wide smile, and a graze of stubble on my cheek as he kissed the air in front of my ear.

How un-American of him.

And sure enough, as I tensed under his invasion of my personal space and he said, "Sorry about last night," I detected a slight accent in his voice.

I opened my mouth to ask which part he was sorry about—torching my friend or running away afterward?—but I was too angry to even get the words out.

It would have been one thing if his daughter had acted frightened and confused, like a proper hostage, and if he had made me hunt him down, threaten him, fight him, torture him, kill him . . . But this? This acting like we were best friends, like I hadn't watched Becca go up in flames after spouting nonsense about how she had to do it for him . . .

No. Just no.

I felt my rage clawing at my insides, begging to be let out. I wanted to take his head off right here, right now, on this damn playground, and then watch the kids kick it around during recess.

Before I could take in a deep breath to calm myself, I shoved him.

Except I did it without moving.

By accident.

With magic.

Like a gust of wind glowing with energy, shooting from my hands to his chest, leaving a charred hole in his shirt and knocking him off his feet.

A delighted chime of laughter rang out through the crisp air, and I looked over to see Carina still swinging, her eyes on me. When her giggles died down, she slowed the swing to a stop and said, "Do it again!"

Ray was groaning and sitting up now, his butt still in the snow, and I swallowed as I watched him.

Okay . . . something weird was definitely going on with me and magic. So many things were wrong with what had just happened.

So many things.

I shouldn't have been able to access that much power in the daylight, for one. I had never even been taught how to attack people like that, two. And three, it had happened without my consent. I'd had no control over that at all.

I looked down at my hands, which seemed normal. But they tingled. And when I closed my eyes and searched inside myself, my scrye felt . . . immense. Powerful. Unwieldy. A little like it had felt when I was younger and the coven was still making me practice healing magic. But nothing else had ever made it feel that way, and it was worse now than it had been then.

Then, it had felt like a foreign being inside me, gently using me to juggle other people's lives. Now, it felt like it would overwhelm me. Take me over. Like it could blow me up at any moment and take the world with us.

"What was that for?" Ray asked as he brushed snow off his backside.

"I don't think she likes you," Carina chanted in a sing-song voice that made me think she was probably one of the bullies in Noah's school.

What happened to the timid girl I met in the alley? I wondered. She hadn't been allowed to interact with me at all then, but I supposed now the jig was up.

I clenched my fists, trying to calm the magic buzzing inside of me.

"Tell me what you did to Becca, and maybe I won't do it again," I bluffed. I didn't know if I *could* do that again, but I did know there were plenty of other ways I could hurt him.

"I did nothing but help that poor girl," Ray said, and Carina bobbed her head up and down from the swings, as if to back him up. "Her son was in danger."

"What? Because she was a stripper, she couldn't possibly have been a good mother? So you needed to murder her to protect her son?" I regretted it as soon as I'd said it, knowing how stupid it sounded. Becca's job may have caused people to look down on her, but it wasn't a likely motive for murder.

I was just still angry about her ex using her work as ammunition in their custody battle, and something about Ray calling her "that poor girl" had rankled me in the same way. Becca had dealt with her share of problems, just like the rest of us, but she'd never been deserving of that kind of pity.

"What's a stripper?" Carina asked, a slight waver to her voice as she held in a laugh. I'd bet anything that tiny demon knew exactly what a stripper was, and she just wanted to make us have to explain it.

Ray had the same idea, apparently, because he turned to her and snapped, "A stripper is who I'll call to strip your skin off your bones if you don't behave." He paused a moment before raising his eyebrows at her.

She huffed once, then stuck out her tongue and started swinging again, humming an annoying song I didn't recognize.

Ray turned back to me. "I didn't murder her. And I know

that any mother who works hard to keep her child is a good one. My own mother abandoned me, just like yours."

I jolted, as if he had sent my magic attack back at me. And a short "What?" was all I could get out.

"You don't remember me, Darcita? We were orphans together, for a time. Until your mother came back for you."

I didn't remember him, no. And my mother had never come back for me. I'd never known her, or my father. Before I could say so, Ray had walked back up to me and reached out his hand, putting his palm to my cheek. I felt the magic inside me concentrate where his skin met mine, tingling and hot, and the energy coursed through me from my face, overwhelming me with its potential.

"Your body remembers me," he said softly.

Anger jerked through me again, and I pushed it down before it made me attack him again, which I had a feeling he might take as proof to his point.

Instead, I swatted his hand away and growled, "My only memory of you is the one that makes you the primary suspect in Becca's murder. So start talking, or I'll just get on with it and take my revenge. You said her son was in danger—from what?" Before he could say anything, my mouth kept moving. "And where the fuck did you take me when I chased you in the alley? You have a cave full of rock rabbits who keep the souls of your victims tied up and burning? What are they, your trophies? Are you some kind of wannabe-god serial killer?"

I knew I should have stopped after the first question, but they'd been building up for so long that I couldn't stop the torrential flood once I'd started asking.

Ray was looking at me like I was crazy, which I kind of hoped was true at this point. It would be nice if I'd gotten it all wrong and there were no gods or serial killers involved, just some fun hallucinations left over in my mind from all the time I'd spent letting a vampire play around with it.

But Ray didn't seem as taken aback as he would if I'd been spouting nothing but nonsense. He tapped his fingers against his side for a moment, then said, "I'll tell you everything I know, but first I need you to look at something for me." He turned back to Carina, who was slowing her swinging again. "The book, mija."

Carina hopped off the swing and skipped over to where she'd left her backpack in the snow. She unzipped it and pulled out a book. For a moment she looked like she wanted to toss it at Ray, but instead she tucked it under her elbow and somberly walked it over to us. She held it out between us, and I couldn't tell if she wanted me or him to take it.

I clenched my teeth, biting back the protest that had been on the tip of my tongue. It seemed like he was doing everything he could to distract me from the information I'd come for.

But there was something about this book . . . I had no idea. It looked old, worn. Nothing written on the cover at all. Some part of me wanted to take it, open it, dive into the pages even though I knew nothing of what I might find in them.

Ray delicately took the book from Carina and came to stand at my side, holding it in front of us as he opened it. "This book belongs to us both." He flipped through the pages so I could see, but all I saw was emptiness. The pages were all blank. "It will only show itself to us both," he explained, and then he pushed the book out further towards me, moving his hands to one side, gesturing for me to grasp the other.

What the hell? I thought. This was clearly nonsense, but in my experience the best way to deal with nonsense was often to indulge it and let it implode of its own accord.

"So if I touch this Book of Nothing with you, then you'll tell me about Becca? Is that the deal?"

"Yes," he said. And it sounded like he meant it. He must really want to collect my fingerprints.

I sighed and grabbed it, then waited a moment in silence for something to happen. When nothing did, I looked up at him and said, "Like this?"

He narrowed his eyes at the pages in front of us, which were still quite blank. "Yes, but—"

"Oh no—nope. 'But' nothing. I'll even keep my hands on this thing while you talk, but if you don't start talking now, I drop the joke book and pull out my weapons."

He sighed, then flipped through a few pages of the book—still all blank—before he looked back at me with disappointment in his eyes. "What have they done to you?" The words came out in almost a whisper.

I just stared at him, not willing to indulge this second round of nonsense. Maybe he really had me mixed up with some other person, or maybe this was all an act to distract me. Whatever the case, I was done playing along.

Finally, he broke away from my gaze and snapped the book shut. Handing it back to Carina, who took it without a word, he said, "Fine."

Carina walked somberly back to her bag with the book. Once it was securely zipped inside, she plopped down on her back beside it and began swinging her arms and legs around to make a snow angel, humming again.

I kept staring at Ray, waiting.

"We came to this city to find you," he said in a monotone voice, his eyes looking off in the distance. "And when we did, we also found Rebecca and her son. I knew immediately what the boy was, so he became our priority. His father would have killed him, you know. For being a half-breed. That was the only reason he wanted custody. But Rebecca had no idea, until I told her. I was only helping her save the boy's life."

If that was true . . . then maybe Becca had been telling Baz the truth after all about trying to hide Noah from his father.

"But why?" I asked Ray. "Let's assume for a minute I

understand why you were stalking me in the first place—why does it matter to you *what Noah is*? He's a child, for fuck's sake. That's all he is."

"He's no more just a child than you are just a bartender."

"Answer the question. You said you would answer my questions." I was losing patience again.

"That is my answer. He is a creature of fire, like you and me and Carina. A *demonio*, but half fae . . . he will never be accepted by his kind on either side. But in our family? Our strength is that we are all different, and the fire of our god binds us. Rebecca would have seen that he will be safer and happier with us."

The fire of our god. So they were witches, too. I'd never encountered a witch before yesterday, and now I was suddenly drowning in them.

I almost opened my mouth to confirm that their god was who I thought it was, the Aztec legend Popo, and that it was his cave I'd been in, but that would only derail the conversation further. I didn't like the way Ray had been talking about Becca and what she would have wanted. "Let me guess," I said instead, "you killed her because she thought that sounded creepy and cultish?"

"No. We hadn't gotten to that part. We were still on the part where I was trying to help her kill her ex-husband."

My face scrunched up in disbelief. "Becca wasn't a killer," I said.

But then, looking at the calm expression on Ray's face— the expression of a man who had nothing to lie about—I remembered the kerosene Adrian and I had just found in Becca's room.

My phone started ringing, the sound coming from my coat. *Bats*, I thought, looking down at my pocketless dress. Normally I kept my phone in my pants. My jacket was only supposed to be for weapons, and I didn't remember which of its many pockets I'd put my phone in.

I awkwardly patted myself down while trying to ignore Ray's eyes on me as I did. When I finally found the little chunk of ringing metal, I accepted the call without looking to see who it was and said, "What?"

"Still haven't learned any manners, I see. Not helping your case, little lady. But hello to you too," the voice on the other end said.

I grimaced and took the phone away from my ear to look at the screen. The cops. But not Adrian. His dolt of a partner. Lovely.

"Hello," I said back into the phone, and then I waited.

"Uh . . ." Dirk paused, probably confused that I hadn't apologized and begged him to show me mercy. "Crane told me to call you," he said, all business now. "Wants you to come to the burn site we're working. Texted you the address. Former residence of a . . . Omar Kanaan. You got that?"

Omar. The name rang wildly in my ears for a moment before finally making it to my brain. That was the name of the man I'd been angry at for so long despite never having met him—Becca's ex. Noah's supposedly murderous father.

"Well?" Dirk snapped over the phone. "Don't make me regret this, witch girl."

"Got it," I said, then hung up as I stared disbelieving at Ray, who was looking at me expectantly.

"What was that?" he asked, as if he didn't know full well.

I frowned at him, lost in my thoughts. If Ray had been helping Becca kill Omar . . . he may not have been the one to kill her, but he'd done something almost as bad.

Omar had been a high-profile politician with a reputation to uphold, just like Simeon, and no matter what he was, I had a hard time believing he would have killed his own son. It was much more likely that was a scare tactic Ray had used to manipulate Becca because he clearly wanted to steal Noah away into his fiery witch cult.

Ray sighed at this point and took a business card out of his pocket. "When you want to see me again," he said, tucking the card into one of the front pockets in my jacket, "come by my shop. And bring Noah—I'll make him something nice to eat."

No chance in hell of that, I thought. If Becca really had torched her ex-husband, then Ray was probably the one she'd been hiding Noah from by sticking him with Baz. And I trusted her instincts.

Ray smiled as he stuck his hands in his pockets. "Don't bother Carina here again. She has enough trouble keeping her grades up without such distractions."

"Hey!" she yelled from her snow angel, which looked more like a blob as she had melted the snow all the way down to the brown grass underneath her. "My grades would be fine if you didn't make me spend so much time—"

Ray snapped his fingers at Carina, and she shut up quickly. Then he turned away from me and walked off toward the street. Carina hopped up with a little snort, snatched up her bag, and waved at me quickly before rushing after him.

The wind picked up and a chill came over me as they left, my stomach rumbling and my eyes beginning to feel just a tiny bit heavy. As much as it scared me to admit it, the magic in their presence had energized me, and my tired body was feeling its loss.

But I'd gone without sleep before, and for much less dire reasons than this. Breathing out my annoyance at the situation, I pulled out the protein bar Adrian had given me, took a bite, and pushed through my fatigue like I'd been trained to do.

It was time to go see what havoc my girl had wreaked on her jerk of an ex.

11

Luckily for my sleep-deprived butt, Noah's father lived within walking distance of the school. And what a walk it was. I had put on my nicest outfit to go into that school, but it still wasn't nice enough for me to look like I belonged in this neighborhood.

There were hardly any cars on the streets here. They were probably all locked up in the garages of these mansions, behind wrought-iron gates and long, winding driveways and lawns that looked like golf courses. It was all smaller than what you would see in California or out in suburbia, of course, because real estate was tight this close to DC, but it was still unquestionably grand.

Even Simeon hadn't lived in a neighborhood like this. He hadn't had a family, so he'd preferred to stay in a penthouse apartment in the city. Now, walking through this pristine, lush, compartmentalized display of houses that seemed more like individually guarded prisons, I realized I would probably prefer that, too.

As I neared the address Dirk had given me, a charred scent infiltrated the air.

I turned a corner and saw flashing lights up ahead, the road suddenly cluttered with official vehicles of all shapes and sizes. No ambulance, though. I supposed that meant there were either no casualties or they had already been dealt with.

The burnt smell wasn't nearly as strong as I'd have expected, and I saw no visible flames or smoke littering the air ahead, so this probably wasn't a fresh crime scene. Which made sense, if Becca really had caused it before her death last night. Maybe this was the second time the cops were visiting, now that they'd linked Omar to Becca.

I remembered Becca coughing on the phone earlier in the day, telling me she was just running somewhere, having gone into the city to help Noah . . . and I'd jokingly asked if Noah had burned down our place. I'd known instantly that Becca had been breathing in smoke. My training and experience had known. But that hadn't seemed like something she would try to hide, so I'd given her the benefit of the doubt and assumed normalcy. Assumed she had a damn cold.

I shook my head, disappointed in myself.

As I got closer to the scene, I began to wonder where the damage was. I'd expected to see burned-out ruins of a mansion like the others I'd been walking past, but the only buildings before me were still pristine. The cars were still far enough away that the other buildings could feasibly be hiding the burn site, but it was unlikely they would hide it entirely. Could it have been burned completely to the ground?

Curious, I sped up a little. Then a searing pain shot up my leg through the bottom of my left foot.

I stumbled, crashing into the trunk of a tree next to the sidewalk. I slid down the trunk, trying not to scream, and looked back at where I'd been walking to see a charred wooden board with a nail sticking out of it—the nail coated in my blood.

Awesome. This was what I got for wearing my pretty boots.

Sleek instead of clunky, but a damn nail had gone right through the sole.

Had there been an explosion with the fire? No . . . that would have created more debris, and I couldn't see any other charred bits of house lying around.

"Hey, are you okay?" a man's voice called out to me, and a second later someone wearing gloves ran over to me, a paper face mask hanging around his neck.

He knelt by me and picked up my wounded foot without waiting for me to answer. He must have seen me fall, because he knew which foot I'd hurt even though the damage wasn't visible.

"I'm fine," I said, wriggling my foot out of his grasp. "Just help me up?" I put my hand on his shoulder without waiting for his response, then hoisted myself up between him and the tree.

When I tried to put weight on my wounded foot, my leg crumpled beneath me. I fell, practically crushing the man who had come over to help me.

"You don't seem fine," he said, picking up my foot again. "Here, let me assess the damage. Then I'll go get supplies and bandage you up."

He unzipped my boot and slid it off before pulling out a pocketknife to cut my stocking away from the bottom of my foot.

I sighed, squinting my eyes in frustration at my not-very-helpful savior. If he hadn't seen me, I could have easily used magic to heal myself enough so I'd be able to walk. The sun was still bright, yes, but healing was the skill I'd spent my entire adolescence mastering. The family business.

It was also the one skill I tried to keep secret. When people knew you could heal, there was no end to the guilt trips—and if you gave in, you'd spend your time doing nothing else. That might be fine for some, but I'd been miserable spending my

108 | ERIN EMBLY

days healing. Just like I would be miserable spending my days stripping. Even when you have the physical capability to do a job, it doesn't mean you have the aptitude.

"How does it look?" I asked the man, resisting the urge to kick him in the face and tell him to go away.

"Hmm . . ." He prodded the tender skin around the puncture wound on the bottom of my foot, and his gloved hand came away bloody. "It looks perfect."

"What?" That was an odd thing to say about a—*Oh, fuck.*

The man threw back his head and opened his mouth, and then . . . he kept opening it. Until his jaw looked completely unhinged and the gaping hole in his face was bigger than his entire head should be. His teeth disappeared entirely, but his tongue thickened and elongated and darted out like a frog's, twisting around my ankle before wrapping entirely around my foot, until it was all but lost in the pink, sticky, disgusting prison.

I clenched my jaw shut, trying not to lose the protein bar I'd just eaten. I could actually see my blood being pulled through the semi-transparent . . . appendage . . . into his mouth. Gross.

"What are you, a vampire frog?" I yelled at the creature, and my stomach stopped doing backflips. Yelling always helped me counter nausea. But the thing ignored me. It just kept sucking the life out of my foot.

Had the market for immortality been tapped so fully that the vampires were now innovating and creating blood-sucking pets? Hybrid vampire shifters?

More importantly, why wasn't it turning into ice? So far I'd only had icy assassins sent after me, which made sense assuming they were all working for the same group, the Sweepers. Did this new devilry mean someone *else* was trying to kill me?

Whatever it was, and whoever it was working for, it was about to be toast.

I had been propped up on my elbows so I could look at what he was doing, but now I laid my back flat on the ground to free my arms. Hopefully, he would think I was passed out or submitting.

Before reaching for my knives, I tentatively checked inside myself, putting a metaphorical finger on the pulse of the magic coursing through me, wondering if I could repeat what I'd done to Ray at the playground. But it wasn't there. The magic in me felt normal—weak.

So I slipped my fingers into my big jacket pocket and pulled out the serrated hunting knife everyone at the Academy had made fun of me for carrying around.

I used it for cutting bread more often than not, yes . . . but it was also much more effective than a regular dagger when it came to cutting certain body parts. I kept it mainly for quick, easy throat-slitting, but it was also perfect for this ridiculous tongue. I had a feeling if I'd tried to stab the thing like I'd stab someone's torso, it wouldn't stop the creature and I might end up stabbing my own foot.

Instead, I jerked myself up and lashed out at the part of his tongue in between my foot and his mouth. In a flash, I'd dragged the serrated edge of my knife crosswise along his tongue and then again the other way. Two deep cuts, but what I really needed was three.

The tongue was hanging on by a thread, and blood—my blood—was oozing out of it. But I didn't get a chance to make the third cut, because at that point the frog-vamp's hands shot up and grabbed mine, like vices around my wrists.

The knife became useless as he slammed my wrists into the ground, leaning forward over me and closing the gap I'd made in his tongue by engulfing the whole mass with his mouth.

Whatever. I could still move my leg, so I pushed it out and rammed it into the back of his throat. I hoped he choked on it.

He didn't. But it did make him gag a little. When he opened his mouth reflexively, I yanked my foot out with a jerking motion.

The tongue tore the rest of the way where I'd cut it, and he screeched, so loud and so high pitched that I nearly dropped my knife to try to cover my ears. But I had more self-control than that. So I rocked my body forward instead, careful not to put any weight on the disgusting mess that was my foot with a severed vampire-frog tongue still wrapped around it.

For a moment it looked like the creature was going to run away, scooting back and moaning incoherent, garbled nonsense. But then its mouth closed, and it clenched its fists around the snow we were both sitting in, and I saw color eerily flush its skin. When its eyes opened, they were bright and hungry.

The thing wanted my blood enough to die for it.

Opening its mouth again to reveal the nub of a freshly grown baby monster tongue, it launched itself at me just as I was launching myself at it.

My knife met its throat before its mouth met my foot, and I sawed. Once was all I needed this time to slit the thing's throat, but I had no idea what it was or whether a slit throat would actually kill it. If it was a vampire, despite the lack of teeth and the whole out-in-the-sunlight thing, its head would need to come off entirely.

So I pounced on top of it, pinning it on its back as blood gushed out of its neck, and I kept sawing until my blade was cutting the ground beneath us. Then I grabbed the head by its hair—no way was I going to touch that tongue—and I tossed it away from us quickly, like it had cooties. It probably did.

Finally, kneeling over the thing's headless corpse, I relaxed a little. Then I heard someone whistle like a catcaller, and I looked up to see Dirk standing on the sidewalk with the creature's head at his feet, a trail of blood indicating it had rolled up to him.

"It sure don't look like you're not an assassin from where I'm standing, missy," he said.

"How did you get to be a cop with no understanding of the concept of self-defense?" I shot back.

He at least had enough good sense to leave the head where it had rolled, though I could see his fingers twitching; the curious little boy inside him wanted to pick it up and ogle it. He walked over to me instead and offered me a hand.

I wasn't above letting him help me up. Trying and failing to stand on my own would have been worse.

Once I was up, I let go of him and used the tree for balance.

"What happened?" he asked, nudging the tongue still wrapped around my foot with his toe. "A kink turned bad? You like long tongues? Getting your toes sucked?"

He winked at me, and my stomach turned over again.

Luckily, I didn't get the chance to punch him because at that point, Adrian ran over. "Hey, are you ok? Miriam called and—" He paused when he got close enough to see the body and my foot. Crouching down, he squinted at it. "Is that a tongue?"

"Yes. Any interest in getting it off me?" I stuck my foot out at him as I asked, hoping he would help me without feeling the need to make any jokes. I really wanted the slimy thing off me, and I honestly didn't want to touch it with my hands.

Adrian peered at my foot for a moment, and his eyes lit up. "Oh, cool." He pulled on a pair of gloves and poked at the tongue. After a glance at the headless body on the ground next to me, he looked back up at us, almost as excited as Dirk had been in the strip club. "I think this is a *palis*."

"Huh? Like a castle?" I jiggled my foot a bit as I asked,

hoping he would take the hint and get it off me, whatever it was.

"No, P A L I S. It's a vampiric creature in the djinn family, documented in Persian folklore. Lives in the desert and attacks travelers in their sleep, drinking from the soles of their feet. Never thought I'd see one here."

"How do you know so much about it?" I asked. Even with my Guardian training, I'd never heard of the thing. But then, I hadn't been the most attentive student when it came to folklore and mythology. We all had our weaknesses, and I preferred to kill first and ask questions later.

Adrian looked up at me. "I spent a lot of time studying for the DoSC exams, years ago, but—"

"But he's too good for them," Dirk interrupted, not a hint of sarcasm in his voice, and I realized it was the first thing I'd heard come out of his mouth that wasn't idiotic or malicious. He put his hand on Adrian's shoulder, and I could see a bit of embarrassment fade from Adrian's face.

"Well, not weird enough might be more accurate," Adrian said, and I understood.

The DoSC didn't like hiring humans any more than the Guardians did. I'd gotten through because of my healing skills, despite my reluctance to use them. Adrian must have had nothing to offer except his basic human intelligence, so he'd studied to make the best use of it he could.

"I know a lot about weird creatures, though," he said, a bit of excitement returning to his voice. "The palis is supposed to be pretty unintelligent, so how did this one get the drop on you?"

Thankfully, he unwrapped the tongue from my foot as he asked, and I breathed a sigh of immense relief when it slipped to the ground next to me.

"Oh, you know—trusty old board-with-nail technique." I pointed to the object in question, still red with my blood.

"Huh. He was even dressed like someone working the crime scene . . ." Adrian seemed mesmerized, distracted. And I was not okay with that.

"Speaking of the crime scene," I said, snapping him out of his thoughts, "what have you found?"

"Ah, well, we were able to access the neighbor's security camera, and—"

"Shut it, Crane," Dirk interrupted. He was suddenly eying me like I was a bomb ready to explode. "Look." He pointed to the ground where I'd been lying, and we all looked to see Miriam's pink mind-reading "squishy" crushed into the bloody snow.

I pulled my hair up to feel the back of my neck and, sure enough, the blob was gone. But instead of relief, all I felt was frustration. I'd walked all the way here, fought off a frog vampire who'd tried to suck my life out through the bottom of my foot, and now these chucklefucks weren't going to give me any information about the crime scene because they didn't trust me without Miriam being able to read my thoughts.

"Oh, come on," I whined. "I didn't do that on purpose. Look, I'll even put it back on." I stooped over to pick up the blob, but I knew as soon as I touched it that it was dead. Flaccid and slimy and dull. "Ew." I dropped the thing and wiped my hands on my legs, forgetting I was wearing a nice dress today instead of my usual old jeans.

"Don't let her on the scene," Dirk said. Firmly. "Not without a squishy on her."

I rolled my eyes, and Adrian twisted his head to the side with his lips pressed together. After a moment, he turned to Dirk and said, "Can't we just—"

"No," Dirk interrupted again. Then he turned to me. "Not a lot you need to know anyway. It was the stripper. She torched the place. Got footage of her hauling and pouring kerosene all over after a two-hour visit. Screams Black Widow. Must've regretted it and torched herself too."

"That's—"

"Not our official theory," Adrian reassured me. "Becca's death is still an open case."

"Good," I said, then shook off my anger. I couldn't let Dirk get to me if I was going to get anywhere with these two. "Look, I didn't want to say this before, but I'll go to the press if I have to."

"The same press that blasted you for killing the blood-sucker last year? What, you miss the spotlight?" Dirk let out a haughty chuckle.

"No, but they might be interested to know the local police and DoSC turned down help from an ex-Guardian on what's now a high-profile case. My reputation's not great, but I was never convicted. Officially, my record's clean. Officially, I'm someone you can't afford to ice out."

Adrian was smiling at me again, but his face flattened when Dirk turned to him, apparently done with me. "I can't deal with this shit right now. Tell her whatever she wants to know so she'll stop bitching. But if I catch her on that crime scene, there'll be hell to pay." Dirk turned to me and snapped, "Press might care if I ice you out, but the higher-ups will have my ass if I let a suspected assassin poke around a crime scene without one of those on." He pointed to the dead squishy on the ground. "Liability and shit."

He spun around and marched off without waiting for a reply, leaving me and Adrian staring at each other in silence.

I was starting to feel a little wobbly now from the blood loss, and from the standing on one leg. I clutched the tree trunk to adjust my weight, and Adrian's arm was under my shoulder before I got a chance to tell him I could hold up my own damn self.

My body relaxed automatically, leaning into his strength to

conserve mine. Well, shit. Complaining now would just be rude. "Thanks," I said.

He peered down at my wounded foot. "Are you okay? Looks like you're still bleeding."

He curved his arm around my back, securing his hold on me. As nice as it felt and as helpful as it was, what I really needed was to get away from him so I could heal myself.

"I'll be fine," I said, trying not to wince as I set my wounded foot on the ground and transferred some weight to it.

When I pulled myself away from Adrian, he looked more uncomfortable than I'd ever seen him, which was saying a lot. He frowned, eyes fixed on my foot.

"Just tell me what you found and I'll get right to a hospital," I lied. I hadn't been to any kind of medical facility since I was a teenager, and I avoided them at all costs. Too many bad memories.

"Okay, well, we do have footage of Becca with the kerosene, which adds up with what we found in her room."

He was still staring at my foot, so I snapped my fingers at him and said, "Eyes up here." When he looked up, I asked, "Do you have footage of Becca actually lighting the fire?"

"No. The fire's point of origin was on the other side of the house. Off camera."

"And she was here for two hours before pouring the kerosene?"

"Yes. She came, rang the doorbell, was let inside, and then came out the same way two hours later. We think she spent at least some of the time restraining Mr. Kanaan."

"He was restrained? So you found his body?"

"We're waiting for confirmation of identity, but yes. We're pretty sure it's him. She had him tied down with flame-proof straps, more than necessary and in an intricate pattern, covered in salt. And he'd been decapitated. The amount of premeditated organization suggests she was afraid of him. We suspect some kind of magic significance, but we haven't been able to pinpoint it." Adrian reached into his pocket and pulled out his phone. "The coroner's people already left with the body; I'll have Miriam send someone out for this one." He gestured to the dead palis at my feet.

But before he could press anything on his phone, a new message flashed on the screen. His face creased and he quickly turned the screen away from me. Not as open a book as he seemed, then. Great.

I looked past him towards the burn site, my mind fixated on what it was they could be hiding from me. Should I trust that Adrian would tell me everything, or should I sneak in now and find it out for myself?

"Hey." Adrian's voice snapped me out of my thoughts. "You don't want to do that."

"Do what?" I asked innocently.

"Give Dirk another reason not to trust you."

I scrunched my face up at him, squinting because he was so damn tall I couldn't look at him without getting the sun in my eyes, and let out a huff.

"I know, he's impossible," Adrian said. "But it gets worse if you fight him and better if you don't. And like it or not, he's not going away anytime soon."

How dare he make such a reasonable argument? I huffed again, looking away so he couldn't see that I didn't mean it quite as much this time.

He cleared his throat. "Anyway, we should figure out why the palis targeted you. It might be connected to Becca's case. Is there anyone you know of who would want to hurt you?"

I almost snorted. "Of course," I said. "Everyone who thinks I'm an assassin, for one."

"Right." He looked down.

I got the sense that he was grasping for something to occupy me with more than anything else. Whatever news he'd just gotten on his phone, it was something he didn't want me to know—or something he wanted to run by Dirk first.

After a brief moment, his eyes snapped back up to mine. "What about Bawdy Baz? Isn't he a kind of djinn? Like the palis?"

"Sure. But he pays me to make sure his business runs smoothly, so I'd say he's one of the last people who would send a frog-vampire with a foot fetish after me."

"Well, he might at least know more about who would have the resources to send a palis after anybody in this area. Why don't you go ask him?"

Adrian gave me a fake-as-shit half smile, and I narrowed my eyes at him. He was clearly just trying to give me something better to do than sneaking into the crime scene.

But he did have a point. Baz might know something about the freakish creature that had carried out this suspiciously premeditated attack against me. I couldn't write it off as belonging to the Sweepers because it hadn't used ice magic and it wasn't wearing one of their ugly pins.

And I could tell that Adrian was uncomfortable as hell trying to manipulate me right now. It wasn't in him.

So I said, "Yep, great idea," and gave him an intentionally huge fake smile. "I'll call you with whatever I find out. Because I'm a team player."

I could practically see my words cut straight through his guilty-innocent soul. This man had never not been a team player in his life, and it showed.

"Bye!" I said cheerily, then waved at him and turned away, taking tiny careful steps to the curb of the street so he wouldn't see how much my foot still hurt. I pulled out my phone and requested a car from a ride-share service to take me to Baz's, even though we were north of the city now and Baz lived in southeast DC.

There was no phone I could call to reach him when he

wasn't at the club, so I would have to actually go see him if I wanted to talk to him.

But there was no way I'd be walking to a metro station in this state. And if questioning my boss about a creature that had just assaulted me with its tongue was the best way for me to learn *something* useful right now, I would have to take it.

12

MY BOOT WAS FILLING up with blood as I sat in the back of a bug with cream-colored seats, trying not to show it on my face. I'd had to slip my ruined shoe back on (after rushing to patch the hole with some chewed gum) when I saw the car and realized I wouldn't be allowed inside otherwise.

Adrian's texts were blowing up my phone already—it hadn't taken him long to cave to the guilt of keeping me out of the loop, I supposed—but I was trying to ignore them for now so I could concentrate on healing my foot enough that I could at least do a better job of pretending it was fine.

It was hard enough to concentrate already with the cheery driver incessantly chatting, speculating on all the gruesome details of the crime scene she'd picked me up at. All she'd seen was some burned wreckage, and she was convinced someone had summoned a demon to open the gates of hell.

At least she had yet to master the art of pausing after asking questions. She didn't seem to expect me to say anything, and that was a small blessing.

I closed my eyes and did my best to tune her out, focusing on the magic in me and around me. Once again, it felt weak.

Like it always did during the day—maybe even a little weaker. I hadn't eaten enough or slept in too long, I knew.

But healing had always been easy for me. I should be able to do it without even seeing or touching the wound. I could feel it. Not just the pain, but the hole in my flesh. The disruption of order. The cells separated and dying, wanting to rejoin. The blood leaving my body unwillingly, wanting to be held in. Millions of cells calling out to me like lost little children, needing guidance.

And I couldn't help them.

The magic wouldn't listen to me.

It was *there*—not a lot of it, but it was there. And it wouldn't move. It wouldn't change. It wouldn't do what I wanted.

I opened my eyes, frustrated, and the world was blurry. My cheeks were wet. The driver's words were muffled and distorted in my ears.

I'd always known this could happen. *The magic isn't mine.* It had never been mine. I'd repeated that phrase like a mantra all throughout my childhood, forced to say it over and over because the coven leaders had known it would be impossible for me to understand otherwise. Once you could sense the magic, it felt like it was a part of you. Just as much as your skin, or your lungs, or your legs.

But it wasn't. And despite my having said the words so much that *they* had practically become a part of me, I had never really understood them until this moment. Until I'd tried to heal a basic wound of all things, on myself—the last thing I would have ever expected to fail at—and had the magic not obey.

"Do you think they have hippopotamuses in hell?"

The driver's words crashed into me as the car lurched to a stop. When I looked up, I saw Baz's mermaid statue staring at me from outside. "What?"

"Hippos. You know, because no one knows if they're really

good or bad. One minute they're all cute, slow and fat and eating grass, and the next minute they're running you down and trying to eat you, and all you wanted was a picture for—"

"No," I said. Firmly.

Finally, the driver paused. "Why not?" she asked.

"Because there's no such thing as hell," I answered. "When we die, we're just gone."

That shocked her into silence long enough for me to get out of the car and slam the door.

It was an unpopular opinion, now that the world was filled with provable magic out in the open. Most people had taken this as confirmation there would be an afterlife, since it was the one magical thing so many had believed in even when they had no good reason to. No one wanted to be gone when they died. Even if it meant contemplating the possibility of going to hell.

But I only believed in what I had seen with my own eyes, and throughout all the vampires and shifters and fae and djinn, and even fucking mermaids, I still had yet to see or hear of any ghosts. There were no necromancers summoning the dead, no fortune tellers holding seances—not real ones, at least. Which was part of the reason I needed so badly to figure out what had happened to Becca.

Not only so I could bring her killer to justice, but so I could know whether it was really her I had seen in that god's realm— her soul, possibly trapped for eternity, burning. If it was . . . it would be a big deal. And not one I would stand for.

My phone buzzed again as I limped up to Baz's door, and I pulled it out to see a string of texts from Adrian. He didn't know how to get to the point, apparently. I scanned through to find the meat of what I needed to know, which was four messages up:

Someone stole Becca's body.

Great. Another thing to add to the list of crazy I had to

make sense of. What could anyone want with that charred corpse?

I sighed. Realistically, this was actually a great lead. The kind of question whose answer could solve the whole case. But I'd never been a great detective. Sure, I'd taken classes in this kind of work at the Academy. But there was a reason I'd worked in security after graduation, and not investigation.

My brain was excellent at assessing threats, preventing bad things from happening when they were right in front of me. But working out why crazy people would do crazy things? When there were this many misshapen pieces of the puzzle? With every new detail I learned about Becca's case, I only felt more in over my head.

I pushed my phone back into my pocket and rang Baz's doorbell.

This time, he opened the door instantly. And for the first time since I'd known him, I thought he looked a bit frazzled. Frantic.

"Oh, birdie—thank the stars. Are you here to pick up the child?"

"That bad, huh?" I asked, stepping in past him. "I always thought Noah was a good kid."

"He is, he is. Quite good. Better than good. But my aunt is . . . Well, it's been a very, very, very long time since she's had a child to care for, and her enthusiasm is . . . astounding."

"Good to hear he's in enthusiastic hands," I said. "But that's not why I'm here."

Baz's face fell, and he grumped over to the kitchen to make tea, almost like a puppet on strings. Open door, let in guest, make tea—a routine he probably hadn't veered from in a millennium.

I followed him, deciding to get right to the point. "I was just attacked by a palis."

That got his attention. He turned around and eyed me

suspiciously, as if I was trying to pull one over on him. "Birdie, do you even know what a palis is?" he asked with disdain.

Without responding, I sat down on the floor of his still-furnitureless kitchen and took off my boot. Blood dripped and smeared all over the tiles, and Baz almost dropped his tea kettle.

"Not on the tile!" he shrieked, running over to me with a towel.

He wiped up the floor frantically, then balled up the towel under my foot. Peering at it, he asked, "How under the stars did you manage to find a palis on this continent? And . . ." He paused, looking up at me with a bit of worry in his eyes. "How did you escape it?"

"I sawed off its tongue and then removed its head."

Baz's eyes got all big and round and buggy when he heard that, and he leaned in close to whisper in my ear, "Let's not tell my Aunt Salma that, little bird. She doesn't take kindly to people who dispose of our kind."

"It was sucking the blood out of my foot!" I yelled at him.

"Oh?" Salma's voice interrupted our argument. I looked up to see her standing in the doorway, her hand on her hip. "Did you encounter one of the creatures I brought over?" She walked closer and leaned over me, crouching down with more agility than a woman with her appearance should have. She pushed the dainty glasses up on her nose as she said, "I sold the last of them a few days ago, so I'm afraid I can't be held liable for anything they've done since then."

At that point, Baz got up and shuffled out of the room, grumbling, leaving me alone with the cheerful old woman.

"You . . . brought vampire-frog-men from the other side of the world and sold them?" I asked her.

"Of course. That was the main reason for my visit. I was trapped in a teapot for ages and only recently freed, but all my assets were stolen in the meantime, so I needed to get back on my feet somehow." She pressed her lips together and peered at me closer. "You aren't DoSC, are you? You have to tell me if you are—so you can't act on anything I said without knowing."

"Don't worry, I'm just a bartender. Former Guardian."

"Ah, so you must have plenty of enemies from your past, and one is obviously a client of mine." She clapped her hands together and stood up straight again. "Maybe you're in the market for some exotic minions of your own, to protect you? I've sold all the palis, but I have other—"

"I think I'll be fine," I said, interrupting her. I really didn't want to hear about all the other creatures she had apparently enslaved. The sweet grandmother persona that had captivated me at our first meeting was quickly falling away, and it was unsettling. Salma seemed to be just as unpredictable as her nephew. "Can you just tell me if you sold a palis to the Sweepers?"

"Let me check." She closed her eyes. A moment later, she opened them again and said, "I did, yes. What did you do to anger them?"

"I honestly don't know."

Baz shuffled back into the room then, his arms full with bottles and cloths of various shapes and sizes. He plopped himself down beside me and grabbed my bloody foot unceremoniously.

"Now birdie, tell me—why haven't you healed this yet? Please don't say you intended to bleed all over my kitchen just to get my attention."

I eyed him carefully, wondering how he knew I could heal with magic.

He knew I could infuse drinks because I'd shown him as a selling point so he would hire me as a bartender. But I kept my healing abilities very secret, and I didn't think I'd used them for anything at all since I'd started working for him.

"Ah, don't worry, birdie, I won't tell," he said, picking up on my wariness. "One look at you and I can see very clearly all you can do. It's part of what I am."

"I . . . tried," I said simply. "It isn't working right now." That was the truth, and all I knew.

He squinted at me and then clicked his tongue. "Oh yes, I see now. She's angry with you." He shook his head at me and then dove into the materials he'd brought, starting to dab my foot with a stinging liquid.

"What? Who?" I asked, but he ignored me.

"You really shouldn't take for granted what you have, birdie. Play nice. Do what she wants. You'll thank me later."

At that point, Salma chuckled. "It seems to be a recurring theme with you, yes? Angering people obliviously? You should probably learn to communicate better."

My own anger level was rising quickly, so I kept my mouth shut.

Baz and his aunt were acting less like the family I'd always wanted and more like the family I'd run away from. Berating me about some made-up nonsense I'd somehow fucked up while doing nothing to help me understand. I was starting to think I'd been monumentally stupid for letting myself get even a little comfortable around them, but then I heard a door squeak open, and Noah poked his head around the corner next to Salma.

"Hi Darcy!" he said in a rush before tugging on Salma's sweater. "Auntie, I finished it. I'm ready for the next one. Come on!"

"Alright, dear," she said, and they disappeared back down the hallway.

I sighed. Noah was happy here, and that was all that really mattered for now.

My phone buzzed again. When I looked down, there was another message from Adrian:

The body wasn't stolen.

It took a great deal of self-control not to crush my phone in my grip. The annoying play-by-play was bad enough, but couldn't he get his facts straight before passing them on to me? Had they seriously just wasted this much time because some intern had mislabeled the bodies and mistakenly reported Becca's as stolen?

The phone buzzed again, and a new message popped up:

It was reanimated.

I stared at the screen, at this point wondering if I had actually been dreaming since yesterday. That was the only thing that could explain this much crazy happening to me all at once.

Another buzz:

We saw her on camera getting up and walking out.

And then another:

Any idea where she would go?

Just then, I heard a crash from the entryway, like someone had thrown something through the window at the front of Baz's house.

"Yep, I think I have an idea," I said aloud as Baz disappeared from in front of me without a word, leaving my foot half-bandaged. It was nice to see where his priorities lay.

After shooting off a quick text to Adrian, I stuffed my phone back in my jacket and stood. The pain had lessened somewhat, probably a psychological effect from the wound having been cleaned and partway dressed, so I was able to make my way down the hallway fairly quickly.

When I got to the entryway, I saw Becca climbing in through Baz's broken window. Actually Becca. Not her reanimated corpse. It wasn't charred and twisted and shriveled and dead—it was my friend, the way she'd been before. She was even wearing the same blue and yellow lacy lingerie set she'd been wearing at work last night.

Which, as it turned out, was not the best outfit for climbing through a broken window. The jagged shards of glass were cutting into her exposed skin, and she was about to track way more blood into Baz's house than I just had.

"Bex . . ." I said, but she didn't acknowledge me at all. And now that I thought about it, she wasn't acknowledging much of anything. There was an empty look in her foggy eyes, and her mouth was hanging half open, and her movements were sluggish. She walked right through Baz—actually *through* him, and he had to temporarily vaporize himself to avoid being knocked over by her—as he tried to block her from coming in.

When he solidified again, he was yelling something about how no one had told him owning a strip club would mean letting naked women bleed all over his belongings all the time. Not in this day and age.

There was a good joke in there somewhere, but now was not the time.

"Bex!" I yelled, somehow hoping she would recognize me —or I would recognize *her*—if I raised my voice loud enough.

But she just kept walking past me into the hallway, and when I stood in front of her she walked right into me, shoving me like a steamroller, refusing to acknowledge my existence. Her blood smeared all over my dress, the green fabric she'd loved so much darkening in splotches of wet brown. And her eyes just kept staring forward, lifeless despite the movement of her body.

I put my hands on her shoulders and braced myself to hold her back, thinking that maybe if I could stop her, she would do something other than walk forward like a zombie.

Oh bats . . . was she a zombie?

Her eyes focused on me for a brief moment when I stopped her, and then she brought her arms up between us and punched me in the chest with both fists.

She was strong. I didn't fall on my ass, but I did stumble out of her way. My instincts told me to pounce on her from behind as she walked past me and tackle her to the ground, but I couldn't do that—not to Becca.

When she reached the door to the basement, she stopped short. Then she turned towards it, and she walked right into it. When it didn't budge, she stepped back a bit and tried walking into it again.

I groaned. Yep, she was definitely a zombie if she didn't even have the brainpower to twist a damn doorknob.

I heard Salma's voice call up from the basement, muffled, "Bassam? What in the world is going on up there? The boy needs to concentrate."

Concentrate on what? I wondered.

As soon as Salma had said his name, Baz disappeared from where he'd been standing next to me, and I assumed he'd gone downstairs to answer his aunt in person.

Becca's corpse, on the other hand, had frozen up at the sound of Salma's voice. Then she let out a terrifying snarl, her mouth opening to reveal the sharpened row of outrageously long fae teeth I had never seen her show to anyone before.

I knew all fae had vicious traits like this that they kept hidden behind glamours—but, well, most of them kept these things *very* hidden. Becca especially would never have let anyone see her like this unless they were about to die.

Would she try to kill Salma to get her son back? She had already killed her ex for Noah's sake, apparently, and that was when she'd had a working brain, or whatever the hell it was that made someone not a zombie.

Invigorated, Becca's corpse took a few steps back from the door and then ran at it, hitting it so hard she bounced off—and the door actually opened towards her after bouncing off its own frame. She ran forward through it and down the stairs into the basement, and I was left standing there trying to decide whether I was really going to go chase my friend and fight her to keep her away from her own son.

I had to. I fucking had to, even if it was the last thing I wanted to do.

If I didn't, Baz and Salma would deal with her somehow. And as much as Noah was already going to be traumatized just from seeing his mom as a zombie, it would be worse if he saw two djinn make her head explode—or whatever djinn did to people who broke into their houses trying to kill them.

I'd never seen Baz violent with anyone before, so I had no idea what he was capable of. But I had a feeling it wouldn't be pretty.

I ran to the doorway and down the stairs just in time to hear Noah shriek, "Mama! You're hurt!"

Becca's corpse launched herself at him and he shrieked again, this time in fear. But Salma had him wrapped in her arms, and Baz was using a broomstick to hold Becca back from them.

A *broomstick, really?* I thought. Becca's corpse was too strong to be kept back by that. But then I saw the faint glimmer of magic running down its shaft, and a moment later it was wreathed in blue smokeless flames.

Becca snarled again and leapt back when the flames touched her, and that was when I finally did pounce on her from behind, knocking her to the ground.

Out of habit, I expertly pulled her arms behind her back while holding her down with my legs. Then I realized I had nothing to cuff her with. I still carried a ton of weapons as a civilian, but no handcuffs. And in this cruel twist of fate, I'd finally happened upon an enemy I really couldn't just kill. She was already dead, for one, and also she was my friend.

"Baz, handcuffs!" I yelled while Becca's corpse squirmed underneath me. He probably had some pink fuzzy ones lying around somewhere, and that would have to be good enough. I wasn't sure how long I could hold her down like this.

Baz did me one better than kink cuffs, though. He tossed

me a jump rope. Once I had knotted it tightly around Becca's wrists, he touched it and it lit up with blue flames, just like the broomstick had.

Becca snarled again, but the flames didn't look like they were doing any damage to her skin, so I relaxed a little. Baz handed me another jump rope, and I looked at him blankly.

"How many jump ropes do you have down here?" I asked, truly wondering why he had any at all.

"Enough for a proper Double Dutch, of course," he said, and I decided not to delve into that particular dark hole. Instead, I snatched the rope from him and flipped myself around so I could get at Becca's feet while still holding her down.

Once her ankles were wrapped with the flaming jump rope just like her wrists, I stood up and watched as she thrashed around on the floor, her gaze never moving away from Noah, who was still standing by Salma and clutching her arm tightly.

"Okay," I said, forcing as much fake cheer into my voice as was humanly possible. "Noah, why don't we go upstairs for some . . ." Damn, I couldn't think of a treat good enough to lure the kid away from his zombie mother.

"Hot cocoa!" Salma finished for me, and I was at once grateful for the thousands of years of experience with children she probably had on me.

I tried to keep smiling at Noah as they walked up the stairs, and when they made it into the hallway and Salma closed the door behind them, I felt my chest clench and my knees weaken. But Baz was still down here with me, so I steeled myself and tried to forget the heartbreaking face of the heart-broken little boy.

"Do you want to do it, or should I?" Baz asked.

I turned to him slowly, not liking the sound of that. "Do what?"

"Cut off her head, burn her, bury her—everything of that

sort. I'd prefer for you to do it, and take her outside first, but I'm not above getting my hands dirty if you're too . . . involved," he said. "I would understand. I've been in your position before."

I rolled my eyes at him. "Oh, so you had a friend die gruesomely for no apparent reason and then come back as a zombie and attack you?" As soon as I said it, I remembered how old Baz was, and I realized the odds were he'd experienced many things that seemed unlikely to someone with a normal life span.

"Yes. A lover, actually," he said. "Although I suppose it wasn't my fault. And this is most definitely your fault." He looked at me with pity, like I would look at a child who'd dropped an ice cream cone in the dirt on a hot summer's day. "Don't worry, birdie, I'll do it."

"No," I snapped at him, stepping in between him and Becca. "No one will be doing 'it.'"

"Well, I can't keep her tied up forev—" He stopped, and I saw cool flames light up behind his eyes. "Do you think she could work like this?"

"I'm going to pretend you never said that," I said as I tried to banish the mental image he'd just given me of a zombie stripper chained to the stage at work like a damn freak show on a leash.

I pulled my phone out of my jacket and sent another text to Adrian.

All I wanted was to get Becca out of this house. Away from her son, who really shouldn't see any more of her in this state. And away from her boss—who, if he hadn't viewed her as an object before, certainly seemed to see her that way now. But I didn't have my car here, so I needed a ride.

I told Adrian to come without Dirk, who probably shouldn't be allowed around a near-naked woman tied up under the influence of zombie-ism. Then I turned to Baz.

"Help me carry her upstairs without hurting her, and maybe I'll be nice enough to help you find someone to replace me at the club tonight."

A look of panic flashed in his eyes for a scant moment, then disappeared. "No need, birdie!" He looked excited all of a sudden. "I'll go back to work tonight. I was only taking time off to redo my house and spend time with my aunt, and with the boy here . . . well, obviously that's not possible right now."

Baz gestured around the basement, which I hadn't paid much attention to before on account of my zombie friend being very distracting.

It was a complete and utter mess. The carpet was torn up in places, the paint on the walls bubbling and peeling, trinkets scattered all over the place—some of which were even warped, as if in a surrealist painting.

"What the . . ."

"I told you, the boy is remarkable. But, well, his abilities are untested and unexplored. To be expected, since he is a rare mix. And my aunt is a curious sort." I must have looked horrified, because he continued, "Oh, there's nothing to worry about, birdie. *Really.* It's good for him. Better he find out early what he's capable of so he doesn't accidentally melt his first girlfriend. Salma has experience with the process."

I narrowed my eyes at him. "Do you know what he is? On his father's side?" I asked, making sure to let him know with my tone that now was not the time for brushing me off.

"Not exactly, no," Baz sighed. "We suspect he's one of us—djinn—but there are many different varieties, so it's difficult to tell. Even if he weren't half fae, it would be difficult."

My phone buzzed before I could respond. Not that I even knew what to say to that.

It was Adrian. Texting that he was here, holding up traffic outside with his cop lights on, so could I please hurry up and bring out the zombie already.

Okay, so he hadn't really texted all of that. But he was probably thinking it.

I put my phone away and moved over to Becca, squatting down to hook my arms under her shoulders. "Get over here, Baz—you'll have to be Brawny Baz today. I'll get her head, you get her feet."

13

THE MUSIC PLAYING from the speakers in the cop car was way too peppy, way too fast, and had way too many instruments. Luckily, it was also turned down way too low—so low that the fact I could barely hear it annoyed me even though I could clearly tell I hated it.

Adrian had apologized, saying he needed to keep it low so he could hear anything that might come through on the radio. This also meant we couldn't do anything to drown out the steady thumps that were coming from the backseat, where Becca's corpse—properly cuffed now—was banging every part of her body against anything that would listen.

"So, did you ask about the palis?" Adrian said awkwardly as we both tried to avoid looking in the rear-view mirror.

I glared at him, hoping to convey without words that this was the last thing I wanted to talk about now.

He didn't get it. He wasn't even looking at me; his eyes were locked on the road, like a responsible driver, which was ridiculous because cops were usually the worst behind the wheel, just racing past traffic with their lights on for the heck of it. We had a zombie in the back of the car, and Adrian hadn't flipped his lights on even once. "Well?" he prodded.

"I did ask, and I got an answer, and it's not related to the case." I looked away from him and back at the road in front of us.

We were driving through Georgetown, which was supposedly one of the few places in the city that had remained largely unchanged in the years since the Opening. Attending university had become more popular than ever now that the world was flooded with young immortals.

I usually avoided this part of the city because I hated driving on the narrow roads through the throngs of pedestrians, but Adrian seemed unfazed by it.

It was the most efficient route to get back across the Potomac from Baz's place, I would give him that. But in this stop-and-go traffic, I knew the people walking on the sidewalks were staring through the windows into our car, and I didn't like putting Becca on display like that. Not in her current state.

"How do you know the palis isn't related to the case?" Adrian asked, refusing to drop the issue.

I sighed. "It was sent by the same people who sent the assassin last year—the one who actually killed Simeon Drake."

"And how do you know *that*?"

"Because they've been trying to kill me all day. Sending witches after me, of all things. I think. And I just learned they recently acquired a palis, or a few."

Adrian glanced at me with his eyebrows scrunched together in concern. "And . . . considering the timing, you think this is unrelated to your friend's case because . . . ?"

"Because they have an obvious connection to me, which is unrelated to Becca. And they've only come at me when I've been alone. And their witches have been using ice magic; nothing with fire. And there's no way such a high-profile political group would risk their necks going after a stripper even if she did hear or see something in the club that she shouldn't have. No need to silence a witness whose occupation alone would be enough to discredit her to the majority of the public."

"Okay, yeah, all that makes sense," he said. "But what 'high-profile political group' are you talking about?"

"Why?" I asked.

"Because Omar Kanaan was one of the Sweepers' most generous donors. So if it's them . . ."

Bats. I was sure Adrian could see in my wide eyes that it was them.

Suddenly I felt like an idiot for making assumptions. My brain really wasn't suited to this type of investigative work. I'd had to make assumptions every day to assess threats when working in security. In that line of work, I'd never had the luxury of taking time to explore every possibility. I'd had to take whatever actions I deemed most likely to result in the safety of my charge, without impeding his ability to do his job.

And the thing was, I could never be certain. There was always a small amount of risk I'd had to accept, because it was impossible to predict the future and it would be counterproductive to lock my charge in a box so no one could hurt him. Safety wasn't worth it for anyone if it came at the price of their freedom. So I'd trained myself to dismiss the doubts that prodded at my conscience when I had every reason to believe I was doing things right.

"What if I'm wrong?" wasn't always a productive question to ask in security, but it was apparently an essential question to ask all the time when it came to detective work. Especially on a complex case like this.

Adrian continued as if I had confirmed what he'd suggested—as if he could read my mind now even without a phone call from Miriam. "Okay, so we should probably go question the Sweepers once we drop . . . her . . . off at the station." He gestured at the back seat with a jerk of his head. At Becca.

I snapped my neck around to glare at him. "What are you talking about? We're taking her home. Look at the state she's in—you can't put her in a room with a bunch of men like Dirk."

"Dirk isn't really that bad, okay? He's all bark, no bite. And there are women at the station, too."

"That's not the point. Hasn't she been through enough? She doesn't deserve to be made a spectacle of any more than she already has been." I turned to look at Becca as I spoke, and for a brief moment she made eye contact with me.

Probably by accident. But it felt like a punch to the gut, because the life I saw behind her dull eyes was so unfamiliar. Like her body had been possessed by something evil and it was moving her around like a puppet.

"Except . . ." Adrian said slowly, as if explaining something to a child. "If she wasn't murdered—which is questionable right now, since I'm not sure exactly how dead she still is—I'd have to arrest her for arson and murder."

"Fuck, I forgot about that."

He gave me a look.

"What?" I said, taken aback by the judgment in his eyes.

"They really let you be a Guardian with a mouth like that?"

"You know what? You can go fuck your—" I stopped short, something outside the car catching my eye.

We had finally made it onto the Key Bridge, which was packed at this time of day, with all the people who lived across the river commuting home from work. And after yesterday's ice storm, the architecture on either side of the bridge was obscured by massive lumps of ice. I'd just seen one of those lumps move.

"Sorry, what is it I can go fuck? I didn't hear you," Adrian said, again looking at the car ahead of him like the goody-

goody he truly was, even though he'd just tried way too hard to prove to me that he could stoop to my level when it came to normal fucking language.

I didn't answer him, narrowing my eyes as we inched closer to the suspicious lump of ice. When we were just a few feet away from it, it moved again. All I saw in that moment was a mouthful of teeth opening, but that was enough for me.

"Get down!" I reached out to shove Adrian's head down below the steering wheel, practically throwing myself over him to keep him there. He slammed on the brakes just as the driver's side window shattered, and something flew over our heads and out the other window. Then the car began to shake.

I lifted my head and twisted my neck to see what had happened, and it was like an ugly replay of my incident with the palis earlier in the day. Another frog tongue, this one wrapped around the roof of the car now.

Only the creature it was attached to, perched on the edge of the bridge, didn't look even remotely human.

It was almost entirely plated in ice, like the wolf I'd killed last night, except the inside of its mouth—including the tongue latched onto our car—was still pink and squishy. Its jaws were shaped like a crocodile's, complete with the terrifying rows of sharp teeth. But it was squatting with a body that looked like a frog's, powerful leg muscles poised to jump at any moment. And it looked like it had . . . fins?

This was some terrible monstrosity of different animals mashed together, like someone had brought to life the subject of a little kid's ridiculous drawing. I almost felt sorry for it.

But then it used its fins to brace itself while it yanked on our car with its tongue. When the car moved, any sympathy I had for the thing got tossed on the trash heap of other useless thoughts in my brain.

"Fuck!" Adrian screeched, pulling out his gun and firing off a couple shots into the creature that seemed to glance right off. While he did that, I reached into my jacket for my trusty hunting knife. I'd already cut out one creepy frog tongue today; maybe it was time to start a collection.

Except the car lurched just as my fingers touched the handle, and suddenly we were in the air, and my knife had fallen out of my jacket and out of my grasp and out the broken window of the car, all in a single breath.

I heard Becca crash against something in the back, and I instinctively grabbed Adrian's arm to keep him from flying out the window.

Then the bottom dropped out from my stomach. I'd expected to come crashing down where we'd been on the bridge, but that was apparently not what the frog-croc monster had in mind.

No—it had swung us over the edge of the bridge, and now we were falling towards what would surely be an icy, watery grave.

My mind seemed to spin for an eternity as we fell through the air, weighing our options, our chances.

It was good that the windows were already broken, but also bad, because it would have been better to get Becca up front with us before breaking just one window, to maximize our chances of getting everyone out of the car before it filled up with water and sank.

Because once our bodies were submerged, there was a very real possibility that some or all of us would simply pass out from the shock of the cold. It would be a good thing for Becca to pass out, because who knew if zombies could even swim. One of us would have to drag her. But if Adrian or I went out, I didn't see how we could all make it.

And that was just the fun, unlikely odds of us surviving the water itself. When you added the monster, which was still very much alive and jumping off the bridge to follow us down here . . .

It didn't look great.

The river seemed to roar at us when we crashed into it, thin splotches of ice on its surface giving way like they were made of glass.

Adrian was quicker than me, sliding open the partition that was keeping Becca trapped in the back while I gasped as the cold hit my lap, rushing in through the windows. I clenched my teeth and willed myself to ignore the freezing jolt, imagining the comforting fires of fantasy hell, reassuring myself that the adrenaline would keep me warm as long as I got my ass in gear.

I was right behind Adrian then, grabbing my zombie friend by her shoulders and dragging her into the front of the car as the water rose quickly. I didn't care what I banged her into as long as I could get her out of this death trap.

When Adrian saw that I had her arms, he grasped at her feet and dove out the window on his side, pulling her behind him. The water rose above my head as he made it out, but even so I could have kissed him in that moment—because it was clear now that dragging a zombie out of a sinking car was in no way a one-person job, and I would have been fucked if he had jumped out without helping. Becca was squirming too much.

I followed him out, holding her torso tightly to make sure she got through the window okay. When I saw him break through to the surface of the water, I let go of Becca so she could float up with him. My vision started to darken as I kicked up to the surface—at least I thought I was kicking. At this point, I wasn't sure whether or not I could still feel my feet.

But then I felt freezing wind rush over my face, and I gasped in a breath, and air filled my lungs.

I caught a single glimpse of Adrian pulling Becca to the shore—expertly, it seemed—before I was yanked back under by something wrapped around my foot. The same foot that had been attacked earlier by the palis.

It didn't hurt, because it was too cold to feel pain, but damn it made me mad. That was my favorite foot. Yes, I had a favorite foot—and a favorite hand, and a favorite boob, because perfect symmetry is an unattainable fantasy. But also because I'd always thought my left foot looked good with the tattoo I had on my ankle, the one shared by all the mages in the coven I'd been raised in.

It was an intricate knot in the shape of a crescent moon, made of delicate lines that snaked their way around each other, highlighting the arch of my foot and the line of my lower leg. It was a symbol to bind us all to one another. A family. Even though it had never been a particularly *good* family, just having it had meant a lot to me as an adopted kid. It still did.

But now it looked like it was going to be some sea monster's dinner. Along with the rest of me.

When I managed to open my eyes underwater and twist my neck toward my foot, I saw the mish-mashed icy fish monster that had thrown us off the bridge, only it looked like it had de-iced itself. Swimming must be more difficult with ice armor on.

It was a greenish, purplish color now, and even through the murky water I could see sharp white teeth not just inside its open mouth, but also along its shoulders and elbows and knees. This thing had a bunch of mouths all over it. Okay, so it was a hungry-bitch sea monster. And its tongue was currently pulling my leg towards its main mouth—the big one on its face.

Nope, that wasn't going to happen. I knew that, even though I had no idea how I was going to stop the thing. My hunting knife was gone.

My gun was still in my purse, which was still in the car. I hadn't even been able to do a simple healing spell the last time I'd tried to use magic. And hell, I was really cold, and my lungs were starting to ache.

Okay, Darcy, think basic. No time for anything fancy right now.

The answer was floating right in front of my face, and I grabbed it right before my leg was shoved into the monster's mouth. A simple stick. Not even a big, sturdy one. Just a damn stick. But it would have to do.

Like I'd seen once in an old sci-fi movie Etty loved, I jammed the stick vertically into the monster's mouth before it could chomp down on my leg.

The thing went crazy. Its jaw was stuck open, and it looked like it had to hurt. It wasn't a particularly wide stick, and I'd gotten it in behind the thing's teeth, so I wouldn't be surprised if it went right through flesh if it tried to bite down.

But with all the flailing and thrashing the creature was doing, its damn tongue still wouldn't let go of my favorite foot. And I would start getting loopy soon from the lack of air, if I didn't pass out from the cold. So I grabbed the thing's teeth and pulled myself more fully into its mouth, so I could reach my foot with my hands.

At first I tried to unwrap the tongue manually, but it was freakishly strong, so instead I reached around it and loosened the zipper on my boot. With a little bit of squirming, my favorite foot slid right out.

Just as the creature seemed to decide it needed to go back to its ice form.

Which, I realized, would be able to snap my silly stick without any problems.

I scrambled to get out of the mouth, and I'd just about cleared it when the stick cracked and the jaws snapped shut. My favorite foot was grazed by an icy tooth as I got away, but I kicked like hell all the same, not stopping to think about the damage.

Hopefully, the thing would be slower to follow me in its icy state—or it would decide I wasn't worth the trouble. Hoping and swimming were all I could do now.

When I made it to the surface, I swam over to the nearest piece of land I saw, which was a rock jutting out in the middle of the water. And when I started to claw my way up onto it, I wanted badly to sink back into the water. The wind on my wet skin seemed like it would suck the life out of me, while the water had started to feel almost warm.

That was a very bad sign. I couldn't remember why that was bad; I just knew it was. And I trusted the part of me that knew things even when the rest of me couldn't remember why. I also knew now that it had been a monumentally bad idea to skip sleeping last night.

"Darcy!" Adrian's voice sounded shaky and scattered over the wind. I looked around and saw him on the shore, about thirty feet away from me, doing jumping jacks of all things while Becca lay curled on the ground beside him, still cuffed.

Okay, so those two were as fine as could be expected. What about me? I looked down to see a massive amount of blood flowing along the rock into the water, coming from my favorite foot. When I twisted my ankle to look at it, I saw a deep gash running right through the middle of my moon tattoo.

My eyes stung for a moment as heat rushed to my face. I didn't ever like getting hurt, of course, but I'd gone through enough that usually I didn't mind it. I never feared permanent damage from minor injuries, because I knew I could easily heal anything less than, say, getting a limb torn clean off.

But this . . . this was the only part of my body that had ever meant something to me. Family. A reminder that there was somewhere I would always belong, even if they weren't perfect and I had left them, even if I didn't want to be a healer, and even if—anything. Even if anything.

I hadn't realized how special that was until I'd lost everyone I'd known as a Guardian. I'd been telling myself it was because

I'd failed, because that at least felt like something I could prevent happening again in the future. But that was dumb. Even without the Guardians' high expectations and a vampire brainwashing me, I couldn't be perfect for the rest of my life. No one could. My zombie friend over there was proof of that.

And I knew that Etty and Becca had only accepted me as their roommate in the first place because I'd threatened the landlord who was trying to evict them for attracting stalkers to our building and gotten us all lower rent by revamping the whole place's security system. I had thought they had become my friends, but you could never really tell with people you worked with. Hell, Becca was apparently an arsonist and a murderer, and I'd had no idea. And without her, Etty and I seemed to have lost our tenuous connection.

The only people I'd ever been sure about were my family, and now this monster had ruined my only tangible connection with them. Even if I could heal it, there would be a scar obscuring the tattoo.

And the monster wasn't done with me yet. Something big was moving towards me under the water, creating waves that pushed the fragments of floating ice out of its wake.

Adrian yelled something at me from the shore, but my freezing, oxygen-deprived brain was having a hard time figuring out how to pay attention to everything happening at once.

I heard a splash to my left, and when I turned to look I saw Adrian had jumped in the water and was swimming towards me.

The idiot.

It was a miracle he had made it out of the river in the first place, and with Becca. I'd been trained to deal with extreme temperatures and extended durations underwater, but he probably hadn't. And he couldn't possibly think a few jumping jacks in between dips into freezing water would keep him alive.

That was, if the sea monster didn't kill him first.

It burst out of the water in front of me, roaring, and I honestly had no idea what to do. There were no molten bunny rabbits to help me here, no pole or stick to use as an improvised weapon, no real weapons except some tiny daggers in my jacket that would do nothing at all to this huge beast in its ice form, and magic . . .

Shit, there was so much magic in me right now.

More than I'd ever felt, except maybe in the obsidian cave, only this time it didn't feel like *too* much. It also, somehow, seemed unconnected to my scrye. Which was why I hadn't noticed it at first.

I wasn't sensing it the way I usually did. I wasn't pulling it from the ambience, or from any external source. It felt like it was *really* part of me. Like it was me. Like it depended on every cell in my body to exist. And like it would defend that existence —and my life—whether I liked it or not.

I screamed. Not out of terror, or anger, but just because I was completely overwhelmed. And when I did, it was like I'd unleashed a storm.

The river parted in front of me, water swept to the sides by a massive gust of wind that shredded and shattered the icy sea monster in front of me.

It looked like an enormous piece of glass exploding out away from me—all except for the pink, slimy tongue.

The one part of the monster not made of ice was sliced into tiny slivers instead, creating a pink mist of blood that coated the glittering shards of ice in the air around it before everything fell to the ground.

I looked around, expecting to find something that had caused all that damage aside from the gust of wind that had come from . . . me . . . But there was only the wind.

Wind as sharp as a thousand knives.

It died down almost as quickly as it had rushed out, and the water came crashing back to the empty space in front of me, the entire river turning into a tumultuous icy soup.

Adrian. Was he okay? I turned to where I'd last seen him swimming towards me, and I saw nothing except choppy waves.

Becca was still curled on the shore, unmoving as the waves washed over her.

Damn it. It looked like I was going for another swim. I would have to get to the shore somehow anyway.

I rolled over into the water. Not very elegant, but I didn't want to put weight on my wounded foot. My whole body felt numb, even worse than it had before, but I forced myself to move.

Just a little longer, I thought.

When I was halfway to the shore, I saw Adrian's soggy head of hair bobbing in the water in front of me, almost washed up near where Becca was, unconscious.

One last push and I'd hooked my arm around his back, pulling him along as I dragged us both to shore. Becca was squirming again now, tugging her arms and legs against her cuffs, and the effect was almost like she was a fish out of water, flopping around. But Adrian wasn't moving.

It was hard to tell with stars in my eyes and numbness overtaking my senses, but I didn't think he was breathing. I pressed my fingers against his neck, searching for a pulse, but I still couldn't even feel my own fingers, so that wasn't going to work.

"Damn it, wake up!" I yelled at him, and when he didn't answer I slapped him across the face. He wasn't allowed to die like this—not after he'd tried so hard to save me and my friend who wasn't even really alive anymore.

Magic. I could do magic again, right? I picked up his hands and wove his fingers through mine, like I used to do with the patients at the hospital. Closing my eyes, I tried to feel what was wrong with him—but I got nothing.

I could still feel the magic inside me, the strange magic that felt like it was a part of me. But it had a mind of its own, and it apparently still didn't want to listen to me.

Okay, help. I needed to call for help.

There were enough bystanders up on the bridge that I was sure official help would be here eventually, but I couldn't just sit here waiting. The phones in my jacket were dripping with water and dead, of course. Both mine and Etty's.

Etty.

"Elephant Bitch," I said, smashing my numb hands together as best I could. They weren't really producing claps, but it was the thought that counted, right?

Then a glorious, glittering goddess appeared in front of me, and I only had the wherewithal to say "Becca's a zombie" before everything went dark.

14

WHEN I WOKE UP, my bed was unnaturally warm and my foot was unnaturally . . . squishy and wet?

My eyes didn't want to open all the way, and my body didn't want to move very much, so I wiggled my foot out from under the covers and squinted at it, my face still half buried in my pillow.

It was blue. Blue and kinda shimmery and jiggly. Like jelly. Like a big, blue jelly dessert. I bet it would taste like fake raspberries. My mouth watered. But I didn't have the energy to bring my foot any closer to my face, so instead I rolled over. I could just go back to sleep and dream about eating blue-raspberry jelly. That sounded better.

My knee touched something hard and warm as I repositioned myself. Something hard and warm and moving. A person? A person in my bed.

Okay, cool. They felt comfy. I inched my way closer to the heat source and reached my arm around, snuggling myself up against . . . Oh, that felt like muscle. Smooth, hard, hot, just the tiniest bit damp with sweat. There was a man in my bed.

Maybe that meant I was dreaming. There hadn't been a

man in my bed since . . . well, since my politician vampire charge had brainwashed me into loving him—and I didn't want to think about that now.

But even so, I was quickly remembering everything I'd been missing. Dream or not, I didn't care. It didn't take too much energy to slide my hand over his chest and what felt like insanely defined abs. Yeah, this must be a dream. He smelled too good to be real. Like a damn forest, with a little bit of gun oil mixed in.

He was moving more now, his arms reaching behind his back and finding me. In one smooth motion, he rolled over and hooked his hand behind my neck, pulling my face so close to his, so fast, that my eyes didn't have a chance to open and my brain didn't have a chance to process anything besides his hot breath on my cheek, and then his lips brushing mine.

And then I was kissing his jaw, drawn by the deliciously rough stubble around his lips, and then the taste of salt on his neck. And when my eyes fluttered open just a tiny bit, I saw more of the blue jelly. Right under his ear.

Mmm, good dream, I thought. Sex and candy at the same time.

I took a bite of the jelly, and it did not taste like raspberries. Rotten raspberries, maybe. With emphasis on the rot.

The door burst open then, and someone was shouting, and bright lights blinded me.

"No, no, no!" a woman screeched, whacking me with a throw pillow in time with her words. "That is not for eating!"

She didn't have to tell me twice. I spat out the chunk of rotten jelly in my mouth, then gagged as I curled up in a ball, bringing my arms in front of me to defend against the pillow.

"Bad, bad, bad!" she screeched again with more whacks, and then she finally relented and dropped the pillow. I heard her breathing heavily as she bent over me to scoop up the chunk of jelly I'd spat out, so I uncurled a little and opened my eyes.

A matronly outfit cobbled together of too many different shades of pink stood over me, white-blond hair in an elegant bun, and old-lady glasses hiding the agelessness of the face behind them.

"Miriam?" I said, gaping at her. "Why are you in my apartment?"

But she wasn't paying attention to me, just carefully poking at the little chunk of jelly as she muttered, "I try to help you, and what do I get? You eat my babies. Horrible, horrible woman. I don't believe for a second that the pink one was an accident. You probably stepped on it after it fell off you."

Cradling the blue jelly in her hands, she rushed over to the other side of the bed, and I turned to see a familiar face staring at me blankly.

He looked even paler than usual, and even more uncomfortable than he'd been in the strip club. And the blue blob of Miriam's jelly stuck to his neck wasn't helping anything.

"What the fuck are you doing in my bed, Crane?" I couldn't bring myself to use his first name after what had just happened.

"I . . ." he said groggily and then coughed. He looked even more confused than I was, and his voice sounded hoarse, like he was an old man near death.

I decided I wasn't going to wait around for him to answer. Instead I threw the covers off myself and jumped out of bed, only to be screeched at again by Miriam.

"Don't you dare put weight on that foot!" She glared at me with menace in her eyes.

Of course, the jelly went all the way from my calf down my ankle and wrapped around the bottom of my foot. Like a living bandage. Was there anything this woman's "babies" couldn't do?

Maybe there was a different color for each ability. Pink for mind reading, blue for healing . . . Ugh, there were probably a lot more colors in her arsenal, and I wasn't sure I wanted to see them in action.

Obediently, I let myself nearly fall over and caught my weight on the nightstand, then hopped across my room as Miriam patted the little chunk of jelly back into the bigger chunk of jelly on Adrian's neck. Then she started softly singing to it.

That just solidified my decision to hop the hell out of this room. When I passed my full-length mirror, I felt a moment of relief that at least I wasn't naked. But this flimsy bra-and-panties thing wasn't much better. Especially with the bouncing up and down.

Hoping that Adrian was too out of it to be paying attention, I grabbed my robe out of my closet and slipped it on, then picked up one of the swords I also kept in my closet and used it as a cane so I could walk a little more normally.

Then I burst out the door into the living room, ready to slice an explanation out of whoever else was here.

It turned out to be Etty, crouched on the sofa with her feet up on the coffee table, painting her toenails.

I let out an exasperated, growly, screamy sound and she jumped a little, then shook her head when she saw me.

"What?" she said. "They don't like nail polish in court, so I had to take it off before I went."

"Why . . ." I started, drawing out the word so I could figure out how to phrase the rest. Why had she put a half-naked man in my bed with me? Why had she invited over the psychic Barbie swamp monster? Why had I been *sleeping* instead of tracking down Becca's killer?

"Because our nails are sorta sacred," Etty said, interrupting my thoughts. "Functional." She made a clawing motion in the air and raised her eyebrows at me as she hissed like a cat.

"Not that," I snapped at her. Then I sighed and dropped myself into the couch so I could give my one good foot a rest.

It was tough to stay mad at her. It was her fae nature to take everything I said at face value, to treat every conversation as if it were a game. And I knew I couldn't blame her for it, even when it was maddening. "Why are a naked detective and a swamp monster playing doctor in my bedroom?" I tried.

"Well," Etty said carefully. "That's because our zombie roommate is in *my* bedroom. And *her* bedroom is blocked off by police tape right now."

I groaned. What, had she never heard of using scissors?

"Okay, maybe a better question is why are they in our apartment in the first place?"

"You and the cop were practically dead from hypothermia and blood loss when you called me. I dusted us all here just to get out of the cold so I could think, and Miriam was waiting for us. She said something about Becca getting arrested if we didn't hide her, and she at least seemed like a competent healer."

I pressed my lips together, thinking. How had Miriam even known to come here? Adrian must have sent her a message before diving back in the river to try to save me. And if we were hiding Becca, Miriam had probably wanted to hide me and Adrian too until we could all agree on a story. He wouldn't be happy about that. Hopefully Miriam had had the sense to cover for him in the meantime. I didn't want to see Dirk on a warpath looking for his missing partner.

My overwhelmed brain was also wondering, yet again, why Miriam was going to so much trouble to keep things from the people she was supposed to be working with. Either she was absolutely terrible at her job, or I didn't know what her real job was. But that mystery would have to wait a little longer.

Etty was back from her fae court, and she'd done something I hadn't thought was even possible. "You said you dusted us here?"

She didn't respond, just finished up her last toenail and twisted the cap back on the polish bottle.

I continued, "As in you magically teleported yourself and Becca and two unconscious humans all the way from the Potomac River to our apartment?"

She finally looked at me, a sour expression on her face. "Don't call it that—teleported. So demeaning. It's not like on *Star Trek*."

"What's *Star*—"

"And yes, sure, that's what happened. But don't go around yelling it unless you want me to be sent back to the fae realm for all eternity. Extravagantly saving the lives of two humans isn't the sort of dust usage my queen would approve of."

I stared at Etty, suddenly feeling awful for unleashing all my disoriented bitchiness on her after she'd so extravagantly saved my life. Especially if it was something she could get in trouble for.

Maybe I'd been wrong about our friendship falling apart without Becca. Maybe Etty was really someone I could count on as more than just a coworker and roommate.

But Etty wasn't a mind reader, so she took my stunned silence as a cue to explain further. Her voice took on a stilted, mocking tone as she continued, "I am the queen's servant and her representative, and so is all the dust I command, and as such all of my actions are subject to her approval." She rolled her eyes. "They already sent a messenger to ask what I needed so much dust for, and I told them I saved a cat from getting hit by a truck. I'm not sure if they bought it."

I bit the inside of my cheek as something clicked in my mind. "Do you think maybe . . . maybe Becca's queen had her dealt with because she didn't approve of Becca's actions?"

Etty gave me the same look she'd given me just last week

when I'd tried to wear an old turtleneck sweater to work on an especially cold night. Criminally offended. "No way," she said. "We're not barbarians—especially not Becca's queen. And Becca would never have done anything that bad, anyway."

"Um . . ." I started. Shit, no one had told Etty what Becca had done. That she was a murderer.

"What?" Etty pressed.

"I thought the same until I saw it for myself," I said. "She killed someone. Noah's father. Burned his house down, with him restrained inside it. Even spilled some kerosene in her room earlier—you can duck under the tape to smell the carpet if you don't believe me."

Etty only paused for a moment, and the blank look on her face didn't stay there long. "Well," she said, lifting her eyebrows. "If she was ever going to kill someone, she chose the right someone."

I only stared at her. She was right, of course, but I had expected her to be more shocked. I supposed that as sweet and innocent as Becca had seemed, sudden murderousness probably wasn't too crazy of a thing to expect from any fae. They were known for being fickle, and Etty would know that better than anyone.

"Still," Etty continued, "the worst Becca's queen would have done is call her back to the fae realm, deem her unfit to consort with mortals."

"Okay," I said. Back to square one. "Well, did you find out anything from your queen? Did you ask her about the wings Becca grew before she went up in flames?"

Etty sucked in her cheeks, like she'd eaten something unpleasant, and then gave me a small frown. "It's a little embarrassing," she said.

I widened my eyes at her. "Last week you bent over naked in front of me to ask if there were any pieces of toilet paper stuck in your lady bits before your shift, and now suddenly you're trying to impress me?"

She chuckled, and it seemed to relax her. "Okay, you're right. Just don't laugh." She paused and looked up at me. "So, fae—all fae—are either born with wings or without. I knew this. Everyone knows this. But it's . . . You know how human parents lie to their children about Santa Claus? Like fantasy stories?"

"Fairy tales?" I prompted.

She grimaced. "Is that really what you call them?"

She had a point. Most fairy tales had nothing to do with fairies at all. "I promise from now on I will call them fantasy stories," I said, crossing my hand over my heart.

"Anyway, it's a common fae fantasy story—"

"You know, in this case, the term 'fairy tale' would be appropriate," I interrupted.

She glared at me. Yeah, I should know better.

"Anyway," she said as she began applying a layer of glitter polish to her toenails. "It's a common *fairy tale* that a fae child born without wings will one day fly. Like your princess with the rats and the shoe . . ."

"Cinderella?" I asked.

"Yes, that one. Rags to riches."

"Are wings a status symbol then?"

"Exactly. Any fae born with wings is revered, blessed, and only those with wings can hold positions of power in court. So when I saw Becca with those wings, even if it was only for a moment . . ."

"You thought of the story."

"Yes. But that was silly of me. It's never happened before, and with the fire and the death . . . My queen suggested Becca might have been touched by a phoenix."

I froze. "She grew fiery wings, was consumed by flames,

and then her body was resurrected and healed . . ." A phoenix seemed to fit perfectly.

"It's not right, though," Etty continued, interrupting my thoughts. "She shouldn't have come back as a zombie. She should have been reborn, truly, with her soul intact."

"Are you sure?" I asked. "How much do you know about phoenixes?"

"Not that much . . . but I know they aren't in the business of creating zombies. They are creatures of fire, creatures of life—not of death. Or *un*death," she added as an afterthought.

"Creatures of fire," I repeated, a bell ringing in my head. That was what Ray had said about Noah, that he was a creature of fire—like everyone in Ray's creepy witch family. What were his exact words . . . all different, bound by the fire of their god? Could Noah be the phoenix? Or his father?

"The point is," Etty continued, "Becca's soul is missing, and that's not right. But she seems to want to get free—maybe if we let her go, she'll lead us to it?" After seeing the look on my face, she added, "We can follow her to make sure she doesn't eat anyone's brains. That's one of your fantasy stories about zombies, right? You don't have to worry; I don't think it's real."

But I wasn't worried about Becca eating anyone's brains. "I think she already did lead us to her soul," I said, remembering that she had immediately gone for Noah. Maybe he had caused her death by accident and botched the job? If he was a phoenix, he was only half—and he was also just a child. "Can you go pick up Noah at Baz's?" I asked Etty.

"Sure, but—"

"Bring him here, but don't let him near Becca until I get back." I stood and started hobbling back to my bedroom. Then I remembered what had just happened in there, and I paused, turning back to Etty. "Can I borrow some of your clothes?"

They wouldn't fit well, but that was a small price to pay to not have to go back in and face Miriam and Adrian.

"Sure, but where are you going?" Etty asked.

"Remember Ray, the big tipper at the club who Becca freaked out about and said she loved right before she died?"

Etty opened her mouth and then quickly shut it, looking confused. "Yeah, I remember him. Becca kept saying she had to tell him what she'd done . . ." She paused for a second, taking in a breath. "She was probably talking about murdering her ex, yeah?"

I nodded, realizing Etty was probably right.

"She never said she loved him, though," Etty continued. "She was talking about Noah when she said that—you were over with Mitch at that point, so you didn't hear. But that was the last thing she said before she went crazy and bit me. That she loved Noah."

All the more reason to suspect Noah might be the phoenix, I thought. "Well anyway, I think Ray might know something about this phoenix, and even if Becca wasn't in a messed-up relationship with him, he owes us some answers."

There was nothing Etty could say to that, so I gave her a short nod of my head. I turned away from her briefly and then turned back. "Etty?"

She raised her eyebrow at me. "Yeah?"

"Thank you for saving us."

Etty smiled. "My pleasure, Darce. But you owe me." Her eyes twinkled with fae glitter.

I hobbled away, telling myself that if I needed to be indebted to a fae, it was at least a good thing I'd gotten one who was willing to lie to her court on my behalf.

When I opened the door to her bedroom, the darkness took me by surprise. Etty usually had tons of tiny little candles and colorful lights glowing all around, and I'd never walked in here and not felt like I was in some sort of holiday wonderland. Like me, Etty thrived in darkness, but only because it accentuated the small amounts of light that made us feel comfortable.

Now, though, the only light in here was streaming in from the living room behind me, and Becca's face looked even eerier in it than it had before. She slowly turned her head to look at me, but her body didn't move. She was lying on Etty's bed, arms and legs still restrained, and it seemed like even more life had been sucked out of her.

The last time I'd seen her, she'd been desperate to get free. Banging every part of her body she could against anything within reach. Now, it was like she'd given up. Maybe it was because we'd taken her too far away from her soul.

I flicked on the lights, hoping to see just a little more life behind her eyes, and instead what I saw felt like a reflection. Maybe it was because I was still half-naked, still had Adrian's scent on me, still felt the intoxicating warmth I'd felt lying next to him in my bed—the warmth I'd always expected to feel next to Simeon, despite knowing that because he was a vampire, I never would.

Things like that hadn't mattered to my brain when I'd been with Simeon. Reason. Logic. Reality. I'd wanted the warmth, and whenever I would look into his eyes they would tell me I would have everything I'd ever wanted, so I would just smile and relax and trust that the world would be what I needed it to be, someday.

It was the same as giving up, really, only more dangerous because it was giving up and hoping at the same time.

Those things had never worked together, and they never would. Sooner or later, they always collided in disappointment. In death.

Simeon was a monster to have done that to me, but he had also done it to himself. And I wondered, looking into Becca's lifeless eyes, if the monster who had done this to her would also suffer because of it in the end.

I fucking hoped so.

My eyes burning, I stepped up to the closet and grabbed a whole armful of clothes out of Etty's active-wear drawer. Loose and stretchy—something was bound to fit me in all this.

I flicked the lights off again before gently shutting the door as I walked out. It seemed like a mercy. Complete darkness would always be better than light when it only had false hope to shine on.

15

It FELT nice to be driving my own car again, even though it was probably still infested with a horde of obsidian rabbits, and even though I was heading back into the city for the second time today—actually, I had no idea if it was still the same day, or how long I'd been asleep. That was probably something I should have found out before leaving.

Damn it, I really was terrible at detective work. I needed to get better at asking questions. I reached into the cup holder for Becca's cell phone, which Etty had made me take in case she needed to call me. It made me uncomfortable to use, like I was intruding on Becca's life, but both my phone and Etty's had been killed in my river battle with the icy sea monster.

Luckily, Etty had an extra she could use—her business phone, so she would always be able to coordinate her shifts at the club to align with her richest customers' schedules. But I'd been a one-phone woman ever since the Guardians had taken my work phone away, so now I was swiping past a background image of Noah and trying to ignore the stinging in my eyes while I looked for the calendar app to see . . .

Oh, bats. I had been asleep for almost two days. It had been afternoon on January seventh when we'd gone into the river, and now it was morning on the ninth. Had I been in bed with Adrian that whole time? Had *he* been asleep that whole time?

I really hoped so. I shivered, not looking forward to the next time I would need to look him in the eyes. Maybe I could just solve the rest of the case with Dirk. Or maybe I could get Miriam to say she'd put some sort of sex magic in those jellies. That would make it her fault, not mine.

Realistically, though, I knew it was my fault. The first thing Becca had said to me when she'd seen me at the bar on my first day, pounding the crap out of an ice bag that had melted a little and refrozen, was that I needed to get laid.

I hadn't listened to her then, because of what had happened with Simeon. But now, with Becca gone, everything she'd said to me in the past suddenly seemed weightier. Wiser. And I did need to do something to ensure that what had happened today never happened again.

I would figure it out. Once I got Ray to tell me everything he knew about Noah and phoenixes, I would never need to see him again, right? So maybe he would do. Anything was better than accidentally almost-banging someone I had to work with. Anything.

Ray was already easing into my good graces, too, because it looked like his shop might actually have a parking lot in the back. It was in a part of town that had been utterly destroyed by riots right after the Opening, but now it was a cheap place for small business owners to set up shop. Ray's was called the Fulgid Forge, and it looked like he might be a . . . really unpopular car mechanic? This building looked like a garage, and there *was* a parking lot, but I didn't see any cars.

Oh well, more space for me, I thought as I slid into the spot that looked the least iced over. If Ray's whole family were "creatures of fire," he shouldn't be hurting this bad for a snow shovel and maybe some salt. It was like he didn't even want customers.

When I got out of the car, the familiar sound of chirping marbles greeted me. I groaned, looking down at my feet, where the shiny black bunnies had appeared again. Not nearly as many as in the garage, but at least a dozen were hopping around my car to melt the ice. If they weren't so deadly and mysterious, I'd be grateful for the help. This would certainly make getting out easier.

I was going to knock on the front door, but a few of the bunnies hopped in front of me and around the side of the building, where I saw a garage door half opened. The bunnies had melted a nice path for me, so I followed it.

When I poked my head under the garage door, I was met by a spiky, scaly, snakelike thing as wide as my thigh. It moved lazily from side to side, sweeping along the concrete floor like a giant dog's tail.

Oh bats, it *was* a tail. Not a dog's, though. I crouched down and moved to step inside, where I saw the tail was connected to a whole damn dragon. With wings and everything. It was breathing fire into a furnace, which Ray stood in front of with his back to me.

I accidentally knocked my head against a chain that was dangling from the garage door, and the jangling sound made the dragon jump. Which was ridiculous, when I thought about it, but hell if I was thinking about anything right then.

The dragon's head snapped towards me, its fire breath directed over to Ray, and both Ray and the beast turned black in a fleeting moment. Like scales turning over and transforming, shiny and hard—obsidian.

The moment was over as quickly as it had begun, and Ray was slapping at his burning clothes and yelling, and the dragon was gone in place of a little girl—almost gone, actually. The girl had a scaly tail.

"Whoa," I said, my hands up in front of me as I watched Carina's tail slowly retract into her tiny, tiny body.

She stared at me with round eyes, her hands pressed to her little puffy cheeks. And when I opened my mouth to say hi, she let out a high-pitched scream and ran. Past Ray, past the furnace, across the room and through a door, which slammed shut behind her.

A handful of the bunnies that had followed me in ran off after Carina and wiggled their way under the door.

"Is she okay?" I asked Ray, who turned to me and shrugged.

"She's just embarrassed," he said. "She doesn't like it when people see her tail. Thinks it's too long. 'Like a monkey' is what she says."

"That's . . . crazy."

"I know. I keep telling her she'll grow into it, but she won't believe me until it happens."

"You saw those rabbits go in there with her, right? Please tell me I'm not hallucinating."

He laughed and bent down to the ground, extending his hand to a rabbit that hopped up and then perched on his shoulder. I guessed that meant I wasn't hallucinating.

"You've been blessed by our god," Ray said as he stood. "You're welcome, by the way. He wouldn't have been able to send the *teporingo* if I hadn't found you first." He reached over to the rabbit on his shoulder and scratched it behind the ears. It let out a delighted chirp, and I narrowed my eyes at the both of them.

"If these rabbits are a blessing, why was the soul of my dead friend burning in the realm where I met them?"

"She wasn't." Ray shook his head. "The cave is more like a hallucination. It isn't a real place, and certainly not one that harbors human souls. It's a vision we call up when we need to talk to Popo, or when he needs to talk to us. It's not like you can call a god on the phone. If he showed you your friend there, he was trying to tell you something about her."

I had no idea what to say to that, beyond wishing this god had used words to communicate instead of some cryptic vision. But then, gods were sort of known for cryptic visions, and for not making much sense in general.

Ray bent over again to pick up something from the ground, the bunny hopping off him as he did.

I walked over to see what he was holding, but the object was unrecognizable. "What is that?"

"Glass. My father made his living crafting drinking glasses for tourists in Mexico. I use what he taught me to make weapons, forged in dragon fire. Inefficient heat source and fragile material, but the magical benefits are worth it. This one will be an arrow, once Carina gets over herself and comes back." He turned to me with genuine curiosity in his eyes. "Will it get worse before it gets better?"

"What are you talking about?"

"She's only eight now, so I'm not sure if she'll be more mature in a few years, or if she'll just find more reasons to—" He sighed. "I don't know much about females."

"Well, I don't know much about dragons."

"Fair enough."

"But yes. I think the general rule of thumb is if she's not a teenager yet, it will absolutely get worse before it gets better." For a moment I wondered if that was what the coven had thought of me when I had refused to keep healing and gone to the Guardians instead. A rebellious teenager who would eventually come around. I hadn't seen any of them in years, so by now they had to know that I never would come around.

Ray put the chunk of glass and metal down on the ground, and the small noise it made broke me away from my thoughts.

"Um . . ." I said. This conversation had gotten away from me way too fast. But at least I had made a tiny bit of headway on the whole "creatures of fire" mystery—one of them was a dragon. *Good job, Detective Darcy.* "Is she really your daughter?" I asked, hoping Ray's answer would tell me whether he was also a dragon.

"Of course." He looked at me as if my question had offended him.

"So, why don't you just finish the arrow yourself?" I pointed at the lump of glass he'd been holding at the end of a metal rod.

"Her mother is the dragon, not me."

"Got it." I knew I should be asking what the hell *Ray* was at this point, but my curiosity got the better of me. "And her mother is okay with her skipping school to help her dad at work? Isn't there some law against that?"

He gave me a cold stare. "It's Saturday. And her mother is not around anymore." His voice made it clear that line of conversation was over.

Damn it, Darcy. I had literally just checked to see what day it was. I needed to get my shit together. But Ray seemed to be annoyed with me now. He had turned away from me to walk across the room to a cabinet, where he pulled out a non-burnt t-shirt and slipped it on over the ashes he was currently wearing.

"Why are you here?" he asked as he started cleaning up his workspace. "You didn't bring the boy—you don't still think I killed his mother? I would never take away a child's mother, not by choice."

The way he said it, tersely, with his fingers gripping his tools just a little too hard—I believed him. And I felt like a bit of a jerk now for suspecting him of trying to take Noah from Becca, whether by murder or manipulation. The idea of it clearly struck a personal nerve for him as a single father, and as an orphan. A supposed orphan.

But that was the job. I took in a breath, focusing on what I came here to find out. "Is Noah a phoenix?"

He stopped what he was doing to look at me again. "Why would you ask that?"

"Because I think a phoenix had something to do with Becca's death. The wings, the burning, and . . ."

"And what?"

"Her body was resurrected and healed."

He raised his eyebrows at that. "If that's the case, why do you care? You have her back."

"Not really," I explained. "She's empty, a zombie. I don't think her soul came back with her."

"Well, you're wasting time trying to track down the phoenix," he said. "That wasn't what killed her."

"How do you know?"

"Because a phoenix's touch only affects those already marked by death."

"Huh?"

"A phoenix doesn't kill. So Becca must have already been dying, past the point of no return, for one to have affected her like that."

My brain was having a hard time processing this. It did make sense with what Etty had said about phoenixes being creatures of life and not death. But the burning had sure looked a hell of a lot like death to me.

Could there be two killers? Becca *had* seemed uncharacteristically sick at the club before she had gone on stage and burned. So without the phoenix, would she still have died some other way? Had someone poisoned her? Cursed her?

"If she's been resurrected without her soul, it means whatever really caused her death might have consumed or imprisoned it," Ray offered.

"Any idea what might do something like that?"

"Beats me. Maybe look it up on the internet?" Apparently he was done being helpful.

"Thanks," I said icily. "I'll do that." My instincts told me to turn around and leave, to go act on what I had learned even though I had hoped he would tell me more. But those weren't the instincts of an investigator, which was what I needed to be right now. "Look," I said after a decidedly awkward pause, "can you just tell me what you and Noah are?" An investigator would have much better tact than that, but I would have to work on that part next time.

He sighed, dropping his tools to the ground with a metallic clang that sent adrenaline running through me for just a moment. And when he turned to look at me, I could see he was pissed. All the cavalier friendliness he'd shown me at Carina's school was gone, and I hated that I found the change disorienting.

My best friend had been murdered—apparently, twice—and this man was still technically a suspect. Angry and suspicious and cold was how he should have been acting towards me this whole time. This at least made sense. But it was unpleasant, I had to admit, when he marched towards me, his entire body a threat, his face darkening as he loomed over me and said, "What am I? Is this a joke to you? I'm a person. A father." He shook his head at me. "If someone asked you what you are, would you even know how to answer?"

"I'm human—" I started, and he laughed in my face.

"That's not the whole story, and you know it," he said.

I didn't know it. Unless he was talking about my magic training. But that didn't make me any less human. It couldn't.

At the blank look I was giving him, he reached up and pressed the palm of his hand to the middle of my chest, at the base of my neck, where I had some skin exposed.

He closed his eyes and bowed his head, and then I felt it again. The same burst of heat I'd felt when I'd first seen him walk into the club. I'd mistaken it then for sexual attraction, but it definitely wasn't that. Not at all.

It was the same magic I'd compulsively attacked him with at the playground, the same magic that had destroyed the sea monster when it had threatened my life. The same magic that felt like another entity entirely, even though it filled me completely, its very existence threatening to overcome everything I was and dangle me over the world like a puppet. And this time, it felt desperate, like something was fighting to restrain it.

Ray frowned. "It's stronger than before, but still broken, fractured . . ." He paused and sniffed the air a bit. "Have you been wounded?"

"Yeah, but I'm fine. Don't tell me you're a vampire." I stifled a groan. Anything would be better than a vampire. I hated dealing with bloodsuckers. Complete tunnel vision with them if you were bleeding. Worse than the men in the club looking at boobs.

"Where?" he asked sternly, not even bothering to answer my dumb question. If he were a vampire, he wouldn't have had to ask where I was bleeding.

With a small frown, I gestured to my left foot, and he was on the ground taking off my boot so fast I almost lost my balance. Almost.

"What is this?" It came out almost a snarl as he ripped off my sock and pressed his rough fingers into the skin around the wound on my ankle.

I fought the urge to kick him, and instead I leaned against the workbench behind me so I wouldn't fall on my ass once he saw the hole in the bottom of my foot. "A sea monster bit me," I said. "After a palis tried to drink me. But it's fine. It's healing nicely, thanks to—"

"No, I meant the tattoo." He twisted my foot over to look at it from a different angle. "And this blue stuff . . ." Reaching around me, he pulled a small knife off his workbench. "I need to cut it off."

He brought the knife to my ankle, and I decided that now was an appropriate time to kick him if there ever was one. But his grip was annoyingly strong on my calf, so I leaned back to brace myself against the bench with my arms and lifted my other foot. The foot with the boot still on it.

I brought it up and planted it right on his chest, shoving him off me and onto his back. For the second time since I'd met him.

Only this time, I was totally cool with it. No way was he cutting anything off my body, and especially not from the part I liked most. Yes, the tattoo was damaged by the wound, but Miriam had told me not to worry before I'd left the apartment, said she could help it heal without a scar, and I desperately wanted to believe her now that my own healing abilities had apparently vanished. Plus, she'd been in my head for so long that she probably knew I would kill her if she was lying to me about it.

It was the only reason I'd consented to her leaving on a thin layer of the healing jelly after she'd come out of my bedroom ranting about how I wasn't allowed to put on shoes yet. It had made my foot feel like a wet slug inside my boot, but it was worth it.

"Agh," Ray grumbled in front of me as he moved to right himself. "Why do you keep doing that?"

"You take a knife to a woman without asking first, and you wonder why she fights back? Honestly, I worry for you. How have you made it this long without landing in jail?"

"Sorry," he said, but it didn't sound like he meant it. "It's just, the tattoo—*that's* the problem." He stood up and cracked his back, then rubbed the side of his ass and winced. "Strong legs," he remarked.

But I would not be distracted by flattery. "The tattoo is not a problem. It's the symbol of my family."

He looked surprised at that. "So . . . your whole family,

everyone has the same tattoo?"

"Yeah," I said. I thought it was pretty clear.

"So they were all witches too?"

"What? No—" I started, but then my butt started ringing, cutting me off. Becca's phone.

I put it to my ear and heard Etty's voice, rich and comforting compared to what I was dealing with now at Ray's, and it immediately calmed me down a little. "Hey Darce, I have the little guy. I'm taking him to the club for now, since it'll be a while before you're home."

"I can be back soon—" I said, but she just kept talking over me. She wasn't very good with phone conversations. And now that I thought about it, I'd never met any fae who was.

"He seemed pretty attached to Baz's old lady, didn't want to leave. So I'm assuming you haven't told him about his mom, and I'm gonna let you do that when you get here."

"I—what about his dad? Does he know his dad's dead?" I asked, suddenly wondering whether I should start saving up for a good child therapist.

"Weird old lady," she continued, ignoring my question completely. "I hope she's not going to be our new boss. Would probably make us dance in sweaters and socks. Baz was happy, though. He wants you to come to work tonight now that you're awake and he doesn't need to escape his own house."

"Damn it." I sighed. "Maybe. I don't know." I needed to figure out what I was going to do next about Becca before I could even think about going to work.

"I told him probably not, since you have to do that thing with Detective Crane."

"What thing?"

"Oh, right, that's what I was calling to tell you. He wants you to meet him now at . . . Sweepers Headquarters? I think. Didn't feel right giving him Becca's number to reach you. I'll text you the address. He's already on his way."

This was just getting better and better. Part of me wanted to be annoyed that I was being told rather than asked to do all these things, but another part of me was happy to have help moving forward.

I still wanted to get more out of Ray, but who knew how long that might take?

And anyway, it would probably be better to meet him somewhere away from his knives. In public. I didn't know what he thought the problem was with my tattoo, and I didn't care. He wasn't touching it.

"Thanks," I said to Etty as I eyed Ray warily. "I'll meet you at the club when I'm done, and we can take the kid home together. But tell Baz I'm not working tonight. He can complain all he wants—he won't fire me."

"That's okay, I'll find someone to make drinks. Have fun with sexy jelly boy," she teased, and I groaned inwardly. Miriam had probably told her what had happened, and now I would never hear the end of it. I hung up the phone without responding, and Ray spoke before I could.

"Noah's dad is dead?" he asked in a hard voice, looking me straight in the eye.

"Yes. Becca torched his place the day she died."

"Damn," he growled. "I didn't think she'd gone through with it. I was at the club that night to try to talk her out of it." After a small punch of frustration to the wall, he looked back at me with brightness in his eyes. "So, Noah's parents are both dead and he needs a new family?" he asked innocently, and I immediately regretted the last two minutes.

"Don't you fucking dare," I seethed.

He lifted his hands in surrender. "Fine, fine—look, I don't want to hurt the kid. Or you. I just want to help."

"If that's true, you can prove it by waiting until I ask for your help," I said, then spun away from him to leave. I dearly hoped I would never need to ask.

THE WORLD FELT wrong as I walked towards the Sweepers' office building. It probably had something to do with the fact that I was on my way to ask polite questions to the people who had been trying to kill me. The people who, at this point, I assumed had something to do with both Simeon's and Becca's deaths.

My legs felt heavy, plodding along, crunching slowly on the salt that had cleared the sidewalks of ice by now, even though Miriam's jelly had effectively numbed the pain from my wounds. My body was trying to keep me from doing this, and for good reason.

The Sweepers were a can of worms, I knew that much, but I had no idea how many worms were about to jump out at me, or whether they would be gummy or bloodthirsty. This was the life of an investigator, though. Shining light into dark places instead of blindly guarding against them.

And as much as I wanted to help Becca and get revenge on whoever had killed her, I had to admit I'd been avoiding shining light on this particular dark place the whole time.

In the past year, while I'd been watching and waiting and

seething, I had always imagined Simeon's killer as the blond assassin, smelling of roses and herbs, who had actually killed him—the blond assassin I'd witnessed cut off his head before it rolled to my feet, eyes still shining at me with false promises. It had never occurred to me that she might have been working for a group so large, that the motive could have been so . . . impersonal. And now, with all my theories turned on their heads and yet another person I'd cared about dead, I didn't want it to be for the same reason.

If Becca had been killed by the same people who had killed Simeon, that meant she was dead because of something I had done, even if I couldn't fathom what.

So I hadn't wanted to believe the Sweepers' attempts on my life had anything to do with my friend. But that was stupid of me, and cowardly, and I was glad Adrian was competent enough to realize what needed doing even when I wouldn't. It was nice, feeling like I kind of had a partner again to check my bullshit, and I started to feel nauseous when I remembered what had just happened between us. When would I stop ruining everything good in my life?

The nausea faded quickly when the scent of coffee and sweet cinnamon invaded my senses. I was only one building away from the Sweepers—I could see their dumb sign with the dumb broom on it—so I ducked into the little cafe next door and relished in the comfort of the aromas and my good luck. I was going to do this, yes, but I wasn't going to just walk in the front door like everyone in the building wouldn't immediately turn their heads and train their weapons on me. That would be just as stupid as my avoidance.

It wasn't very crowded at this time of day, and the redheaded barista stared at me with wide eyes as I walked up to the counter. She looked like she had seen a ghost, which meant she probably recognized my face from all those unflattering news stories last year.

Her hair was up in a messy bun, and black feather pendants dangled from her ears. I narrowed my eyes at her, trying to figure out if I'd seen her somewhere before. She felt familiar.

She came to her senses quicker than I did, a cheerful smile replacing the look of terror on her face so quickly it left me wondering if I'd imagined it.

"Let me guess!" she said in a charming British accent, and her enthusiasm immediately reminded me of Becca. That must be why she seemed familiar to me.

"Hmm? Guess what?"

"Extra-dark mocha cappuccino?" She gave me a hopeful look, biting her lip a bit nervously.

"Sure," I said. I needed to order something anyway, so why not?

With a bright smile, she skipped away from me to make the drink, and I stood there wondering whether she was even going to charge me. The counter beside the register had colorful papers scattered around, what looked like abstract watercolor paintings.

I felt my heart tighten a little as I was forced to picture what her life must be like. Aspiring artist, working at the cafe to pay the bills, clearly empathic but not driven mad by it—yet. Happy. Peaceful. Innocent.

I'd never known any life like that. Not even when I was a child. I'd been thrust into hospital rooms with dying patients as early as I could remember, asked to juggle life and death amid blood and gore while the other children were juggling balls outside. What would I even make if I had the space in my life for art? I supposed I had, this past year. And I'd been creative with my bartending. But not with the wholesome enthusiasm I saw in this girl. I'd done it with only half my heart, maybe even less. Always distracted, feeling sorry for myself, plotting my revenge.

Maybe that was what Becca had meant when she'd said I needed to get laid. Maybe what I really needed to do was lighten up a little, give myself permission to enjoy *something* in life without feeling like I should be doing it better.

The warm memories of Becca coursing through me seemed to get stronger when a steaming cup of nutty-smelling, foamy coffee slid towards me. I looked up and the barista was smiling at me, unnervingly wide, and holding out a card.

"It's lovely to see you again!" she said. "You know, I was worried."

I took the card from her with a frown on my face, confused. For the life of me, I couldn't recall ever having met this woman. I opened my mouth to ask how she knew me, but she started talking again before I could get anything out.

"Oh, this one's on the house," she said, breezing through my confusion, and then she winked at me. "You'll be back."

"Thanks," I said, looking at the card.

Minnie Davidson, Diviner.

"I have a studio upstairs," Minnie chirped. "Tea leaves are for the ancients—I'll paint your future beautifully, even if it's tragic. All lives are works of art."

I guess she's older than she looks, I thought. And she was probably just pretending to know me, to get me to hire her. "Um . . . can you point me to your restroom?"

She did, without losing her bright smile.

I sipped the coffee on my way there, and it was like Becca's presence was still there with me as the warmth from the drink made its way from my lips to my fingertips, comforting my soul.

Invigorated, I tucked Minnie's colorful card into my jacket, already deciding I liked her. Clearly, this was my biggest weakness. Any annoying person could worm their way into my heart just by handing me yummy coffee. But I knew then that

Minnie was right—I would be back. If she didn't ban me for life because of what I was about to do.

I ducked into the hallway leading to the restroom and then made for the door to the stairs instead. It swung open easily, without a creak.

Excellent. I didn't even have to break any locks. Hoping things would be a fraction this smooth once I made it to the building next door, I climbed the stairs. Curiosity tempted me to peek into Minnie's studio at the top of the first flight, but I kept going without stopping. I would have plenty of time for that later.

After two more flights of stairs, I opened the door to the roof and took in a breath of the crisp air. I loved the feeling of the wind in high places. The higher, the better. It was cold, yes, but also comforting. Pressing against my skin like an infinite blanket that never stopped moving. If I fell, I might die, but it would feel like the wind was cradling me, rocking me to my death as one might rock a child to sleep.

Yeah, I was crazy. But I needed to be crazy to do some of the things I did on a regular basis without letting fear overwhelm me. Like jumping from the rooftop of one building to another.

After a brief look around to make sure no one was up here smoking, I reluctantly set down my unfinished coffee and did exactly that. One smooth leap, with my still-strong leg muscles, and for a moment I was flying. The wind embraced me, whispering words of strength into my skin. Telling me I could do anything, go anywhere, be anyone. I might be rusty in combat, and aim, and investigative work, but this one superpower would never leave me.

The intoxicating feeling left me as quickly as it had taken me over, when my feet hit the pavement and my body rolled forward to absorb the shock. And when I uncurled myself to stand up and get my bearings, a familiar face welcomed me.

Adrian stepped forward out of the corner he'd apparently been hiding in and gave me a little wave. He looked a lot more alive than the last time I'd seen him, and the jelly was gone from his neck, but the two days' worth of light stubble he'd grown while asleep with me was still there. And seeing it only made me remember the intoxicating feel of it grazing my cheek.

Damn it. I could have used the rest of Minnie's mocha right about now.

"Hey," he said. "You're lucky it's me here and not Dirk, because that . . ." He gestured his head at where I'd just jumped from. "That definitely wouldn't have helped your case in his book."

I brushed myself off, discreetly making sure all my weapons were still in place, and the corner of my mouth turned up in distaste. "What are you even doing here? Aren't you supposed to be inside?"

"Yeah, well, the Sweepers have cameras outside, and they spotted you going in next door," he said. "It was either me up here waiting for you or them."

"It's just a precaution," I snapped. "I'm sure they won't admit it, but these guys do want me dead for some reason. Badly."

I really wished I could get rid of the bitchy tone in my voice, but it refused to leave me. What I needed to do was apologize to this guy, because he was honestly better at this shit than I was, and for Becca's sake we needed to work together.

But it had shaken me more than I'd thought, our sleep-hazed encounter. It had brought back all the terror of losing myself I'd associated with Simeon. The terror of becoming useless again. And my defenses had put themselves way, way up, even though I knew they wouldn't help me here.

"Oh, I know," he said, unfazed by my bitchiness. "They tried to kill me too, remember?" Before I could respond, he kept going, and a little excitement crept into his voice. "You know, that creature was another thing I never thought I'd see—not in this day and age, and not in this region. Cipactli, a sea monster documented in Aztec mythology that was said to have been there when the earth was created. The gods actually created the earth from its body, supposed—"

"Aztec, you said?" I interrupted. Never mind that it was crazy for him to even know what that thing was, or that he seemed to want to nerd out about it after it had come so close to ending us . . . my stomach had dropped as soon as he'd said Aztec.

"Yeah. That mean something to you?"

It did and it didn't. I knew now that Ray and Carina were minions of an Aztec god. The same god's molten bunnies had been following me around and were still lurking in my car. And I had seen a vision of Becca's soul in that god's realm . . . But how could a volcano god be connected to all these ice witches? The sea monster had been plated in ice, and the ice magic had led us here, to the Sweepers, and not to Ray.

"Maybe," I said, in the interest of saving time. Hopefully, we would know more after talking to the ice-cold murderers downstairs. "Let's just go in and see what they say."

No one tried to kill us on our way in. Maybe Adrian and Dirk had cleared the way earlier, or maybe all the Sweepers' minions were smart enough to hide from me. Either way, I found myself a little disappointed. Even now, I wanted to avoid this conversation—I wanted to just fight the problem to make it go away.

"You'll have to accept our deepest apologies, Miss Pierce," a small, young, meticulously put-together woman said to me when we walked into her office—which, as it turned out, was the most un-officelike office I'd ever been in. It looked more like a garden.

Green things grew out of pots and over trellises everywhere I turned, flowers were blooming in every color, and there was even a fish tank built into the floor in the corner of the room, made to mimic a pond.

The woman had her back to us when she spoke, with Dirk inspecting some flower beside her, and she sprayed something out of a mister onto the tall plant in front of her before she turned to face me.

"I was just showing your associate here some of my rarer specimens," she said, her bright blue eyes catching in the light, offsetting the harsh look of her sleek black hair and her sharp gray suit. "Although, of course, all natural life is becoming rarer these days." She cocked her head to the side and gave me a half smile as she offered me her hand. "I'm Shelby Wren, President of the Sweepers Society for Natural Rights. Pleasure to meet you."

It was only when Adrian widened his eyes at me from her side that I gritted my teeth and shook her hand.

Not that it meant I was accepting the bitch's apology. I wanted to snap at her about how sorry doesn't cut it when you try to kill someone and they kill all your pathetic assassins right back, but that wouldn't get me anywhere useful. So instead I said, "What exactly are you apologizing for?" Get her to admit what she did. My interrogation teachers at the Academy would be proud.

But she only smiled at me and said, "For assuming the worst of you, of course."

Dirk let out a little chuckle at that, then quickly averted his eyes from my gaze, and I choked down a comment about wondering whose side he was really on.

Shelby moved over to her desk, which I'd almost over-looked because it was covered in so much foliage, then sat down and rested her chin on her hands as she continued, "After what happened last year to Senator Drake, I'm afraid we couldn't help but suspect you when one of our esteemed donors was assassinated in his home a few days ago and we found he had ties to your *other* associate."

Did she mean Becca? I gulped, trying to keep my jaw from dropping at the brazenness of it all. But she wasn't done.

"I'm just glad Detectives Crane and Quincy were able to pinpoint the real culprit before we could take any action against you. You look like an absolute dear; I almost can't believe now that we thought you were a killer."

I opened my mouth, but nothing came out. Part of me was trying not to laugh at her calling Dirk by his ridiculous last name. Mostly, all I wanted in that split second was to prove to her that I *was* actually a killer, no matter how dear I may look.

But she was clearly just trying to get under my skin, distract me from the fact that she was both admitting she'd tried to have me killed and denying it at the same time—and it was working.

Luckily, Adrian stepped in and saved me from myself. "That's actually what we'd like to talk to you about. We're trying to gather as much information as possible about Omar so we can ensure we have the right culprit."

"Oh, you aren't sure?"

"We're . . . quite sure about Rebecca Linden as the arsonist, but she herself was murdered shortly after Omar. It's likely their deaths are connected, which means it's likely Rebecca wasn't the only culprit in Omar's murder. We're investigating both cases."

"I see." Her eyes drifted over to me for a moment, and I could tell that if there was any part of her that had actually believed in my innocence for a moment, it was gone. But she couldn't say it, because my supposed innocence was the only thing keeping us from accusing her of trying to have me killed. And now she might need to keep trying.

"So, what can you tell us about Omar?"

"Well . . . he was our most generous donor, by far. Still, not everyone here was happy to be associated with him. He was, of course, not human. Not a natural creature in any sense. But . . . he was one of our most important allies, just for that reason. He knew he was a threat to humanity, and the others like him as well. Too old, he said, too powerful, and getting more and more reckless as the years went by. He said he'd spent his life watching others of his kind be driven mad and wreak destruction, and that he would do whatever it took to ensure it never happened again."

"He wanted to eliminate his own species?" I asked.

"I think so, yes. Of course, I told him many times that we in this society are not in the business of *eliminating* anyone. We are not killers."

She offered no further explanation on that count, and I gathered that was because she had none. It was an outright lie. Legislation may be their official starting point, but I'd seen these people's propaganda and rhetoric. Genocide of everything they deemed "unnatural" was the logical conclusion. And already they seemed to be trigger-happy with assassins.

Fuck it, I thought. This wasn't a court; I could ask leading questions. So I said, "Is that why all the assassins you hire are non-humans? Non-natural, as you would say?"

She smiled, and the twinkle in her eyes told me her answer was yes even as she said, "I have no idea what you're talking about. But if you've run into multiple assassins and all have been non-human, I'm not surprised. The violent tendencies of the supernatural are exactly what my organization hopes to protect against."

"And yet you were happy to take money from Mr. Kanaan? A . . ." I squinted and looked at Adrian, realizing I still didn't know what type of non-human, non-fae, possibly-djinn Omar had been.

Adrian just shrugged.

"You don't know what he was?" Shelby asked, seemingly happy to take back some of the control in our exchange.

"Do you?" I shot back.

"Of course. And it's the only reason I'm talking to you in the first place. The only reason I care about finding his killer. He wanted to die anyways—I have no need for vengeance. But the others of his kind . . . they will be looking to avenge him. They must. It's a compulsion, rooted into their makeup. That's why he needed our help to find a way to neutralize the rest of his kind without bringing their wrath down on all of humanity."

"So, he was . . . ?"

"An ifrit."

"A type of infernal djinn," Adrian supplied, enlivened now. "Inherently evil. One of the myths I read about them suggested that they often act as vigilantes, following murdered souls to their murderers and then trapping the killers' souls in eternal torment and flame."

"Like hell walking on two legs," Shelby finished for him, venom in her voice.

"But if they only go after murderers . . ." I started, confused at why this was so evil. Killing murderers was one of my favorite pastimes, personally.

"They don't," Shelby said. "Murderers are like dessert for them. Icing on the cake. Evil souls are the most delicious to an evil creature. But Omar told me there's always collateral damage. Especially when it's one of their own that's been murdered. When that happens, they go on sprees. Rampages. Devouring souls indiscriminately until they're sure they've gotten the killer. Sometimes even beyond that, extending their rage to anyone and anything the killer ever loved. To further torment the offending soul."

"And that's why you want so badly to find out who killed Omar . . ." Adrian said.

Shelby squeezed her eyes shut and whispered, "I'm amazed we're all still alive. If I were an ifrit looking to go on a rampage against humans who may have killed Omar, this would be the first place I'd try."

"So you thought if you could find his killer first, that could save you," I said. "And you thought his killer was me, because I'm friends with Becca and she had a motive."

"And you have a history of assassinating—"

"I don't, and you should fucking know that," I snapped, getting up. I could play nice when need be, but this was the one person I couldn't tolerate insinuating I'd assassinated Simeon. This was the woman in charge of the society who had actually had him killed.

She looked shocked at my response, but she quickly looked away from me and composed herself. When she turned back to us, her expression was cold, hard. "I think we're done here," she said. "I hope you can find everyone involved in Omar's death and make that information very public—and do it soon. Because I don't want to be trapped for eternity, burning inside an infernal djinn's private hell."

My insides went cold when she said that, and not only because it appeared I'd been wrong about some kind of after-life existing. I should have made the connection much sooner in the conversation, but once again, my brain worked slower when distracted by anger.

A trapped soul, burning for eternity . . . We were all still alive because the ifrit avenging Omar already had the soul of his killer in its private hell. Becca's soul. That must have been what Ray's god had been trying to show me outside of the obsidian cave, all those burning souls trapped along with Becca's.

But if what Shelby had said was true, why hadn't there been any collateral damage?

I shook my head. Whatever luck had kept the ifrit from coming after me and the Sweepers, and probably everyone who had ever associated with either Becca or Omar ever, I was about to spit in its face.

I stood and looked to the side to avoid eye contact with Shelby. "I recommend . . ." Bats, this made me sick to say, but it would be such a dick move not to. "I recommend that you close up shop for the day. And maybe the next couple days, too. Send everyone home, take a vacation. Enjoy your damn life."

"That's crazy," Shelby protested. "Why for the love of the earth would I do that?"

"Because I know why we're not all dead yet. The avenging ifrit already has its killer's soul. And I'm going to steal it back."

17

SOMEONE WAS BLOWING up Becca's phone as I sped through traffic behind the wheel of a police car after deciding to leave my slower, bunny-infested ride behind. Adrian was in the passenger seat, and Dirk Quincy was in the back. Neither had been happy about the arrangement, which was probably technically illegal, but both had been too afraid of me to protest.

Dirk still thought I was some kind of assassin witch, and Adrian had seen whatever it was I'd done to the hungry-bitch sea monster—Cipactli, he'd said—that had tried to kill us. And after our meeting with Shelby, I wasn't willing to mess around in the least.

When I'd refused to explain to them where we were going or why, Dirk had mumbled something about residual squishy effect and called Miriam—who, as far as I could tell, had told him to just shut up and be cool. Ridiculous as she was, I might be starting to love that woman.

I'd flipped on their stupid lights and sirens and floored the gas, hoping that all the annoying drivers who normally plagued my existence would have good enough reflexes to get out of my way.

So far, it was working. But when we hit traffic on the bridge, Adrian took advantage of me slowing down to start talking at me again.

"Not that I don't love suicide missions," he said, "but I've always thought they should be a last-resort kind of thing, so I'd love to know if you have some plan that doesn't involve all of us burning for eternity in infernal fire."

I glanced over at him briefly, goaded into it by the cars in front of me doing a terrible job of getting out of my way, and immediately regretted it. He didn't look scared so much as innocent—that ineffable false innocence again that no cop with his experience should exude. And my instincts made me weak wherever innocents were concerned. So I answered him, even though talking to anyone was the last thing I wanted to do right now.

"We kill the avenging ifrit before it can kill us," I said.

"Uh . . . out of curiosity," Dirk piped up from the back, his voice heavy with sarcasm. "How exactly are you gonna kill something like that?"

I gritted my teeth and pressed a little harder on the gas, even if it meant pressing harder on the brakes just a moment later. "You two are going to tell me how."

Dirk pressed his face close to the bars separating the back seat from the front and said, "Lady, if you think we get paid enough to fight ivrai . . . ifra . . . demons and monsters and whatever the hell this thing is—"

"I think you know exactly how Becca managed to kill Omar, who was an ifrit. The same thing should work on this one."

"Ah . . ." Adrian started.

"I know you were keeping something from me at that crime scene," I interrupted. "I don't know what and I don't know why, but you're going to fucking tell me now if you want to live through the night."

Their combined silence sent a strange uneasiness into my gut, and then the buzzing from Becca's phone made it worse, so I reached into my pocket to grab it. Tossing it to Adrian beside me, I said, "Who the hell keeps calling?"

"Bawdy Baz?" he said. "Seven voicemails and a few texts."

That was worrisome, considering how much Baz hated phones. I wondered whether he even knew I had Becca's phone. He must. Not even Baz would try this hard to contact a woman he knew was a zombie.

"Well?" I prompted. "What does he want?"

"He wants to . . . to know where 'the boy' is."

"What the hell? Etty said Baz was there when she picked up Noah."

"Should I just call him and put him on speaker?"

"Go for it," I said, somewhat reluctantly.

I barely heard one ring and Baz was already chattering on the other end of the line, talking so fast I could barely make sense of what he was saying.

"Slow down!" I yelled, and he stopped.

"Ah, birdie?" he asked after a brief pause. "Is that you?"

"Well, you didn't think this would be Becca, did you?"

"No, I thought—I was trying to reach the tall one who took the boy. Is she with you? I need to find the boy—I absolutely must—It's a matter of life and death and—"

"Calm down, Baz," I said. "Etty said she was taking Noah to the club for her shift today. But what's so important that—"

"What?!" he screeched. "What club?"

"The club she works at. The club I work at. The club you work at. The club his mother worked at . . ." I was across the bridge now and getting closer to the club in question, where I would be going after a quick trip home to pick up Noah myself, who was my best chance at finding the ifrit who had stolen his mother's soul. After all, he was half ifrit himself. And my patience was running thin now.

"No, no, no, no, no, no, no . . ."

He kept going with the noes, over and over, and I had to yell "Baz!" at the top of my lungs to get him to stop. "What the hell is going on, Baz?" I said once I thought he might be listening.

But the line was dead. He had hung up on me.

"Any idea what that was about, little lady?" Dirk piped up from the back. "Cause it didn't sound like anything good."

Adrian gently put the phone down as I chewed on my tongue, and then he said, "Noah?"

Somehow, the tone of his voice was enough to get across what he was implying. Noah—the boy I'd just acknowledged was half ifrit himself. Could he be *the* ifrit we were looking for? The ifrit who had murdered his mother and stolen her soul? Becca *had* gone straight to Noah when she'd been revived as a zombie, and we'd already suspected she might have been trying to lead us to her soul.

And from what I'd heard about ifrit nature from Shelby and Adrian, the urge for vengeance would be instinctual, probably enough so that Noah could have killed his own mother without realizing he was doing it. And now . . . now that he wasn't being distracted by Salma's lessons, Baz was worried Noah would continue on the path of vengeance, starting with the club.

My fingers clenched the steering wheel so hard they turned white. I had been planning to kill the ifrit who had trapped Becca's soul—hopefully with Becca's body present. That plan had seemed logical enough.

Except . . . could I do that to Noah? Could I kill him to save Becca or avenge her? She wouldn't want me to. I knew that as sure as I knew my own name. But I also knew the kid, and I knew what he was going through, somewhat at least. I might be able to stop him without killing him, but only if I could get there before Baz—who would surely not be merciful. No time to stop at home for Becca first.

"Call Miriam," I said, picking up the phone again and thrusting it back in Adrian's direction. "Tell her to bring Becca to the club, as fast as possible."

Adrian slipped the phone through the barrier to Dirk in the back, and then he just looked at me. "Are you thinking what I am?"

"That it's the kid? Yeah." I said, my eyes quickly moving back to the road. "So, good news, we might not have to kill anything. Bad news . . ."

"If we do, it'll suck a lot more," he finished for me.

"Yeah," I said. "But I still need to know how to kill . . ." I couldn't finish the sentence. *How to kill my dead friend's little boy.* "What did Becca do in that house that you don't want me to know about?"

Adrian glanced back at Dirk quickly, who was distracted by what sounded like Miriam giving him a lecture through the phone. Then he said, "You're not going to like it."

"I don't have time to worry about what I'll like right now—just tell me."

"Okay." He took a deep breath. "It was some kind of black magic."

He said it like it was something to talk about in hushed voices, in hidden spaces, lest it hear you and come after you. Black magic, the boogieman of post-Opening civilization.

Now that everyone knew magic was real, the populace needed something to fear beyond the obvious predatory vampires and shifters, who were generally really good at PR.

Black magic was the thing. The stuff of demons, devils, folk who wore too much eyeliner and killed chickens and all that. It was nonsense, really. No real magic users actually did that kind of thing, as far as I knew. It would be horribly inefficient. And despite the infernal djinn I'd just learned about, there was no devil to worship, no underworld teeming with demons, no one divine embodiment of evil—the multitude of gods that had toyed with the mortal world once upon a time had handled good and evil and everything in between without any help from below.

How could I be so sure? Well, I'd been forced to toy with mortality enough as a child to have a much more solid understanding of these things than anyone ought to. I'd followed many souls to the edges of death and guided them back to reality, and I'd seen firsthand that there was nothing resembling life after death. Everyone I'd saved, I'd saved them from the same thing—a void. Absolute nothingness.

I never wore hats, but if I ever found myself in something that looked like fire-and-pitchfork hell being tortured by something that looked like a demon, I'd eat my boots. And then I'd find a way to fight my way out and kill whoever had thought it would be funny to play that kind of joke on me.

"Black magic," I repeated to Adrian, trying not to let him feel too much of my disdain. "What makes you say that?"

"Runes drawn on the ground in blood, within a circle of salt, and a sacrificed . . ."

"A sacrificed what?" I pressed.

"A baby goat," he whispered, and I tensed.

Goats were Becca's favorite animal. And a baby . . . If she'd really done that, it would have broken her heart. Not to mention about a billion fae laws, probably. But why would she? And where would she even have gotten the goat?

"Why would you keep that from me in the first place?" I asked. I really had no idea why they would. It was interesting evidence, whatever it meant, and if I were them I would have wanted an extra brain working at it.

Adrian looked back at Dirk before answering and found the man asleep with his head against the window, Becca's phone fallen to the seat beside him. I wondered if Miriam had some kind of siren magic to sing him to sleep over the phone, or if we'd just gotten lucky.

"He's really afraid of you, you know," Adrian said.

I frowned. "Seriously? Dirk thought if he mentioned black magic to me that I'd—what? Voodoo him to death?"

"Kind of? Probably. Subconsciously . . . Maybe," Adrian stammered. "But his official reasoning was that we should hold back some details to catch you in a lie. He suspected you helped Becca with the arson and murder, especially when we couldn't see on camera who actually started the fire."

"And you suspected me too? Or you just didn't have the balls to tell your partner he was being an idiot?"

Adrian opened his mouth and then closed it, fists clenched. After a moment, he said, "A little of both." I raised my eyebrows at him, and he continued, "Okay, mostly the latter. I knew you wouldn't have helped Becca—you would have just handled things on your own had she come to you for help."

He was right about that, and I squirmed a little in my seat, uncomfortable at him predicting my hypothetical behavior so accurately.

"I'm good at reading people," he said, without waiting for a response from me. "It's how I know Dirk wouldn't hesitate to fuck me over and get me fired if he thought he couldn't push me around. He needs to feel like the boss. And I need this job."

I wrinkled my forehead at him. "Never thought I'd hear anyone say that about being a cop these days. I'm sure you could make more money else—"

"Look, I don't want to talk about it," he said quickly. And then, probably assuming (correctly) that I wouldn't drop it, he banged his elbow on the barrier to wake up Dirk.

"I said I don't know whose turtle that is!" Dirk yelled as he sat up with a jolt.

The look on his face in the rear-view mirror was hilarious, and I'm sure I would have laughed had I not been on my way to possibly having to murder my best friend's adorable little boy.

"You're in luck," I said, putting my game face back on. Dirk might need to feel like the boss of his partner, but I liked his healthy fear of me just fine. "No turtles where we're headed. But we might need a goat." Trying not to smirk at the clear horror in his expression, I dug into my pocket and then slipped Ray's business card back to him. "Call this number and tell them to bring one to the club."

There was no way Becca had come up with any "black magic" on her own, especially nothing involving goat sacrifice. And Ray *had* said he'd helped Becca with her ex. I was hoping with every fiber of my being that I wouldn't need to ask them what to do with the damn goat to kill a six-year-old ifrit boy, but I hadn't made it this far in life by being unprepared.

ETTY WAS DANCING when we got to the club, and the exuberant look on Dirk's face when her golden crop top flew past him was enough to put a slight damper on how happy I was to see her.

"Darcy, thank god!" someone shouted at me from across the dark, bustling room. A busy night tonight. When I turned towards the voice, I saw Mitch looking at me with round, desperate eyes as he frantically moved glasses and bottles around behind my bar.

Right. Baz had changed his mind about covering for me before he'd had his meltdown and decided Noah needed killing. And apparently Mitch had a rock-solid work ethic, despite having no actual skill in bartending. It almost warmed my heart to see him try so hard.

"Dirk," I said, elbowing the man next to me in the gut until he tore his eyes away from my fae roommate, who was getting nakeder by the second.

He jumped away from me as if I'd nudged him with a gun

instead of my elbow. Wow. Adrian hadn't been joking—this guy really was terrified of me, and trying to hide it.

"What?" he said, the venom of fear-tinged embarrassment in his voice.

"I bet you can make a mean drink, yeah?"

He perked up a little at the compliment, rubbing his side. "Well, I mean—"

"Great, that'll be your cover for the night. Get over there and work the bar." I turned to Adrian. "And you—talk to Mitch. Make sure he's ready to evacuate everyone if things get dicey."

"Shouldn't we just go ahead and close the place now?" Adrian asked.

"Not if we want to have any chance of getting Noah out of this alive. Baz will be here soon, and if the place is empty, there'll be nothing to stop him from just waltzing over and killing the little boy in the back. But with his customers as witnesses . . . he'll at least pause first."

I looked over at the stage as Etty clacked her heels together loudly, the sound catching my attention. Her eyes found mine and, disguising the motion with a graceful body roll, she used her head to point me to the dressing room. Then she smiled at a couple women who had just tipped her and cooed something at them that I couldn't quite make out.

I had almost forgotten—ladies' night tonight. The second Saturday of every month, women got in without paying a cover. That was why it was so busy. It had been my idea, and Baz had gone for it without understanding I'd envisioned it with male dancers. It ended up being a surprise success, and we quickly became popular for being one of the few clubs that catered to non-hetero women.

Ladies' night had become one of my favorites, especially because sometimes we *did* bring in a male dancer or two, but right now I wished it were any other night. This was already going to be a delicate endeavor, trying to get Baz not to kill Noah and Noah not to kill everyone in here—and the last thing I needed was another variable. The ladies might sometimes be more fun than the men, but they were also more challenging; none of us had as much practice with them as with our regular clientele.

Oh well. Whatever the circumstances, I had to get it done. Taking a deep breath, I walked across the floor and slipped into the dressing rooms, where Etty had pointed me.

Instead of the usual cacophony of music and chattering, all I heard were snores.

Well, shit. Now I could see why Etty had wanted me to come back here. Everyone was asleep. Noah in the middle of them all, on the one couch we all shared, his face peaceful and angelic, a hot-pink blanket laid over him.

Kat was literally curled up at his feet, looking more like the little boy's pet than the ruthless bloodsucker I knew she was. A couple other dancers were slumped over in their chairs, and one was even lying on the floor, sucking her damn thumb.

I felt a yawn fight its way up my throat, and I immediately clamped down on it, trying to focus on the glimmers of magic around me to infuse myself with energy. But the magic still wasn't listening to me, and I felt my eyelids getting heavy, my knees weakening . . .

"Gah! Noah!" I yelled as I crumpled to the ground, and he stirred. "Wake uuuuu . . ." The yawn finally escaped, hijacking my entire neck and mouth before I could tell the kid to get his ass up and stop doing this to us. Because he was doing it to us.

Even though I couldn't control the magic in the room anymore, I could still sense it. Becca had been a master at fae evocation, the ability to magically implant thoughts and emotions into the minds of others. She'd never needed to infuse drinks like I did. It was her natural ability. Instinctual.

She'd probably had to work for years to be able to control it, and Noah probably would too.

Perhaps he'd already been working with Becca on it and her absence had triggered him to lose control, or perhaps Salma had awoken this ability with whatever others she'd been toying with over the past few days. Hopefully nothing too deadly.

The muscles in my jaw and neck relaxed again as Noah sat up, rubbing his eyes, and I braced myself for his inevitable anger at me for not being able to protect his mom. After all, if Baz was worried Noah would go ballistic, the boy must have found out about his mother.

"Hi Darcy," he said in a sleepy voice, not the least bit murderous. "Is my mom here yet? I'm hungry."

"I can get you some food," I said, carefully avoiding his question. If he didn't know yet . . . I would need to find a way to tell him as gently as possible. "What do you want to eat?"

His eyes focused on me, the last remnants of sleep falling away from them as he gave me a little smirk. "Lobster!" he yelled with deviant glee. He'd just begun to learn which foods were expensive and which were cheap.

And suddenly I felt a little devious and gleeful as well. I had to admit it was a nice change of pace. Some of the dancers had woken up now, and they were starting to get back to their primping and chatting, but Kat was still curled up on the couch.

Like alcohol, this kind of thing must hit vampires slower and harder. A vampire's heart is stronger than almost anything else's, but their other organs kinda suck.

I bounced my eyebrows up and down at Noah while holding my finger to my lips, then snatched up a tube of fuchsia lipstick from the table next to us.

Then I drew a vagina on Kat's face. With vampire fangs coming out of it. Bitten Kitten—Toothy Pussy. I chuckled. She could thank me later for all the extra tips she'd get from the ladies tonight.

Noah just looked confused at this point, tilting his head and squinting his eyes at what I'd drawn. "Is it a lobster?" he asked.

"Nope," I said, sobering up and regretting my life choices in a way I hadn't done in years. I forced a smile back on my face. "And while I'd love to go dive into the ocean to catch you a lobster right now—well, the ocean is too far away for that. How about some red gummy fish instead? That's pretty close. Same color, same habitat, all that."

He looked at me suspiciously for a moment, then slapped his hands on the couch as he jumped up and said, "Yes, please!"

I banged open Etty's locker, where I knew she always kept candy, and started rooting around for the bag of sweet fishes that should be in here somewhere. Then I heard the back door open, the entrance no customers knew about that led straight into the dressing rooms, and I jerked into action, spilling candy all over the floor as my hands sprang out of the locker to reach for my weapons.

If this was Baz—

"Baaaaaaaaaaaaaaa," the tiny, white, fluffy monster bleated as it hopped over to me and nipped at some of the gummy worms on the ground. Soft fur brushed against my hands, and tears nearly came to my eyes with the overwhelming urge to wrap my arms around the sweet, adorable creature when . . .

Ah, Noah. These were his emotions. I could tell because he'd just run over and tackled the baby goat in an aggressive snuggle. Just like Becca would have done if she were here.

"Darcy! Is this where you work?"

I looked up to see a gleeful Carina, no longer in her school uniform and no longer with her . . . dragon bits exposed. She looked older somehow as herself like this, in a sweatshirt and jeans, and I wondered for the first time if she was really only eight years old.

"Yep," I said, to answer her question. "Does your father know you're here?"

"Nooooo," she said slowly, with round eyes. "He's still pissed about whatever happened with you. Or what didn't happen. Locked himself in his office. Brooding or whatever. But he wouldn't let me come here before when I wanted to see it, so . . . maybe keep this between us?"

"I will if you will," I said, then glanced over at the other child in the room, the one currently cuddling the creature I'd been considering sacrificing to kill him with. And for the second moment in the last five minutes, I regretted my life choices in a way I hadn't done in years.

"Sounds good," Carina chirped. "Okay, here's the rest of it." She dropped a bag on the table next to me and said, "Page sixty-two of the book. And don't worry—if you don't get it right on the first try, I have more." She licked her lips and jerked her eyebrows at the goat with a wink, and my toes curled when it dawned on me just why a dragon shifter apparently had easy access to a never-ending supply of goats. Gross.

"Well, thank you—"

"Ah, and we were out of sacrificial daggers, so I brought you a mace instead."

"A wh—"

"But that should be better, right? Harder to make a mistake with a mace. It'll kill anything you swing it at."

"Sorry, I think I'm missing something," I said. "Why do I need your mace? I have plenty of weapons of my own."

"But you don't have any forged in dragon fire, right?"

"No, but—"

"That's what you'll need for the ritual. Not to kill the goat, silly," she said, shaking her head at me. "To call forth the spirit of an ifrit and infuse some of its essence into. That's what the whole ritual is for. You need a weapon infused with an ifrit's essence to kill another ifri—"

At this point, I grabbed Carina's arm and swung her small body towards me, wrapping her up in what I hoped looked something like a hug so I could cover her mouth and drag her into the bathroom with me. The last thing I needed right now was a perfectly happy Noah getting triggered by overhearing us plotting to kill him.

Once we were in there, she rubbed her mouth where I'd pressed my hand over it, then just kept talking. "I was saying, you need a weapon infused with an ifrit's essence to kill another ifrit. You sacrifice the goat, you use its blood to mark out the sigils for the ritual, which is a summoning. It summons an ifrit and then traps a tiny piece of its essence in the weapon. Which is forged in dragon fire and made at least partially of glass. Because glass is the best material to trap essence with." She finally paused and looked around. "Why are we in here? Is this where the poles are? Can I climb one?"

I ignored her question. Something about this didn't sit right with me. "But . . ." I said. "If ifrit are all compelled to avenge their killed brethren . . . Wouldn't summoning one just before killing another be suicide?"

Carina shrugged. "Sure, I guess. Maybe that's why Ray kept trying to convince your friend to use Noah's essence instead of doing the summoning."

"Of course." I groaned. Suddenly it all made sense. Becca wouldn't have wanted to involve Noah in killing his father, for so many reasons. She would have done the ritual to keep him out of it, and to save him from his father, even knowing it would probably get her killed. That must be what she'd been ranting about right before she died . . . She'd wanted to tell Ray that she'd done the summoning instead of using Noah, because she loved Noah too much.

"Hey, maybe that's who killed her, then?" Carina piped up,

breaking through my thoughts. "The ifrit she summoned with our ritual? I mean, not *our* ritual, really—we just found that book at the library. But you know what I'm say—"

"Great, thanks Carina," I said as I pushed her out of the bathroom, through the dressing room, and then quickly out into the cold. "Tell Ray I'm going to come by later to murder him, yeah? Now that I know just how he helped my friend get herself killed. Ifrit aren't the only ones who know how to do vengeance."

"Hey, I helped too!" Carina said just before I slammed the door in her face. Good fucking riddance.

The noise startled Noah, who looked up at me with a smile as the floofy monster in his arms let out a particularly loud bleat.

The good news was that this sweet little boy hadn't killed his own mother and, as far as I could tell, had no plans to kill anyone else. So I wouldn't need to kill him. The bad news was that now I was most definitely going to need to kill a bigger, stronger, more murderous ifrit, and I had no idea who.

18

Etty nearly crashed into me as I came through the dressing room door back onto the floor of the club. After swerving and catching her balance (which could only be magic, with how tall her heels were), she grabbed my arm and hauled me into a private dance room.

"Why did you bring those cops here?" she snapped at me, taking me by surprise. This fierceness in her eyes, the claws cutting into my bicep, and the sharp words . . . I'd seen Etty like this before, but never quite this intense. She was pissed at me, and it was much more serious than any of the roommate spats we'd had.

"I'm sorry?" I said. "I thought we might need all the help we can get. They're just looking out for Baz now. I think he's coming to kill Noah." Etty's fingernails dug deeper into my arm as her eyes narrowed, and I continued, "Long story. Baz thinks the kid is going to destroy his club, but it's more likely some other asshole is coming to do that job. Whoever it was that killed Becca."

Etty sighed. "Why can't it ever just be a normal level of shit in my life?" she asked.

"I've been asking myself that all week."

"Look," she said. "You have to get Noah out of here. I'm . . . I'm supposed to be his guardian, with Becca gone. She asked me last week, and . . ." Etty loosened her grip on me a little and looked away. "I promised her I would take care of him."

"I have to talk to Baz first," I said quickly. "Otherwise he'll just keep coming after me until he gets his hands on Noah. Wait . . ." I had finally registered how weird it was that Etty was looking away from me. She never did that. Always made eye contact. It was one of the things I liked about her, how unapologetically intimidating she was all the time. The sense of unshakable confidence she exuded. "Why didn't you tell me before that Becca wanted you to take Noah?"

She looked at me again, but her eyes were soft, wandering around my face instead of boring into my own eyes. "I . . . was going to. But I'm not going to be able to keep my promise to her now," she said. "It's my queen—she didn't buy my 'saved a cat' excuse, and she says I've been using too much dust for mortal interests. I've been ordered to return to the fae realm."

"For how long?"

"Indefinitely."

"But—she can't just make you go!" My head was spinning now, and I felt dizzy from a sudden sense of emptiness inside me, like I hadn't eaten in days. Which, to be honest, I hadn't really.

Even if Etty and I weren't exactly friends, I was about to lose the only roommate I had left. Both gone in a matter of days. There would be no one to have coffee with, no one to bitch with after a bad day, no one to laugh with about stupid nothings, no one to worry about, no one to protect. It would be like losing Simeon all over again. Alone with my guilt, only now the guilt would be triple-fold. "It's my fault, isn't it? I asked you to go talk to your queen. And then I called on you to save me at the river . . . and you dusted us all back home. Oh my—"

"It's not your fault," Etty said firmly. "It's my queen's fault. That woman is too stuck in the past. Yeah, I have mortal friends now—that's what happens when you're posted in the mortal realm for a few decades." She touched my cheek and looked at me with eyes softer than I'd ever seen on her. So much so that I actually believed she'd just called me her friend. Then she punched me in the tit. Gently, but not as gently as I would have liked.

"Ow!" I yelled. "What was that for?"

"Look, if it wasn't you, it would have been some other mortal I used too much dust to help. Stop making everything about you, you narcissistic ass."

I thought about punching her back, in her own tit, but it wouldn't have had the same effect. Hers were a lot smaller than mine, and I would have had to reach up to an embarrassing degree, since she was towering over me like always. So instead, I punched lower. And I was only a little disappointed when she caught my fist before it could make contact with her crotch.

"Did you not hear me?" she said in a low, tense voice. "We don't have time for your feelings right now."

I dropped my hand, in shock. It was like hearing my own words thrown back at me. Just a few days ago, after Becca's death, I hadn't had the patience to deal with Etty's feelings. Or anyone's. Not even my own. But guilt and shame were feelings too, and lately I'd been letting them get to me. Letting them distract me.

Etty must have seen my face harden, because she put her hand on my shoulder and said, "Good. Now, I was supposed to report back yesterday. But I needed to stay until I could make sure Noah was safe with you. That means—"

"With me?" My head was starting to spin again, this time with frantic thoughts of Becca. Not that I couldn't handle taking care of Noah, if it came to that—but it would be so much better if I could get him his mom back.

Etty completely ignored my outburst. "*That means* my queen will have notified the authorities of this realm to apprehend me." At my blank stare, she said, "The cops, Darcy. The cops you brought in here tonight. They're going to fucking arrest me and have me hauled back to the fae realm."

As if on cue, a beam of neon purple light shined on Etty's face, sparkling in her eyes as the curtain was pulled back and Dirk stepped in, saying, "Ladies, ladies . . . what kinda party we having in here?"

"You can't just barge into the private rooms, Dirk," I said, a knee-jerk reaction, enforcing the rules of the club like I'd done a million times over the past year.

But Etty had already grabbed him and put him in a dust trance, with the claws of one hand digging into his forearm and the claws of her other hand flirting with the delicate skin over his throat.

Dirk's eyes went white, rolling back into his head, and his lips parted as all the muscles in his body went slack. Etty held him in front of her as if expecting to be shot at. But I knew that wasn't going to happen.

Adrian knew what was at stake tonight—so, even if there was an APB out on Etty, I doubted his priorities were screwy enough that he'd let himself get distracted by a wanted fae who wasn't harming anyone. And I was willing to bet some sexual-favor-wink-wink bluffing was the worst Dirk would have done.

But, it appeared, Etty wasn't in the mood to take risks. I couldn't blame her. "Okay," I said. "I'll keep Noah safe; don't worry. But until we can talk down Baz, this is the safest place for the kid." This club was probably the one place where Baz would think twice before doing anything destructive. "Just put the cop down and get out of here. I can only keep them off your back if they don't think you're trying to kill them."

Etty looked down at Dirk, a little bloodlust in her eyes. She wasn't a vampire, but the fae from her court were creatures of the desert—so they tended to dessicate their enemies with their claws, sucking out not just the blood but all the fluid in a body. Similar enough to a vampire in my book. Not that I would ever say it to her face.

After a brief moment, she dropped Dirk on the velvet lounge chair and said, "Fine." Then she licked her lips, still looking at him.

I shook my head. This was taking too long, and I didn't like being in here behind the curtain, with no eyes on Noah and only Adrian out there keeping watch. So I took a step toward Etty and punched her where I'd been meaning to do so before. This time, she didn't see it coming, and it caused her to yelp and jump back a little.

"Go home," I said to her once she was looking at me. "You'll be safe there for now, and I'll help you dodge whoever you need to dodge as soon as I have a lid on the situation with Noah."

Trusting her, I pushed the curtain aside and made my way back onto the floor, eyes scanning for Adrian.

He was still sitting at the bar, with his back to Mitch, who must have refused to hand over the reins to Dirk. The sandy-haired detective raised his glass to me, and I was just about to head back to the dressing room to check on Noah when the front door burst open, daylight streaming in as Baz sauntered through.

The small man closed his eyes as the door shut behind him, then turned transparent. The whirling colored lights from the stage passed through him, distorting higher and wider as his mist-like form grew in size to be gigantic. As gigantic as the ceiling would allow—and it was a high ceiling. When he re-solidified, I found myself wondering whether I'd climbed a damn beanstalk.

Still, no one had really noticed him, as distracted as they all were by business as usual. That changed when he opened his whale-like mouth and bellowed, "Where is she?" His voice was so loud, the ground shook.

She? I wondered. But my thoughts were drowned out by the screams suddenly bouncing around the room. Women ran in every direction, haphazardly. The dancers knew to head for the back door, but the customers were blocked from the main exit by the giant genie standing in front of it. And since it was ladies' night, there was a lot less false bravado in the room than there normally would have been.

It seemed I'd grossly overestimated Baz's desire to not disrupt his business.

I took a step towards him, steeling myself to confront yet another creature I had no idea how to get the better of, when I heard bleating behind me through the screams.

I turned to find that, sure enough, Becca's curious little child had been drawn into the room by everyone desperately running out of it.

"Uncle Bassam!" he yelled in a voice full of glee. "You're so big! Can you teach me to do that one?"

Noah started to jog towards the giant Baz, and I plucked him off his feet when he tried to run past me. "Not right now, Noah, okay?" I said as I tried to pin his flailing limbs and settle his weight on my hip. The kid was heavier than he looked, but I felt better with my arms around him, the touch assuring my nerves that he was safe. It wasn't like I could fight the giant in front of me with my fists anyway.

Baz grunted a little when he saw Noah and took a step towards us.

I shifted my body to put myself between Baz and Noah before yelling, "Baz! You can calm your gigantic genie tits—the kid isn't going to hurt anyone!"

Baz only repeated his earlier question. "Where is she?"

"Who?" I asked.

"Salma. She'll be looking for the boy. And she'll destroy everything in her path to get to him."

"She's not here," I said slowly. "But why . . . ?"

"Because his idiot mother killed one of Salma's kind," Baz said, his voice becoming lighter and faster as he misted over again and shrank back to his normal size. "I only just found out. The boy was keeping her distracted, but once he was gone, she—"

"She's an ifrit?" I interrupted, already kicking myself for not putting it together sooner. Salma had mentioned she'd been trapped for eons and recently summoned . . . of course, it was Becca who had summoned her, when she was killing Omar.

"Well, yes," Baz said, "And like I warned you earlier, she doesn't take kindly to those who kill her kin. Without the boy to distract her, she'll be in a murderous mood, and I think she wants him back."

Fuck, I thought. I looked at Noah in my arms, and the baby goat dumbly standing by our side, completely unfazed by everything that had just happened.

I couldn't kill the goat. I couldn't summon yet another ifrit. That would just perpetuate this vicious cycle. But I could do what Becca wouldn't and use Noah's life essence to try to kill Salma. Or maybe Baz's would work—he wasn't an ifrit, but he was still a djinn. And he was directly related to Salma.

The ringing of a phone broke through my thoughts, and I turned to see Adrian put his cell to his ear and say, "Shelby? What is it?" He jerked the phone away from his ear as she screamed into it, then hung up just a moment later and yelled at me across the room, "We have to get back to the Sweepers'."

Well, shit. Salma must have decided she wanted vengeance more than a child to distract her. I didn't know whether that was a good thing or a bad thing. On the one hand, at least she was going after people I didn't care about—but on the other hand, they were still people, and I remembered what Shelby had said about the boatloads of collateral damage. Plus, there was no way to be sure Salma wouldn't come to find Noah once she'd had her fill. Not unless I took her out first.

Baz seemed to understand what was going on without being told, because he misted himself right through the wall of the club as Adrian ran out the door.

Without putting Noah down, I dodged back into the dressing room to get the supplies Carina had given me. It was time to see what this ridiculous glass weapon of hers could do.

19

I TAPPED on the glass of the driver's-side window as Baz stumbled out from the back of my car. We'd been squeezed in there together for the ride over to DC; meanwhile Adrian drove and the baby goat slept peacefully curled in a ball on Noah's lap in the front seat. It would have been better to take Adrian's cop car, of course, but Etty had apparently slashed the tires while making her getaway. And Dirk had somehow gone missing, too. But as long as Etty kept him alive, that was probably for the best.

I would have been more pissed at her about it all had my car not shown up on its own, driven by the horde of obsidian bunnies who promptly disappeared again as soon as we opened the doors. At this point, I wasn't going to question it, and I'd told Adrian as much. At least not now, while we had a much bigger problem to face. Those bunnies had helped me once, so now I would have to trust that they weren't leading us all to our doom.

Baz swung the door shut and pulled the palm of his hand to his mouth, wincing as he licked his wound. Big baby. Giant baby. It was only a small cut, and he was acting like I'd chopped his hand off. Even if I had, he could probably just grow another.

Adrian rolled down his window and craned his neck to peer at Baz, who was teetering dangerously on the sidewalk as he paced in circles. "Are you sure this is a good idea?"

"He's fine," I said. "Just being dramatic."

"I . . . am not being . . . dramatic," Baz yelled at us in a slurred voice between spinning in circles. "Evil witch . . . stole my soul!"

I ignored him and shrugged at Adrian. "I only took a little." Turning to Baz, I raised my voice and said, "Don't forget what you can have in return."

The dazed djinn stopped in his tracks. Looking up at me, he whispered, "All of Salma's souls." As if he'd forgotten. Maybe he really wasn't putting on a show—maybe my taking some of his life essence really had taken some of his . . . sanity? That was a troubling thought. But it just meant I'd need to hurry and kill Salma before he could do anything too insane.

"Yep," I said, resisting the urge to pat him on the head and toss him a treat. "Let's go get it done then." To Adrian, I said, "Just take Noah somewhere safe, okay?"

"Sure, okay, but—"

"And if you don't hear from me in an hour, maybe take him to another planet," I said, cutting him off. It was supposed to be a joke, but he didn't look amused. He looked worried, and then annoyed in the next instant, and then he was shaking his pretty head at me and driving off.

I took in a deep breath of air and fingered the handle of the glass mace I held at my side, which had turned a deep sapphire blue after our hasty ritual in the car. Hopefully, that meant I'd done it right. And hopefully, Baz's marid essence was good enough to kill an ifrit.

He'd rambled a bit about family politics while I'd been working in the car, and from what I could gather, Baz had always been an oddball in his family, most of whom were ifrit and looked down on him. Apparently, the marid couldn't steal human souls like the ifrit could. But all djinn enjoyed *consuming* human souls—so Baz's family had fed them to him when he was younger.

He said he'd quit the stuff when he'd moved away from them, he didn't really need it, it wasn't natural, he didn't like himself when he was on it—yada, yada, yada. Turned out the New World had made a great rehab center for his soul devouring addiction when he'd first come over here.

But now, in whatever state I'd put him in by taking some of *his* soul, it was all he could think about. Cracking his Aunt Salma like a damn egg and eating up all the souls that spilled out, souls she'd stolen over the course of her long life.

And I would let him do it, too—as long as I could keep him from eating Becca's.

I'd told Adrian to drop us at Dupont Circle, a couple blocks from the Sweepers' headquarters, to keep from driving Noah directly into danger, but even this far away I could hear the screams. My toes twitched. I wanted to run, but Baz wouldn't be able to keep up. *Who cares, though?* I thought as I looked over at him. If I'd done it right, I had all I needed from him in the mace.

He was currently hugging a fire hydrant, so I gave him a firm smack on his backside and yelled, "Follow me." Then I pounced. My legs sprang into action, eager to be in what felt like their natural state—a state I didn't give them nearly enough opportunity to be in anymore. I ran so fast that the wind rushing across my cheeks almost made me feel like I was flying.

And then, suddenly, I was in the air.

Pain seared through my ankle—my favorite ankle—again as something sharp wrapped around it and jerked my entire body upward. I gritted my teeth and clenched my fingers around the mace, determined not to drop it. That would ruin everything. Once I was sure I had it gripped tightly, I tried to ignore how small everything below me was starting to look. Then I arched my back and twisted my neck to see what had picked me up.

Above me, gleaming black scales covered the enormous body of a dragon, its wings beating lazily as it soared upward. The end of its spiny tail was wrapped around my ankle.

"Carina?" I yelled up at it.

She roared at me in response, and then her head morphed into that of a little girl's in about the creepiest display of shapeshifting I'd ever seen.

"Take off your shoe!" she bellowed at me, so loud I worried whether her dragon lungs would blow out her human vocal cords—though I knew better than to try to wrap my head around the mechanics of shifting like that.

I also knew better than to argue in a situation as ridiculous as this one, so I used all the core strength I had in me to lift myself up and grab my foot, unzipping my boot and letting it fall, probably never to be seen again.

Carina's dragon face reappeared for a brief moment to roar at me again, and then the little girl's head was back and bellowing, "No—the other one!"

I grimaced. She wanted me to take off the boot her tail was wrapped around? That didn't seem like it would end well. She must have gathered what I was worried about, because at that point she swung me up towards her feet and wrapped her claws around my torso. Extra security—great.

"Do it!" she yelled, and I suppressed the urge to roll my eyes.

"Fine," I muttered, reaching around the spikes on her tail to unzip the boot protecting what was left of my favorite foot and Miriam's jelly.

When it fell, Carina's voice reverberated through my ribs. "Is the tattoo gone?"

"What? No. Of course not. What the fuck, Carina—" I shrieked as she whipped her tail back around my ankle, the spines slashing into my flesh and tearing haphazardly. Blood sprayed into my eyes, flung by the wind, and I suddenly felt grateful I still had the mace in my hand. The mace Carina had given me just an hour before.

Trying to ignore the searing pain coming from my foot, and trying not to think about whether or not I would ever be able to walk again, I let out a growling scream and swung the mace up into the dragon's belly.

But it didn't connect. It was falling away. I was falling away with it. She had dropped me.

"Darcy, fly!" she yelled.

If I survive this, I'm never having kids. That was the only thought I could manage as I hurtled towards the concrete city below.

So much for me being family. Ray must have decided he wanted me dead after all. And the fact that he'd sent his eight-year-old daughter to do his dirty work just made it sting even more. I couldn't have seen this coming. Could I have?

At this point, I had next to no faith in my ability to see anything coming. But at this point, it didn't matter. There was no way I could survive this. At least I would go out falling through the air. Cradled by the wind.

Flying.

I closed my eyes, trying to enjoy my final moments in this world, but even that was impossible in the next moment as a fiery pain shredded through my scrye. It felt like someone was ripping me open with a molten weapon from the inside out.

I gripped the mace even harder as I screamed—so hard I might have crushed the glass with my bare hands—and swung it around behind me.

But no one was there. Whatever it was had stayed behind me somehow. And now it was jerking me out of my plummet, causing my stomach to lurch. My legs dangled below me, taunting me. With no ground beneath them, they were useless.

But then the pain dissipated, almost as quickly as it had come, and wind rushed past my face—in the wrong direction. Instead of falling, I was moving up again.

I twisted my neck to look behind me, and I nearly dropped the mace out of shock at what I saw.

Wings. Feathered, flapping—fucking wings. Coming out of my back. Using my muscles to move, and without even asking me first. Majorly rude.

Carina swooped in circles above me, then below as she lowered herself to the ground. She shrieked with delight when she passed me, then roared in the next breath.

I didn't know what she had done to me or why, but I was going to kill her. I relaxed my shoulders and then tensed them again, searching for control in my new appendages. When I found it, the wings stopped flapping for a moment and I began to fall. But then I tipped forward and relaxed a little more, and they found their rhythm again as I carefully lowered myself to the ground.

I landed running on the pavement because I'd come in a bit too fast, but as soon as I could stop the flapping, I was on my ass. One of the wings had caught on a lamp post and toppled me over.

Blinking, I pushed my hair out of my eyes. Feathers floated above me, in rich brown hues. And then Baz's face was hovering above mine as he clapped his hands together.

"Ah, birdie! I see you've finally made friends!"

"What?" I choked out.

"Good job. Salma hates flying things. Come, come—let's go get her!"

He ran off, leaving me looking like a toddler as I tried to

clamber to my feet—a monumental task, now that my center of gravity was all wrong. It was starting to feel better quickly, though.

A man was jogging towards me now. Ray. He offered me a hand, but I didn't take it. He may as well have run up to me to finish the job. I didn't think he'd intended to kill me, but I also didn't think he'd known it was a sure thing that I'd magically grow wings after his daughter dropped me out of the sky.

The weight of the wings was gone now, so I turned my head and reached out to touch the feathers. My fingers went right through them. Not solid. Or at least not solid anymore. They must have been solid when they'd been keeping me in the air.

"They'll come back when you need them," Ray said. Then he frowned. "Probably. There are ways to control them, but no time to teach you now."

"Just enough time to see if they would keep me from going splat?" I said, venom in my voice.

"Ah." He took back his hand and crossed his arms across his chest. "You would not have 'gone splat.'" He repeated my words with distaste. "If removing the mark didn't work, Carina would have caught you."

"What do you mean about my . . ." The words dried up in my throat as I leaned over and moved my hands to my ankle. My favorite ankle, which no longer looked like mine at all.

It was bare. No tattoo, no scars, no blood, no wound. I brought my hands to my sticky, crusty face and scraped off some of what I was sure was my own blood. My fingers came away red. So I hadn't imagined Carina's claws ripping through my flesh.

"Without the mage mark, you'll have access to your full potential. Well . . ." He paused as I looked up at him. "It will take a while and some training and some sweet-talking for you to really access your full potential, but the healing and the flying should at least be good enough to help us now."

"Help us?"

"The, um, ugly creature attacking all those people a few blocks that way?" He pointed. "When Carina told me what she gave you and then I saw the ifrit all over the news, I figured you would be here." He grinned and stuck out his hand again. "Can't have you dying on me yet, hermana."

I took his hand and let him pull me to my feet.

"I was kinda hoping I'd have to catch you," Carina said as she emerged from behind a corner. "But it's good you can fly with us now." She jerked her head at Ray. "I was starting to think he was wrong about you being family."

My head spun with questions, questions and frustration at being literally tossed around in the dark. But now was not the time. Baz was out of sight now, no doubt running towards the screams. And if he got there before I did, he might tip Salma off about me and my blue mace of destruction.

"Come on then," I said. Gripping the mace and hefting it above my shoulder, I began running towards the action myself.

The screams died out before I reached them. But by that point, I didn't need to follow them anymore. I knew where I was. And the giant fiery beast with horns standing in the middle of the street would be a pretty damn good sign, even if I didn't.

It was still wearing shreds of the grandmotherly sweater dress Salma had been wearing the last time I'd seen her, but the glasses were gone now, replaced by enormous glowing eyes, burning like the pits of hell. Its knees were bent in the wrong direction, like all the demonic creatures of storybooks, and it even had a tail sweeping out behind it, knocking over anyone who dared come close.

Bodies were strewn about around the creature, both human and shifter, most of them Sweepers if the piles of magical ice covering the area were any indication. It was melting fast, though, with all the fire. The Sweepers' building itself was nothing but flames, flickering out of every window as the smoke rose and blocked out the setting sun.

None of that shocked me. But the other beast did, the one fighting the fiery demonic thing I assumed was Salma. It was another ice creature, bigger than any of the others I'd seen— proving that the Sweepers *had* stopped coming after me before doing their worst, just like Shelby had said.

This one was a bear. Not quite as big as the ifrit, but still much bigger than a normal bear. At least two stories tall when standing on its hind legs—which it currently was as it swiped its icy claws at Salma's chest. When Salma threw a ball of fire at it, it did a better job of dodging than I could have expected in my wildest dreams. It was apparently a ninja bear, and a damn powerful shifter.

"Is that . . ." Ray trailed off after pausing to catch his breath. He and Carina had run after me, using their legs rather than their wings, because I'd convinced them it would be a bad idea to show up before me and my magical mace. Carina was still a couple blocks behind us, but she wouldn't be long.

"Mmm hmm," I said. "A big evil ifrit and a giant ice bear. Looks like everyone else is dead by now, so it might be best to let one of them win before going in." Yeah, the Sweepers weren't actively trying to kill me anymore, but that didn't mean they wouldn't try again later, and I really didn't want to *ever* fight this ninja bear.

"No." Ray frowned, looking at the burning Sweepers building rather than the battling monstrosities. "That symbol. The broom. And the ice . . ."

"It's the group's symbol," I said. "The Sweepers. Death to all non-humans, magic is evil and unnatural, blah blah blah. Big hypocrites—or they hate themselves. Plenty of them are shifters with ice magic."

"Not just any ice magic." Ray's voice grew louder than it had been just a moment ago. Harder. I looked over at him and saw his face red, jaw clenched, an angry vein in his neck pulsing.

"Uh . . ." I started.

"They're witches," he said. "Witches of the Aztec god of frost and death. Itztlacoliuhqui. Our god's rival."

At this point, the demonic-looking Salma bent down low and then sprang upwards, jumping onto the roof of a building next to the burning Sweepers headquarters. The bear had a clear advantage in a close-ranged fight, so she must be trying to get far enough away from its claws to throw a solid burst of fire at it.

The bear, however, hooked its impossibly strong claws into the side of building, and it was up on the same roof in barely two strides.

Carina finally caught up with us, panting and moaning as the clacks of her shoes slowed to a stop.

Ray growled beside me. "Itztla won't stop until the entire world is barren, devoid of all warmth and life," he said.

"Sure, I guess that makes sense," I said slowly. "Convince a bunch of magic-haters to start with the non-humans—the toughest ones to kill. After that, wiping out all life is a piece of cake." It definitely explained all the ice, and the Cipactli that had come after me and Adrian at the river.

"Is that . . ." Carina breathed out heavily.

"Yes, apparently," I said. "But okay, this death god is obviously playing the long game, and the bear is on our side in this particular scenario—"

"We can't let any servant of Itztla live. Not under any circumstances." Ray clapped Carina on the back and then crouched down on the ground. Wings sprouted from his back, just like the ones that had sprouted from mine. They seemed to be phantom wings as well, not tearing through his flesh or his clothes, yet still somehow connected to his muscles and bones.

Does it hurt him like it hurt me? I wondered. If it did, he hid it well, not even flinching as the appendages unfolded. The feathers in dark earth tones had a shimmery quality to them, making me want to squint if I held my eyes on them for too long. It was almost like looking at something hidden behind a pocket of immense heat, the light in the air just slightly distorted. Like the wings were moving even when they were still.

Ray was up in the air just a moment later, with Carina making a reluctant face as she looked up. For a second I thought this was my opening for reasoning with her, but she didn't even look at me. Despite her reluctance, she was already covering herself in black scales. Her spiny tail struck the ground, letting rubble fly around us as she sprang into the air, her bat-like wings catching her and sending wind rushing past me as she flew towards the battle of monsters.

Well, bats, I thought. I should follow them, but no wings were magically appearing on my back this time, and I didn't know how to make them.

That was okay, though. I'd found my own way up to the rooftops here just earlier today, and I could do so again.

Actually, it looked like the monsters had jumped onto the same roof I'd used before to get over to the Sweepers' building without walking in the front door. The one with the little cafe at the bottom, which was now . . . still open. The lights were on inside, glowing a little brighter than they had when I'd run up a few minutes ago now that the fire next door seemed to be dying and the sun was on its way down.

Before I could run over, something grabbed my arm, almost making me drop the mace. I turned to see one of the Sweeper men I'd thought was dead, kneeling beside me with a crazed look in his eyes.

"Help me," he said, clutching desperately at my forearm. He was strong, and I had to fight to not fall over into him.

"Hey, okay, okay—where are you hurt?" I said as I braced myself.

He stood, until his sweaty face and chattering teeth were level with my own. He clearly wasn't well, but I couldn't see any physical injuries or burn marks. He grasped my shoulders. "You have to kill me," he growled. "I've stared into the eyes of hell. I have to—I love them . . ." He squinted his eyes shut hard and then let go of me as he rubbed his face. "Don't let it take them from me . . ." He let out a scream then, gripping his face so hard I thought he might tear out his own eyes. "I have to—"

I hit him over the head with the blunt handle of one of my knives. There was something unsettling about the way he'd been acting, something that sent a heavy dread down to my gut. It felt too familiar—the sickly appearance and delirious words reminding me of Becca at my bar, just before she'd died. Could Salma have done the same thing to him that she'd done to Becca? Taken his soul? Maybe it was a slow process, leeching away over time instead of being consumed all at once. Maybe if I killed this man like he wanted me to, he would get to keep what remained of his soul.

You can't keep your soul if you're dead, I reminded myself. No—I couldn't save the souls of Salma's victims by killing them any more than I could have saved Becca's soul by killing her. Whoever had set her on fire and resurrected her body had proven that well. Salma was the one who had to die.

20

I JERKED the door to the cafe open. It chimed above me as the scents of coffee and spices washed over me, still as strong as before even though the room was crowded with people this time. Not patrons, from the look of it, so much as refugees. The place was filled to the brim with people who looked like they'd narrowly escaped a fiery death. Blood, bruises, singed bits of clothing, terrified faces and tortured sobs—some people as delirious and sickly as the man outside.

And in the middle of it all, untouched by any of it, the same barista from before stood at the counter, smiling at me brightly. Minnie. "There you are, love!" she said. "Here's your mocha. Might be a bit cold, now. I thought you'd be here sooner."

"Do you never turn off the fortune-telling gimmick?" I snapped at her, annoyed that anyone could be so cheerful amid so much destruction.

"Not really," she said without losing an ounce of her cheer.

I walked up to the counter and took the mocha from her, because I never let personal feelings come between me and a mouthful of good coffee when I needed it. I took a sip as I started making my way to the back, towards the stairs.

"But in this case," Minnie called after me, and I paused to look at her. "It was your friends that tipped me off. I don't just sit around asking my crystal ball about you at all hours of the day. You're very lovely, but I do have a life." She winked at me, then nodded her head towards the stairs. "They're up there, in the studio."

It unsettled me how much I *didn't* want to punch her right now; the mocha was that good.

Invigorated, I ran up the stairs and popped my head into Minnie's studio to see who she was talking about.

Two women having a picture-perfect tea party, it turned out. Before this moment, I wouldn't have thought a zombie would be capable of sticking out its pinky finger while sitting with perfect posture, but then Becca always had been extraordinary. That and she was covered in splotches of Miriam's purple jelly, on all her joints and extremities, and Miriam was sitting across from her probably controlling her like a puppet.

I was so happy to see her here that the weirdness didn't even bother me. I'd had Adrian call Miriam when we left the club, but I'd been worried she might not be able to get here with Becca in time.

Miriam dropped her teacup when she saw me and, like a slightly delayed mirror image, Becca did the same.

A high-pitched squeal filled the room as Miriam jumped up and batted at the hot liquid soaking into her pants. I grimaced Becca lifelessly matched her movements.

After a moment of clear frustration, Miriam composed herself and walked up to me. "Where is it?" she said carefully, slowly. The words felt like a threat.

I wondered what she was talking about for a second, then

followed her eyes down to my bare feet, ripped pant leg, and lack of any wound or tattoo—or blue jelly.

"Uhh . . . I'll find your squishy once this is all over. Just please, can you follow me for now and stay safe? I need Becca close when I kill this thing, so her soul can find its way back."

"I didn't just mean my squishy, young lady," Miriam said sternly. "Why is your tattoo gone?"

"It—" I stopped, then narrowed my eyes at her. "What do you care about my tattoo?"

But a tremor ran through the building before she could answer, and I spun around to keep running up the stairs. Miriam had a lot to answer for, and none of it was important enough to keep me off the roof of this building for another second.

I let Minnie's mocha fall from my fingers as I pounded my way up the final flight of stairs, only feeling a tiny bit bad about the mess it would cause. My free hand extended to shove open the door to the roof while my other hand tensed on the mace behind me.

When I burst out into the orange dusk, the wind was dotted with embers. Little flecks of heat burned at my cheeks, my hair, my jacket. But somehow the feeling wasn't unpleasant. In the same way falling through the air had always felt natural to me, these little burns felt natural now.

With a glance behind me to make sure Miriam and Becca were following, I stepped forward. Leaving the door cracked, I signaled for them to wait under cover.

I walked slowly around a bend to get a view of the full roof, which was empty. They had gone one roof over by now, it seemed. But not all of them . . . I didn't see the bear anywhere.

It was just demonic Salma standing on the roof, with Ray and Carina flitting around her in the air, Ray trying to draw her attacks while Carina breathed fire at her. If I had to guess, I'd say that in this case, it wouldn't be very effective for them trying to fight fire with fire. An eight-year-old girl against a woman who might well have been around since the beginning of time? My money was on Salma.

Lucky for Carina, more of my money was on me.

I ran up to the edge of the roof and stopped for a moment, focusing my eyes to gauge the distance. Something below caught my eye, and I looked down to see what remained of the bear lying mangled in the alley. The thing was almost half melted, whole limbs missing along with odd chunks, but it was still ice—and still a bear. That meant it was still alive. Otherwise it would probably be nothing more than the charred, bloody pulp of a human, like the wolf boy I'd killed in my garage.

And as long as it was alive, I was willing to bet its magic would heal it. I shook out my neck along with my dread at one day having to fight that thing, then stepped back and ran at the ledge.

Maybe I can drop Salma on top of the bear—kill two birds with one stone. I leapt into the air as I thought it, into the wind's familiar embrace. And again, the air caught me, jerking me out of my glide by the wings that had suddenly, involuntarily appeared behind me. It didn't hurt this time, but still—I didn't like it. *Maybe this means I should stop thinking about things in terms of killing birds.*

I managed to at least stop the wings from flapping, which allowed me to glide most of the way over to the other roof and catch myself with my feet. But as soon as I did, Salma shot a burst of fire at me.

On instinct, I dropped down to the rough concrete of the rooftop and rolled around, trying to put out the flames. But after a moment, I noticed the only things hurting me were the sharp rocks I was rolling around on.

The fire wasn't even burning my clothes. It was just

diffusing into the air around me, slowly, as though being pushed back by a gentle wind coming out of my pores.

Of course—the thing inside me that had helped me against the ice monster at the river was the thing inside me that was giving me wings now. And that thing could do incredible things with wind.

But it didn't stop the claws that came crashing down at me in the next moment as Salma realized her fire had done nothing against me. I rolled out of the way just in time, and then Carina was swooping in low. I couldn't tell if she was trying to save me or get a shot at Salma while the demonic woman was distracted by me, but either way it didn't work.

The claws on Salma's other arm caught the dragon's wing, tearing through the muscles and causing Carina to dip and spin out of control in the air. She roared and blew fire haphazardly in every direction as she fought to stay in the fight. Dumb girl. She would die if she stayed in the fight in this condition.

I gripped the mace and climbed to my feet. Salma's gigantic claws shot at me as soon as I did, making me jump over them and then roll to the ground. I almost stabbed myself in the eye with the mace in the process. Frowning, I put the glass weapon down. I would need it for the kill, so I didn't want to let it out of my sight—but I needed to weaken Salma before the clunky weapon would be any good to me.

With a knife in one hand and my little gun in the other, I ran up close to Salma, effectively dodging her claws now that I was unburdened by the heavy, unfamiliar weapon. Ray was flying down as I moved in, hopefully to help Carina get out of the way before she could become ifrit food. He hurtled himself into his wounded daughter, sending her soaring away from the fight, towards the edge of the roof.

I dove underneath Salma, between her monstrous legs, legs that looked more goat-like than human, and emptied my magazine straight up into her torso as I attempted to cut where I thought her tendons might be.

She let out a roar and stumbled—yes!—but her claws closed around Ray in the same instant. His screams overwhelmed all other sounds in my ears, even though they couldn't have been louder than Salma, and then all I could hear was the crunching of his bones.

I stood paralyzed behind Salma as blood spurted from Ray's body when her claws dug into him, and then as she dropped him off the side of the building to the street below. I couldn't feel his pain in my body, but I could feel it in my scrye. Like someone had let loose a molten avalanche into the core of my soul.

I screamed and dropped my weapons, falling to the concrete and curling into a ball. It was like the cave with the obsidian, the torturous feeling of malicious, angry magic, more than I could handle.

Through my tears I caught a glimpse of the black scales on Carina's wing. She was clinging to the corner of the rooftop, Ray's push not enough to have thrown her all the way off.

And she was half-shifted back to human at this point, screeching her little head off, sobbing and paralyzed in fear just as I was paralyzed in pain.

Seeing her face set a spike through my heart. That little girl and her constant bravado, her thorny attitude that was probably just like mine when I'd been her age. She was too young to be reduced to this. If she survived, she would never be the same. That pissed me off. But I would be even more pissed if she didn't survive. I wanted her to live so I could whip her ass back into shape afterward.

I yelled out incoherent sounds as I pushed through the pain and took back control of my body.

My hand shot out towards Carina and, without my wings even moving, wind began to swell around me. It rushed at

Carina like it had rushed at the icy sea monster—hopefully not with any slicing power this time.

Bats, it felt so wrong to be using magic I didn't understand, but I didn't have much choice right now.

The little dragon girl was shocked from her sobs by the force of the wind, clinging even harder to the building for a moment to keep from blowing away. But when she looked up at me, she understood. She let go just as Salma threw a claw towards her, narrowly escaping the same fate as her father. My wind blew her away—whether to the ground below or to another rooftop, I couldn't tell. I needed to get Salma's attention so she wouldn't go after the girl.

"Hey, old lady!" I jabbed a knife into her thigh when she turned towards me, as high up as I could reach, then left it there as I darted for the mace.

She was already stumbling and slow from my bullets and cuts, but this wouldn't last. By the look of her legs, she seemed to be healing quickly, so I needed to act fast.

"I think I changed my mind about wanting some exotic minions," I yelled at her. "How much for you to be my bar bitch?"

That seemed to piss her off nicely, although she didn't say anything. I wasn't sure if she could say anything in this form beyond screeching and roaring.

I clutched the handle of the mace and flung myself out of the way as she followed me with her claws. Once she'd swung her arm past me, I pivoted quickly and caught it with my mace. The weapon slammed into her wrist, and the force of it nearly dislocated my shoulder. She jerked away from me with a gritty whine.

Ouch. "Oh, come on," I forced out through gritted teeth. "You can wear something with sequins, light my drinks on fire, and get me extra tips from the men with demonic granny fetishes."

I hoped my taunts would hide the fact that my confidence was faltering. That had only been her wrist I'd hit—a long way from anything that could kill her—and the hit had hurt me far more than it had hurt her. I couldn't keep trying to do damage to her extremities. I needed a head shot. But she was so huge that there was no way I could reach her head unless I climbed her.

Or flew. Maybe Ray and Carina had been right to force these wings on me right before coming here. I tensed the muscles along my back, trying to will the wings to work, hoping they would know what to do. And they did, kind of.

They jerked me upward, miraculously doing a decent job of helping me dodge the swings of Salma's remaining working arm, which were coming faster and harder after my taunts.

But the movements felt so sudden and unnatural to me that it was making my stomach lurch and my brain spin around in my head. I was getting dizzy quickly, which wasn't ideal considering I still wasn't close enough to her head to land a shot.

Okay, so I couldn't rely on my hand-eye coordination right now. What if I flew up high and dropped myself on her?

The force of the mace would be stronger that way, so precision would matter less. But if it didn't kill her in one shot, I would be at her mercy . . . no way could I dodge quickly after letting myself fall directly on top of her.

It was a risk I would have to take.

If I didn't kill her now, who knew how much of the city she would destroy before stopping? Regardless, everyone I knew would probably be included.

Trying to put that possibility out of my mind, I poured all my trust into the foreign appendages on my back, letting them lift me higher than I'd ever been, out of reach of the monster below me.

Then, before she could stop to figure out what was happening, I folded the wings and fell, hurtling downward in a deadly dive with the mace filled with Baz's essence over my head.

She locked eyes with me before I could reach her, and time seemed to stop.

The wind rushed past me as I fell through the sky, but I wasn't getting any closer to the beast below me. Her gaze felt paralyzing, not to my body but to my scrye, like she had her claws around it and was trying to snatch it out of me.

Then I remembered the words of the crazed man I'd had to knock out on the street earlier . . . He said he'd stared into the eyes of hell . . .

Shit. This granny demon was trying to steal my soul, right out through my eyes. It felt like she already had a good grasp on it, too. If I didn't kill her now, I would end up just like those poor souls Ray's god had shown me tied to spits, perpetually burning. For eternity.

I made sure the mace was lined up with her face, and then I shut my eyes. It wouldn't save my soul at this point, but it at least broke me out of her trance and got me moving again. I braced for contact, squeezing my eyes shut as hard as possible and hoping with everything in me that I would hit my mark.

The mace connected. The shock of the impact rushed up my arms and into my shoulders, making me scream. Then the pain spread to my back—to my wings—and suddenly I was flung through the air before crashing to the ground.

I opened my eyes to see I had gotten part of Salma's face. One of her eyes was hanging out of its socket, and her cheek looked like ground meat. But she was far from dead.

She had plucked me off of her by the wings and thrown me down, her clutches still tight around my soul as my body broke around it.

She stepped forward towards me as I lay crumpled on the ground, the bloody mace beside me. And suddenly she looked human again, the old granny full of warmth and love, looking down at me with a soft smile that only made her mangled eye seem more grotesque.

She pressed her delicate, wrinkled hands over my eyes. The world went dark, and I heard her voice inside my head. "Come to me, little bird," it said, all sweetness and soothing.

I tried to get up, to break away from her, but I couldn't move. It wasn't the wounds I knew I must have, because I felt no pain. It was like she'd disconnected my consciousness from my body. She was still trying to take my soul, and now it felt almost inevitable that she would.

I could hear her lick her lips—could almost feel it as it sent revulsion through what was left of me.

"I've never had a phoenix spirit before. So scrumptious . . ." Her voice became deeper, sinking further into my consciousness as I imagined I sank further into hers. "I can almost taste all the souls you've touched."

Horror filled me as I tried to process her words. I couldn't focus on anything past "phoenix." My mind was paralyzed now, not just my body, as I replayed the night of Becca's death over and over and over in my head. My hands on her drink when Ray walked in—the jolt of energy. His wings that matched my own. Phoenix. It was me. Us? Me. Me who burned Becca. Me who resurrected her soulless body. No, not me—the thing inside me.

I wanted to crawl out of my skin. Or I wanted to tear the thing out of me, despite the fact that Salma seemed to be doing just that.

I tried to remember Ray's words, when the lying bastard was telling me all about phoenixes as if I hadn't had one living inside me all along. He'd said Becca would have had to already be dying for the phoenix to burn her. Salma had already gotten hold of her soul at that point— that was why she'd been delirious. I told myself this, repeated it to myself, tried to bang it into my damn brain even as Salma continued to suck all my thoughts out of me.

But regardless of whether I'd actually killed her, I'd been the one responsible for my friend's agony as she burned. I'd been the one responsible for the fucking indignity of her body prancing around as a zombie for the next few days.

My misery filled Salma with enthusiasm, and I felt my soul slip away from me further and further with every negative thought. This wasn't helping. Shelby had said evil souls were the tastiest to ifrit, and right now I was brooding on everything evil in mine. It must be exactly what Salma wanted.

I steeled myself, trying to recall Etty's words after she'd punched me. That I needed to stop making everything about me.

I dug into my mind, deep into the spaces Salma had yet to reach, thinking of all the coffee and laughter I wanted to share with Etty if I could keep her from getting fae-knapped. All the puzzles I wanted to see Noah finish, the life I wanted to see him create, the stars I wanted to see him explore. Minnie and all the mochas she had yet to make me. I thought of Adrian and Miriam and Dirk, all trying to do the right thing in their own ways, to find justice for Becca and keep killers off the streets. Even Baz, with all his bitching, had tried to help, and I wanted to get through this so I could go back to working for him at the club that had been my safe haven when no one else would employ me. I knew it was a refuge for so many others, as well.

And as the warmth of the thoughts of all these people and all their potential began to filter through, I felt the vice grip loosen around my soul and some feeling return to my extremities.

Then the ground began to shake. I tried to sit up as Salma's hands came away from my eyes, but my body still didn't want to respond, and the most I could manage was to crack my eyelids. Salma was morphing back into her demonic form and clutching at her mangled eye as she tried to keep her balance. Was this an earthquake?

I finally managed to lift my head and prop myself up as I fully opened my eyes. And then I saw the side of the roof crumble away behind Salma.

Baz's giant head peeked over the top. He looked hungry, tired of waiting for me to get him his meal. I didn't know where he'd been all this time or why it had taken him so long to find the fight, but I'd never been so happy to see him in my life.

Salma turned around to look at him and I pounced, reinvigorated as my body finally obeyed me and moved before I had time to think about what I was doing. With all the force I had and some that I probably didn't, I swung the mace into the back of her leg, low to the ground. It connected so hard that it embedded itself into her muscle, and I was forced to let go of the weapon as it swept her off her feet.

She fell over the edge of the roof, landing on the concrete below, with something big and bright sticking out of her chest. I squinted to see it was a stop sign that had impaled her. Yuck.

Well, that was one way for the universe to tell you to stop your bullshit.

I looked over at the roof I'd left Miriam and Becca on and gestured for them to come close. Fuck if I knew how they were going to get down to where Salma was, but now was the time.

I turned back to the downed giant below me and saw she was still moving, albeit slowly. Baz had dislodged the mace from her leg and was standing over her, weapon in hand, hungrily moving in for the kill.

"Hey, wait!" I yelled. "Baz—Bawdy Baz! Stop! You have to let me do it—remember?" If he killed her, he would probably devour all the souls inside her. Including all those of the delirious people on the street and in the coffee shop who weren't dead yet. Including Becca's. Maybe even including some of mine.

Baz ignored me and lifted the mace over his head. He licked his lips. And then he stopped as Salma begin to shrink again. The demonic fiery giant morphed back into the old lady I remembered seeing playing with Noah. The old lady I had liked. And hopefully, the one Baz still liked.

He paused. A moment of hesitation, and it was all I needed.

I jumped off the roof, letting my wings open to soften my landing. It didn't quite work as I had intended, and I felt like a dumb little kid jumping off a roof with an open umbrella or a handful of balloons. I had to improvise a roll at the last second, and pain shot through my already wounded shoulder as it hit the ground at a bad angle.

"Bassam," Salma croaked as I stood. Her hand reached out towards him. "Don't let the child become like this."

I couldn't see Baz's face from where I was behind him, but he still had the mace raised in the air. I stepped up and put my hand on his elbow, lowering it.

He looked at me, then back at Salma. He was confused, still not himself, still intoxicated by the prospect of consuming all those souls inside her.

"Like me . . . like you." Her fingers made it close enough to just brush his arm, now that it had been lowered. "It was a mistake to feed you like we did, when you were a child. But . . . what is it they say? Misery loves company." She eked out a crooked smile, and blood began to dribble from the corner of her mouth. "We were all empty inside—so filled with constant wrath, constant hunger, constant loneliness. We were made to serve a purpose, and we did, but beyond that . . . Beyond that, we had nothing. Omar was right. The world would be better off without us. And maybe the child should die . . . but maybe he can be different."

Salma reached out further now, shuddering in pain as the metal impaling her sliced deeper, and she grasped Baz's arm. Her fingernails dug into his skin, and he blinked, a tiny bit more alert. "Kill him if you have to, but whatever you do, don't feed him. Let him never know the taste of another's life inside him." Her eyes moved to the mace, then briefly to me as I gently worked to pry Baz's fingers away from it, and then back to Baz. "Let him never look at someone he loves as you are looking at me now."

Baz's fingers went limp. He dropped the mace so quickly I couldn't get my own fingers around it. It fell to the ground, a mere three feet—like a gentle nudge compared to everything it had just been through in my hands—and it shattered. Thousands of tiny pieces littered the concrete, every one of them laughing at me and how idiotic I had been to go into battle with a weapon made of glass.

Well, yeah . . . that was what I got for trusting a little girl as my blacksmith. That and an utterly useless pair of wings. I knew I should have called bullshit on the whole "my magical fiery dragon breath makes glass not act like glass" thing.

Except now I *needed* Baz to kill Salma for me. And now it didn't look like he wanted to anymore. What a wonderful time for him to grow a conscience.

Maybe she would die anyway. She *had* just fallen off a building and been impaled by a stop sign. And I had technically hit her with the mace, even if it was just in her leg and her eye. If I hadn't, the stop sign probably wouldn't have hurt her at all; she probably could have just turned her body to mist like Baz did all the time.

The best thing I could do now was make sure Becca was close. I could fly up to the other building and get her down. But when I looked over, she and Miriam were already on the ground. They'd climbed down the stairs, like civilized people.

A car honked its horn from across the street, and I looked

up to see Noah running past me towards Becca and Miriam. Adrian was honking at him from the driver's seat, yelling at him to come back.

Damn. He'd had *one job*. Why the fuck had he driven Noah right into the danger instead of keeping him away?

"Mama!" Noah yelled gleefully as he ran up to zombie Becca and threw his arms around her legs. Then I noticed the little black creatures trailing after him. Obsidian bunnies, and once again they were crawling out of my car.

A swarm had begun to overtake Adrian, and he scrambled out of the car as the rabbits seemed to multiply out of thin air.

Wonderful. If I lived through this, I would definitely need to get a new car that hadn't been infested with magic rodents who obviously had an agenda. Although, they had helped me before. And if they really were Popo's minions, this Aztec god of Ray and Carina's could be trying to help me again.

I ran over to Noah, who had already disentangled himself from his squishy-covered mother. Becca stood lifeless, stiff as a board, not even looking at her son. After I'd seen her run face-first into a closed door multiple times to get to him at Baz's house, her stillness now was even more disconcerting than that.

Except she hadn't been trying to get to her son at all then, had she? Now that I thought back on it, I realized Becca had been after her soul all along—after Salma, who had been making a show of protecting Noah from his mother while I played right into her hand.

Damn, I could have prevented so much destruction if I'd realized then what was happening. Of course it hadn't been coincidental that one of the "assassins" sent after me had been one of Salma's minions. If the palis truly had been working for the Sweepers, he would have had some ice magic to show for it.

But no, I'd been too busy feeling relieved that someone capable of taking care of Noah had shown up right when I'd needed her—right when the threat of having to care for him myself had been hovering over my head. I'd been so scared of having yet another person be reliant on my protection, after Simeon, that I'd let it make me even more incompetent than I already was.

Well, no more.

If Becca had been after Salma all along when she'd broken into Baz's house, it stood to reason that was where she would pick up again if Miriam released her. Maybe she really could take back her soul for herself.

"Miriam, we need to get your squishies off her." I stepped forward to start plucking them off, but then I noticed Noah's face. He was squinting at Becca with a blank expression.

"Mama isn't in there," he said.

"No, little guy. She's—" His hand darted out and snatched a knife from my belt.

Normally I was pretty good at reacting quickly to unexpected attacks, but this was beyond the realm of unexpected even for me. My fingers seemed to move like molasses through the air, aiming for Noah's arm when he was already well on his way away from me, running towards Salma.

By the time I caught up with him, he had already plunged my knife into her eye—the one I hadn't already taken out with the mace.

The blade went straight through her skull, all the way up to the hilt, and then it started to glow with an energy that passed through Noah's arm and into Salma's eye.

There was no way she would live through that, not if Noah really was half ifrit. Aside from Baz, the kid was the only one here who could still kill her. Hopefully, all the "training" she'd been giving him recently would help him do it.

I scrambled into gear, giving up on the idea of yanking off Miriam's squishies from Becca. Instead, I bent down and wrapped my arms around her legs, tipping her over my good shoulder. She didn't object, and I prayed that whatever adrenaline was keeping me going would be good enough to get me through this last feat of strength.

By the time I got to Noah, he was in some kind of trance. His hands were splayed over Salma's face, one over each ruined eye socket, just like she'd done to me. His eyes were shut, chin lifted towards the heavens, mouth slightly parted and mumbling incoherent whispered words.

I dropped his mother at his feet and stood helpless, unsure what to do. Miriam caught up to us, heels clacking on the pavement, and she knelt down by Becca. Baz stood on the other side of Salma, whimpering now, his head in his hands as he paced the length of her body.

"No, no, no, no . . . Can't eat them . . . Too late . . ." he whined, and I looked at Noah again. Was he . . . ?

Fuck. He was eating Salma's souls. Eating them right out of her dead eyes. He must have known intuitively to go for the eyes, the boy ifrit drawn by instinct in a way Baz never would have been. This was exactly what Salma had warned against—exactly what she'd asked Baz to not let happen.

I'd stood by, right here, fussing over my zombie friend while her son used my knife to turn himself into a monster. Because that was what he would become now. Not only an ifrit compelled to avenge the deaths of the murdered, but an ifrit with a taste for human souls. And I'd seen in Baz just how addictive that taste could be.

I grabbed Noah under his shoulders and yanked him off the dead woman.

He screamed. A long, low, wailing scream. Not a boy's scream. The scream of a thousand souls, escaping through the lips of a boy. The scream of hell inside a child. If I hadn't seen evidence of this afterlife before, now I had heard it.

I wanted desperately to unhear it.

He brought his hands to his face, to his eyes, and the blood from Salma's face stained his cheeks red.

"Darcy—behind you!" Miriam's voice turned my head just as the Becca zombie shoved me aside and ran to her son. She practically fell on top of him, stifling his scream, and silence fell on all of us who watched. Even Baz stopped whining, and in that moment the world seemed to darken.

Dusk had crossed over into night, and soon the stars would begin to twinkle. Magic buzzed around me and in my scrye, familiar power at my fingertips now, finally—now that it was all too late.

I stepped forward to the pile on the ground that was Becca and her son. Reaching down, I gently pushed Becca's shoulder to roll her over, off Noah, thinking that maybe I could heal her with all this power around me. But her eyes were dead now, truly. No light inside them, not even in the dark of night. Noah, though—he was looking at me with all the life she had lost.

"Hey Dumbo," he said to me with a smile. It was what Becca had called me sometimes, when she wanted to get a rise out of me. Some kind of elephant joke I'd never understood; she'd said it was before my time. The fae aged so slowly, I'd always thought of them as immortal. Not anymore.

I smiled back, shakily. "Bex?"

"Who else would it be?" Noah asked. I glanced over at Salma's dead body and then back to the little boy in front of me, who had followed my eyes. "Okay, there are a lot of people in here—but I'm the only one Noah can't boss around, so . . ."

"I seem to recall him being an expert at bossing you around."

Noah's mouth curved into a smile. "When it came to having cookies for dinner, yeah. This is a bit bigger than that."

"A bit."

"Bex, he—"

"I know. I was afraid of this happening all along. It's why I didn't use him to kill his father in the first place. I would have been alive still, if I had, but . . ." The boy shook his head.

"I'm sorry, Bex. I should have stopped him, and now . . ." Now I would have to kill him. How do you tell that to someone's mother, looking right at you through her son's eyes?

"Now what?" Becca said through Noah. Then she seemed to sense what I meant. "Oh Darcy, give me a break. You're not going to kill my kid."

"You think I can't do it? The least I can do now is clean up my mess. I can't let this happen again." I gestured around at the destruction Salma had caused.

"Then be a fucking responsible adult and tell my son No when he wants to start gobbling up people on the street. Give him a cookie instead. Teach him manners."

"I . . ."

"And it isn't your mess, Dumbo. You're not responsible for every bad thing that happens around you. The world doesn't revolve around you."

Etty had said the same thing to me, just hours before, and it had saved me from Salma just moments ago. But I knew now that they were both wrong. I *was* responsible for every bad thing, because I couldn't live with it otherwise. It was why I'd become a Guardian in the first place, and it was why I'd been so eager to let them fire me when I'd failed. I hadn't been able to keep the bad things from happening, and I could only cope by running away from them.

And now . . . now I was so terrified I couldn't keep a child from becoming a monster that I was willing to murder him in cold blood to prevent it.

Batty hell, Becca and Etty were at least right that I needed to get over myself.

"I'll be here too, okay? Even if you can't hear me," Becca

said to me through her son. "And Etty knows all about self-control. Have you ever seen her dessicate a dude?"

"No . . ." I said, although I couldn't promise she wasn't doing just that to Dirk right now.

"That's because she taught herself how to control her impulses. Not because she doesn't want to every damn day."

Noah's mouth opened wide for a moment, his eyes shutting as his face contorted into a twisted yawn—like he was some sort of robot, glitching.

I tilted my head and leaned over to get closer to him. "Are you okay? Bex?"

"I have to go," her voice said faintly when it returned. "It's chaotic in here, but . . . so much nicer than the other place. It's filled with everything Noah loves. Stars and birds and fish and clouds . . . He needs his body back. Darcy?"

"Yeah?" I asked reluctantly, not wanting her to go. I supposed Noah had at least saved her from Salma's eternal fire, but I had hoped for so much more than that.

"Burn my body again, okay?" she said weakly. "Not with magic this time. I know you love me, but resurrecting me to walk around all zombie-like is undignified. I'm not a play-thing." She narrowed Noah's eyes at Miriam.

I cringed, reflexively shifting the muscles on my back as I remembered the feel of the wings and what they meant about me. What I'd done to her without even realizing it. "Sorry," I whispered.

"What are you sorry about, Auntie Elephant?" Noah said to me with his own voice, an innocent lilt in it that I wasn't sure he deserved now that he'd just put my knife through an old lady's eye. Without waiting for my response, he yawned again and fluttered his eyes, falling into me as he whined, "Can I go to bed now?"

And Becca was gone, just like that.

21

THE APARTMENT WAS empty when I got home. I had refused to get in an ambulance when responders had arrived at the scene, and Adrian and Dirk had been kind enough to keep me out of handcuffs as well. Baz hadn't been so lucky on that front, considering he'd harbored and aided Salma—not to mention the building he'd singlehandedly brought down.

My shoulder was still completely mangled, and I'd probably broken a rib or two, but everything else was scrapes and bruises. Those, I'd been able to heal on my own pretty easily. But the magic inside me was still resisting anything bigger.

Now that I knew it was some kind of sentient being—my birdie friend, as Baz would say—I could only assume turning off my magic was its way of throwing a tantrum.

Maybe it wanted me to go to the hospital, but I'd been avoiding hospitals for years. I was sure it was difficult for doctors in places like that, everyone looking at them with all their hopes and worries, all their gratitude and blame. But still, most people understood doctors weren't magic.

Me, though? I used magic to heal. So no one could ever understand when it didn't work. I'd learned early on that the only thing worse than me relying on my magic was for other people to rely on my magic.

Ironic, since now my best option was relying on Miriam's magic. My shoulder was covered in blue squishies, which were making me feel a bit loopy, but nowhere near as bad as before. I hadn't lost as much blood this time, and I hadn't lost consciousness.

"Etty?" I called out as I walked into the living room. Noah's hand held tightly to mine as he walked beside me. He'd refused to leave my side since Becca had gone, and I needed someone to take him off my hands so I could . . . I didn't even know what I needed to do next, but I couldn't think with this soul-eating kid attached to me.

No one responded to my call, and when I peeked inside the bedrooms, they were all empty.

Etty wasn't here. But she was supposed to be here. She had left the club to avoid being caught by the cops and sent back to the fae realm. She had said she needed to stay to see Noah safe. That Becca had asked her to take care of Noah. And I had asked her to wait for us at home.

Had Dirk somehow gotten the better of her?

Okay, Darcy, don't panic. Maybe she'd gone to run an errand or something. I turned around to look at our message board.

I'm off to fairytale land, it said. And below that: **If I grow wings, I'll fly back**.

It was written hastily, no hearts this time. And the way she'd phrased it, I knew there was no hope she'd be back. She just hadn't wanted to write something so depressing.

I squeezed Noah's hand without thinking, and he yelped. With wide eyes, I looked down at him. I'd just lost both of my roommates in the space of one night—both of my friends. This little boy was all I had left of either of them. And he was completely reliant on me. Without Etty, there was no one to hand him off to. No one Becca would have approved of, at least.

"Sorry, Noah." I let go of his hand.

"That's okay," he said cheerfully, not looking quite so tired anymore. Then he ran over to the coffee table, where the hummingbird puzzle was still laid out just as he and his mom had left it.

I sighed. Once a Guardian, always a Guardian. That was what they'd always told us at the Academy, and I had never really understood it until now. Apparently my habit of failing time and time again wouldn't stop people from relying on me for protection, so I should probably just stop fighting it. I might not be great at the job, but I was still this kid's best hope.

Fine, then. I snorted in a deep breath of air. "Want to get hot cocoa and donuts for breakfast in the morning?" I asked. There was a popular place I'd never been to right by the hospital. "If they have a red one, I'll make it look like a lobster for you."

Noah nodded at me happily as he worked to fill in the hummingbird's head. Maybe Becca was right. Maybe it wouldn't be that tough to teach this kid manners. Maybe his fae side would lend the ifrit side more self-control than Salma had been able to command.

Or maybe, in a few years, my soul would end up behind those cute little eyes of his right alongside Becca's, in his cute little hell filled with stars and birds and fish and clouds.

We would have to see. I had sworn to myself, after Simeon, that I would never protect another monster like him. It had almost become an obsession, so important that I had been afraid to protect anyone, monster or not. But if I was going to keep being Guardian Darcy, I couldn't afford to be afraid. Even when it was my soul on the line, I would need to remember that the job was about mitigating risks, not avoiding them.

Just like I would need to suck it up and drag my ass to the hospital. Because the alternative was risking that Ray and Carina might both be dead before I could talk to them, if they weren't already. And now that I had a little soul-sucker relying on me, I needed to know exactly what was inside me and how to control it. There was only room in this apartment for one monster at most, and I needed to make sure that it wouldn't be me.

I FELT like a teenager again as I walked through the sterile halls of the hospital under the fluorescent lights, all of them flickering minutely. I shivered, chilled and sweaty at the same time. Noah's hand was slippery in mine, but the boy didn't seem to care. He was fully absorbed in the "lobster"-filled dregs of his hot cocoa, and he would follow blindly wherever I led him.

"Miss Pierce," someone called weakly from inside a room as I passed by. I paused, then backtracked a little to look inside.

I nearly didn't recognize the woman who lay on the cot, which wasn't surprising since she was only about halfway there. Both her arm and leg on her left side were just . . . gone. Bandaged stumps were all that remained, and the look on her face reflected the rest.

Sagging cheeks, puffy eyes, limp lips pressed together hard, all obscured behind tangled strands of short black hair.

"Shelby," I said. "It was you." The ice bear who'd had her left side melted away. It was a testament to her immense power that she was even still alive, but I supposed even a shifter that strong couldn't regrow limbs. That was what she got for turning herself into ice.

I could see the benefit, from the perspective of the god who had convinced her to do it. The ice made for strong attacks, more durable creatures—but they were only durable until they shifted back, and not so great against fire magic under any circumstances. She wouldn't have lost those limbs if they had been burned rather than melted, but she also wouldn't have lasted as long in the battle.

"Rarrr." Shelby the ferocious bear eked out a chuckle with her mocking roar, and then it turned into a coughing fit.

I couldn't help but smile. I couldn't help but like this woman, even though she'd been the one trying to have me killed while I'd been chasing after Becca's killer.

"I'm sorry, Miss Pierce. Truly, this time," she said.

"For what?" I asked innocently.

"I'm not sorry enough to answer that question. But you know. And you won't have to worry about us anymore. The Sweepers are mostly dead, burned—melted. Probably without their souls. Our god doesn't care at all. I think he wanted us dead all along, just after everyone else."

I took a deep breath. "You know I'll never be able to forgive you, for Simeon Drake." Part of me wanted to add my ruined career to the pile, but I couldn't blame her for that. She was responsible for having Simeon killed—but I'd lost my job because I'd failed to stop her. That part would always be on me.

"I . . ." She looked at me with sad eyes, real pity in them. "That really wasn't me, Miss Pierce. Even if we were in the business of having people assassinated . . ." She lifted an eyebrow, which seemed to say they absolutely had been in that business. "We wanted Senator Drake alive."

"Why could you have wanted him alive? He was against everything you stood for."

She shrugged. "That's politics. He was a terribly powerful vampire, and everyone knew it. Manipulative. Completely removed from the majority of human voters. Having him in power only made people more afraid of his kind. Not to mention he'd promised to back some of the supernatural regulations we were pushing for."

A strong sense of déjà vu washed over me at her last sentence. I vaguely remembered Simeon telling me about those proposed regulations, and that there was another powerful vampire who wouldn't stand to be policed by his dinner. But the memory was foggy, just like so many of my memories of my time with him.

"What made you think I was the one who had him killed?" Shelby asked.

"The ward your assassin had on her. The first one you sent after me, on Tuesday. The mage." Possum and her floral potpourri. "It was the same ward I smelled on the woman who killed Simeon."

Shelby shook her head. "Sorry to disappoint you, but there have never been any mages in my employment. Mostly just shifters. I've never known a mage with enough self-hatred to do what we did. But that comes with the territory when one day you're a little girl on a camping trip, and the next . . ." She looked away, and I could guess what had happened the next day. Little girl turns into bear, kills and eats her parents? Something like that, probably.

Those stories had been popping up more and more frequently now that brand-new shifters were protected from being prosecuted for their actions under the law. One of the laws Simeon had helped bring to fruition. They were victims, new shifters who had been turned without consent, and to hold them accountable for what they couldn't control would only bring more pain.

But legally forgiving them brought a different kind of pain to the world, and I could see that pain in Shelby's eyes. She knew she wasn't innocent. She wanted—needed—to be punished. I couldn't help her with that.

And she couldn't help me. I knew she was telling the truth. In the back of my mind, I had wondered why the first assassin to come after me was the only one with that stinking ward.

Whoever had sent Possum with that ward and that Sweeper pin, whoever had killed Simeon, they must have had a mole in Shelby's group. Must have sent that assassin deliberately to make me think it was the Sweepers all along.

They would only have done that for one reason, and that was fear. Fear of me. Fear that I would eventually figure out who they were and come after them. And now, I knew I would.

I had nothing more to say to this woman. I needed to go find Ray or Carina, if either of them were still alive. But something was wrong. There was nothing in my hand. No slippery little fingers waiting to be led along.

Bats, I'd lost the kid already.

I bounded into the hallway and thought I saw his bright green shirt turning a corner. *Lots of souls ripe for the picking in a hospital*, I thought. I hated thinking it, but I couldn't help it. I knew all too well just how vulnerable the souls in a hospital could be.

I reached into my pocket as I ran, grabbing the green squishy Miriam had given me when I'd asked. If I was going to take care of a tiny soul-eater, I wasn't going to do it without a way of incapacitating him. And I was fresh out of dragon-forged glass weapons infused with djinn essence.

But when I caught up to him, heart racing, tense fingers ready to slam the squishy in his face, he wasn't trying to steal anyone's soul. A little girl's heart, maybe. He stood by Carina's bedside, giggling with her as he offered her a sip of his hot cocoa.

The look on her face caught me off guard, and I realized this was the first time I'd ever really seen her smile. But then this was also the first time I'd seen her not . . . working?

You couldn't really call what she did with her father 'work,' since she wasn't being paid. Witching, then? She had stalked me, forged weapons on the weekends, fought to the death against witches of her god's rival . . . No wonder Ray had said her grades were suffering. I realized then just how bad a parent Ray really was, and just how much I didn't want to be any part of their "family."

Not that I'm much better, I thought as I loosened my grip on the green squishy in my pocket and stepped forward into the room.

Carina's smile faded when she saw me, and her eyes hardened. Noah looked up and yet again smiled with more innocence than he should have had, for everything he'd been through. Seeing him there right next to Carina, I knew I needed to try to be more like Becca and less like Ray. But of all the things I'd ever known I would need to do, this felt like it might be the hardest.

I took my hands out of my pockets and waved at them. "How are you doing, my dragon goddaughter?" She wasn't a fairy after all, and not a demon either.

"You blew me off the roof of a building and I landed on cement," she said. "How do you think I'm doing?"

"Sorry for saving your life." I rolled my eyes. She didn't look that bad. She'd been plated in obsidian scales when she'd fallen. Most of the damage was probably from Salma, on her wing, which didn't technically exist now that she'd shifted back to her little girl form. "Where's your dad?" I asked.

She got quiet then. "I don't know. They won't tell me."

"He's in surgery," a voice said from behind me.

I turned around to see Adrian, looking like a damn runway model compared to all of us with our bandages and bruises and blood-crusted unwashed hair. Okay, the unwashed hair was just me. I found myself happy to see him, even if he had screwed up the one job I'd given him. It wasn't really his fault, not with those obsidian rabbits taking over my car, and he'd certainly done enough to help beforehand that it evened out the scale.

"Probably be in there all night," Adrian continued, talking about Ray. "He was in bad shape."

"You should find him," Carina said loudly, and when I turned back to her she was staring at me. She seemed like she wanted to say more.

After a brief pause, I gave Noah a nudge towards Adrian and said, "Hey little guy, why don't you show the detective where the hot cocoa is? He looks like he needs some."

Adrian walked towards me instead of leaving, ignoring Noah tugging on his arm, and bent down slightly so his face was close to mine. I froze, my eyes darting from side to side as I wondered what the fuck he was doing.

In a low voice, he said, "You can't work your magic on drinks without touching them, right?"

"No," I said slowly, still not sure where he was going with this.

"Good." He stood up straight again and peered down at me without backing away. "Because if you have some ulterior motive for trying to get a drink in me, you should know it's not necessary."

"Fuck, Adrian. It's hot cocoa. What ulterior motive could I . . ." His eyes bore into mine, and I stopped, remembering how strange he'd acted after I'd thought about messing with his drink in the club. Did he still think I'd made him magically lusty for me? Of course, I probably *had* done that just by thinking about it. Because the magic inside me had started going wonky when Ray had walked into the club that night—when I'd been making Adrian's drink.

I swallowed, suddenly wanting to run far, far away from this room and this man. "It's not necessary," he'd just said. That could mean he found me so revolting that no amount of magic in his drink would do the trick, but the way he was standing and staring at me said it was more likely the opposite.

"Come on," Noah whined, tugging harder at Adrian's arm

now. "You have to get a lobster in your cocoa so we can watch it melt."

Adrian busted out a confused grin, finally breaking his gaze away from me as he looked down at Noah. "I don't know what that means, but I'm excited to find out," he said.

I took in a shaky breath, grateful for the interruption. "Careful what you wish for," I said, and I managed a small smile as they left the room.

Carina gave me a look of disgust when I turned back to her and sat by her side.

"Why are you all so weird?" she asked. "Lobster?"

I chuckled. "This coming from the girl who gobbles up baby goats."

She stuck her tongue out at me, then looked away. "You really should go find my dad," she said.

"Okay, but why?" I asked. "What didn't you want to say in front of them?"

"He'll heal better if you're there." She let out a tiny huff. "It's why we came all the way to this stupid city in the first place."

"Why will he heal better with me there?" I was so tired of all the vague bullshit coming from this girl and her father. "What's the connection between us?"

She shut up then, scrunching her face at me, and I recognized it as the same look she'd given me after being caught stalking me when I'd saved her from Possum.

"Why doesn't he want you to tell me?" I asked.

"Because he wanted to show you. I don't think he thought you'd believe it any other way. The book was supposed to work, but he said it didn't because of your ugly tattoo. And then once we got it off . . ." Her eyes lit up, probably as she remembered tossing me to my death from hundreds of feet in the air. "There wasn't enough time then. And now . . ."

"Did he say anything else about my tattoo? Why did it . . ." I didn't even know how to phrase the question.

But Carina shook her head. "I don't know. He might have said, but it was boring and I wasn't paying attention. Look, I don't know that much anyway."

"Then tell me what you do know. I won't help him if you don't."

"Fine." She huffed again. "You guys are . . . hosts? I think that's the word."

"Hosts? For what?"

"Some kind of phoenix spirit. Just one, though. It lives in both of you at once. It always needs two, a brother and a sister. Usually twins, I think. It follows our god now, but it's much older than him. From somewhere far away. Like I said, I don't know the whole story. I just know it doesn't like being broken apart. So Ray's always had it tough, without you. He's useless to our cause because he can't control his magic. And when he and my mom split . . . they wanted to kick him out. But then I would be alone—that's why we came to find you. He needs you close if we're going to stay together."

I groaned. I'd missed about half of what she'd said because she'd said it so fast, but it didn't matter. It wasn't enough. I needed to know more—so much more—if I was going to get rid of this thing in me, this hot-tempered bird who had hijacked my body and burned my friend.

And to know more, I apparently needed Ray alive.

22

I WATCHED faceless bodies in scrubs dig into Ray's flesh from behind the glass outside the operating room. I could barely even tell it was him, from this far away and with his body so obscured. His face was covered in tubes, and there were so many lacerations on his mangled limbs that his skin didn't even look like I remembered it.

But it was him; I could feel the bird. And maybe something more. As much as I hated it, it wouldn't surprise me if we really were related. A brother—maybe even a twin like Carina had suggested. I'd always wanted something like that when I was a kid. And I'd never known who my parents were, beyond the community of mages who'd raised me. So it was possible.

I touched the glass gently, wondering what would happen if I just smashed through it and fought my way to him. I'd have to take on some surgeons armed with scalpels, but I liked my chances. The only problem was that they didn't deserve to die, and I wasn't great at dropping bodies without also murdering them.

But I'd pissed off more than a few people just getting here, and they weren't going to stop surgery to let me try to heal him with magic. The clinic I'd grown up in had no doctors at all, only mages; but in most hospitals, magic was still scoffed at as unreliable at best, and a huge liability even when it worked. Because who could say that the cancer you found yourself with one day had nothing to do with the magic some mage lady used to heal your broken arm years before?

I sighed, and the squealing of wheels rolling by made me turn my head. Someone in scrubs was rolling a cart towards the door to the operating room.

A quick glance around confirmed that no one else was paying much attention. But still, how to incapacitate an inno-cent who was just doing their job?

Before I could think much about it, I had already cleared the distance between us and pulled the green squishy out of my pocket. If Miriam had thought it safe enough to use on Noah, it was probably safe enough for this guy. Or at least I hoped so as I jammed it over his eyes, killer me having enough sense to leave his nose and mouth free for breathing.

He stiffened immediately, and I caught him under the shoulders before he could fall to the ground. Then I dragged him behind the cart he'd been pushing and started stripping him. He was a small man in loose scrubs, and I was a curvy woman in tight pants, so this just might work.

After a fair share of awkward moments that luckily no one saw, he was in my outfit of jeans and leather jacket—minus most of the weapons—and I looked like a puffy blue alien. I slung his arm over my shoulder and dragged him as gently as possible over to a bench against the wall, where I laid him down with his hands over the squishy on his face. He kind of looked like he was taking a nap. It would have to be good enough.

I shrugged my shoulders and went back to his cart, rolling it into the operating room.

No one said anything to me. Or at least I thought no one

said anything to me. I couldn't understand the nonsense they were saying, and they were all speaking with their eyes down anyway, so I had no idea who anyone was even talking to.

Oh well, better work quick before they realize I don't belong here. Working quick was easier when I knew what to do, which I didn't. But I could . . . oh man . . . I hated myself for even thinking this, but I would have to *wing* it.

I was so thankful Miriam wasn't in my head to hear that. I made a mental note to stop with the fucking bird puns before I could slip and say one out loud.

Trying to clear my mind, I snuck in at the operating table by Ray's feet and covertly touched my wrist to the side of his foot. I couldn't use my fingers because they were covered by the gloves I'd stolen. His skin felt cold against mine.

I took in a breath and closed my eyes, and my heart sank as I realized I had stepped back into my old life. In a hospital, touching a dying patient, trying to ensnare their life force and keep it in their broken body. That had always been my job, the thing I could do better than anyone else. Now I wondered if it'd had something to do with the phoenix hitch-hiking inside me. Was that why I was so gifted when it came to maneuvering between the realms of life and death? Was that why my adoptive family had wanted me in the first place?

Regardless, that wasn't what I was doing now. All I needed to be doing now was connecting the thing inside me to Ray so he could heal himself. Probably.

I looked inward, at my own scrye instead of feeling for his. And I found it burning. Not a destructive burn, though. An effusive burn. It led me to his, which felt like nothing more than the glowing embers of a candle wick with not enough wax.

That was all it took.

Birdie was happy now, apparently. Appeased. Ray's wounds

healed almost instantaneously—too quickly for anyone's comfort.

One of the surgeons screamed, his hand disappeared up to the wrist in Ray's chest, which had closed up around it. And all those broken bones . . . I had a feeling they would need to be re-broken and set in better positions if Ray was ever going to move like a human again.

Bats. Too much healing. Birdie might not be as appeased as I'd thought. Or maybe it just had a sense of humor. I was at least satisfied now that Ray would live, so I got the fuck out of that room before anyone could question me. Now it really felt like I was a teenager again.

I tore my leather jacket off the paralyzed guy and bolted; everything else could be replaced. All I could think about was getting out of the hospital. As far away as possible. I'd done what I'd come here for and more, and I couldn't stand another moment of these headache-inducing lights.

Adrian could bring Noah home later. I wasn't sure if I trusted Mr. I've-Probably-Never-Even-Used-My-Gun-Before Crane to keep Noah safe, but hopefully Noah wouldn't really need protection anytime soon.

What he would need today was someone to keep him from doing anything stupid or evil, and I trusted Adrian to be that person.

Right now, I needed to be alone. I needed to run.

AFTER THE HORROR show at the hospital, and after a shower had failed to take my mind off it, there was only one place I wanted to be.

The streets in Old Town weren't empty like they'd been the day Becca had burned. Ice had slowly melted to reveal wet bricks, and the tree branches that had glittered like magic now only looked soggy and dead. But neon lights made up the difference, and drunk people were scurrying around the neighborhood like ants.

And there was no assassin following me this time, so that was a plus.

If I ever came across Shelby again, I would probably need to make a show of hating her so whoever *had* orchestrated Simeon's death didn't figure out I knew it wasn't the Sweepers. But I didn't want to think about that now. I didn't want to think about anything now except hustling for tips and playing back-up for whatever dancers were ballsy or desperate enough to come to work tonight.

Who knew if our club would even stay open, now that Baz was locked up? I didn't know what I'd do if we closed.

Kat was perched on a stool by the door when I walked in, taking covers and checking IDs while Mitch flitted about behind the bar. The room was crowded with customers, far too many for the number of dancers that were here working. The news had gotten out about what had happened to Becca, and probably even the connection between our club and the Godzilla-ifrit who had wrecked a whole city block in downtown DC.

People loved to see a train wreck, and probably even more so when it came with tits and ass on display.

Well, good. I needed to lose myself in work tonight, so I was happy to see there was plenty of work to be had.

Kat stroked my arm with her long nails and purred at me when I tried to walk past her. "Hey, little bird."

Batty fucking hell. The last thing I needed was another predator—a vampire cat lady, at that—looking at me and seeing a juicy feathered snack. I didn't know if Baz had told, or if she could smell the phoenix magic, or what, but this was not going to work.

My hand darted out to her neck, squeezing just hard enough and fast enough to shock her without making a scene.

"Try anything and you'll be the next one to burn," I said. "Only I'll do it the old-fashioned way and cut off your head first."

She didn't look as intimidated as I'd hoped, just raised her eyebrows and gave me an impressive amount of side eye for someone who couldn't move her head.

"Calm down, fire feathers. I was just teasing. I like you too much to eat you."

I let go of her. "You . . . like me?" This was the woman who had been coming in and dancing her shifts for months without ever saying more than a word at a time to any of us. I didn't know she had it in her to "like" anyone. Not to mention I'd drawn a fanged vagina on her face last time I'd seen her.

"Yeah." She shrugged, the most human gesture I'd ever seen from her. "The guys don't tip as well when Mitch is working the bar."

That was probably true, because Mitch didn't know how to put magic feelings into cocktails like I did. Not that I would be doing any more of that anytime soon. Now that I knew what was inside me, I would be keeping my magic to myself even more than before. Heaven forbid some terminal cancer patient come to the club for some innocent fun and end up reborn in flames because I accidentally "touched" their tequila with a little too much oomph. Nope—not happening. I'd have to find another way to open wallets.

I had no idea what to say to Kat, since I honestly wasn't convinced she hadn't been body-snatched since yesterday, so I just said, "Okay," and walked over to the bar.

"Oh good," Mitch said when he saw me. "I was supposed to be in charge if you didn't come back."

"What? Says who? Did you hear from Baz?"

Mitch ignored me as he finished off an Old Fashioned and slid it over to a man sitting at the bar, who gave me a big wink and a little wave.

"What the hell is Dirk doing here?"

Mitch wiped off his hands and then raised them in the air, ducking out from behind the bar. Coward.

"Hello to you too, pretty little witch," Dirk said as he raised his glass to me.

"I'm not a—" *Fuck, I might actually be a witch.* "What do you want?"

"Officially . . . I'm here to give you this." He slid a thin envelope across the bar to me.

"What is it?"

"You can't read?" He squinted at me. "I knew there was something funny about you." He shook his head. "She can kill but she can't read."

Dirk no longer seemed afraid of me in the least, and it was unsettling.

I tore open the envelope and read the words "Dear Birdie" scribbled in handwriting so florid it was almost illegible. "From Baz?" I asked without looking up. From what I could tell, it maybe said "sorry," and the rest was anyone's guess. "What the fuck does it say, and why are there so many swirly flowers and hearts around the letters?"

Dirk shrugged. "He wants you to cover for his ass. Not sure how long he'll be locked up or when he'll go to trial, but I know there'll be no bail. Not with what he is and what his auntie did."

I frowned. "So I'm just supposed to . . . What? Keep working? Keep everyone working without a paycheck?"

"You'll get your pay. I think. Go see him yourself if you're so concerned." He took a sip of his Old Fashioned and made a face. "That boy don't make 'em like you do."

"Is that all?" I asked.

"Nope." He left it at that, swiveling his seat around to watch the stage. Etty's music was playing, but it was some newish girl on the stage dancing to it, a lizardy iguana shifter

258 | ERIN EMBLY

with a crazy tongue. Dirk leaned back and gestured down the bar, then grunted, "I'll holler when I need a top-up."

I hadn't thought that man could get any more aggravating, but it seemed I was wrong. He sat there the entire damn night, through my long shift, taking up a seat at my busy bar and watching the dancers on stage without tipping anyone a single damn dollar.

He'd racked up a hefty tab by the end of the night, and I took pleasure in handing him the black bill holder with a bright smile on my face. I didn't put it down in front of him; I wanted to make sure he took it.

He did so, without hesitating, slipping something inside and handing it right back to me without looking at the amount. A little disappointed that I hadn't gotten to see him squirm, I turned around with it to face the register. When I opened it, I nearly dropped it on the ground.

A Guardian badge was staring back at me, with Dirk Quincy's smug face pictured on it. Underneath that was a credit card.

I turned back around, glaring at him, and he just lifted his eyebrows. "What? You didn't ID me. I could arrest you for that, you know."

I turned back around and ran his card. I hadn't liked dealing with this fucker when I'd thought he was nothing but an incompetent asshole, and certainly not after he'd disappeared with Etty and she'd failed to come home, but now . . . He'd been toying with me the entire time. So masterfully I'd never suspected a thing. This was bad and it could only get worse.

When I handed the bill holder back to him, he looked me in the eye and smiled. "I've got an extra-special tip for you tonight, little lady." He slid a small box across the bar to me; it looked like it could have chocolates or fancy cookies inside. But I knew it didn't.

This was Guardian protocol—not one I'd ever encountered on the job, but one I'd learned about at the Academy. It meant he had a mission for me. A covert one, and I'd never been slotted to go into covert ops.

I opened the box to take a peek, then shut it after seeing a squishy pink blob inside, along with a tiny data drive. I squeezed my eyes closed, then looked at him. "Miriam too?"

He patted my hand condescendingly, refusing to break character. "Oh, I'll bring her something nice next time; don't you worry."

I pocketed the box with Miriam's squishy in it, feeling like a complete asshole. All of Dirk's complaints about my witchy wiles, my assassin ways, even his carefully acted fear of me—it had all been a ploy for the Guardians to get that mind-reading blob on me. Miriam was nothing but a lie-detector test dressed up as my unlikely ally. All her odd behavior suddenly made sense.

I hadn't expected it because I'd known the Guardians couldn't have kept me on after Simeon, even if I could have proven my innocence. To the public, I would never be trustworthy again, so it would be a bad look. But public opinion meant nothing when it came to black ops. If the Guardians thought they could trust me, they still had a way to make me useful.

And now, it appeared, they were cashing in. Cashing in on the blank check to my life I'd written them by virtue of going to their school and signing on to their service. Once a Guardian, always a Guardian. Everyone knows it. I'd been naive to think I could get out of it by letting them think I'd betrayed them. Not that "getting out of it" was ever what I'd wanted, not really—but damn, I could at least use a break.

After the past few days, all I wanted to do in the near future was make drinks, keep the club running smoothly, and figure out how I was going to live now that I had a tiny soul-eating child to take care of.

I could see in Dirk's eyes that it wasn't going to be that simple.

He turned away from me, took a step, and then doubled back holding a finger up. "Ah, and next time?" He leaned in. "I think I'll have a Bloody Mary. Hope you know how to make it a good one."

Battiest of all the bats—that meant vampires.

I forced a big smile and said, "Sure thing. I'll make it extra bloody for you."

As I watched him walk out, Kat caught my eye from across the room and held my gaze while she licked her lips.

I ducked under the bar and leaned my head against the cool steel of the refrigerator, closing my eyes.

Etty had said it best, and damn I missed her so much already. "Why can't it ever just be a normal level of shit in my life?"

If Becca were here, I knew she would tell me that a normal level of shit would be boring.

Well then, for her sake, I would have to make this fun.

AFTERWORD

Thank you for reading Fractured Flame! If you enjoyed it, please consider leaving a review. I'll be eternally grateful if you do!

For more information about me and my books, check out my website:

www.erinembly.com

Want more to read now? Check out *Assassin Divined*, a prequel novella about Minnie that explores a little bit of Darcy's past with Simeon.

Turn the page and read on for the description and first chapter.

ERIN EMBLY

ASSASSIN DIVINED

A FIREBIRD UNCAGED PREQUEL NOVELLA

ASSASSIN DIVINED

A FIREBIRD UNCAGED PREQUEL NOVELLA

No one expects the tiny ginger barista to deal in stolen magical merchandise...

But then, no one expects me to divine their future, either—and I do that just as well. Sometimes too well.

Sometimes, I see things no one wants me to see. And sometimes, those things do a bloody good job of trying to get me killed.

My name is Minnie, and all I want is what any girl wants: to be left alone with a pile of cash. You know, to make up for all my evil deeds by opening a cafe, where lost souls can come for tea and nibbles and divine advice.

But piles of cash never come easy, and this one is wrapped in a frightening package that might just be the end of me yet.

I know I can achieve my dream—but can I do it without selling my soul in the process?

CHAPTER 1

"A beautiful death," I murmured. The muddy green remnants of tea leaves blurred at the bottom of the mug I held in my hands. Their form gave way to an aura, a scent, a glow and a feeling inside me—all culminating in the words I had spoken without thinking about them first.

Again. *Damn it, Minnie. Dumb as a mouse.* When would I learn?

The man sitting across the cornflower-blue table from me in the empty cafe had begun to sweat a little. With annoyance or terror? Who knew?

Okay, I knew. It was both. I'd terrified him, so he was rather annoyed with me now.

I should have asked for payment before the session.

I smiled. *Teeth bright and glowing as lovely as his death, I'm sure.*

"Quite beautiful," I added, as cheerily as I could, before he could start yelling at me. "Smelled like roses. And you know, I didn't get a clear sense of when it would come for you. So it's really a win/win. If it comes soon, at least it will be pleasant. And if it comes in twenty years, or . . . sixty," I amended, because there was no harm in letting him think he looked young, "then you really can't have asked for anything more out of life."

"Anything more than death?" he said, his face hardening.

"Everyone dies, love. Not beautifully, though. You really are a lucky one." I didn't miss a beat. I had quite a lot of experience putting the positive spin on bleak readings. I couldn't keep my mouth shut when the tea leaves had their hold on me—not yet. I was working on that. But once they'd had their say, I usually managed to say just the right thing.

This time was no different, apparently. The man's eyes had softened a little. And his . . . Oh my, his teeth had gotten longer. A vampire? Fuck me.

"I already am a beautiful death," he said, and I cringed.

All my muscles tensed at once, without invitation from me, like in that first moment every morning when sleep gives way to life but consciousness hasn't quite got its grip yet. I begged my consciousness to return and it obliged, a tad, allowing me to push my chair back from the table minutely as I stared at him like a little lost lamb.

I was not prepared to deal with a vampire today. My eyes shifted quickly over to the very clear (or so I'd thought) "No Vampires, Please" sign on the door of the cafe, and he chuckled.

"Sorry. I'm not familiar with your customs," he said, playing the American-abroad card. Which was bonkers, really, because this was London—we all spoke English.

But he still wasn't sucking out my blood or ripping out my throat, and his vicious incisors had begun to retract slowly back into his gums.

"Well, then . . . I suppose you have nothing to worry about. Unless you meet someone beautiful who smells like roses!" I said the last part with way too much enthusiasm, the kind that comes after roller-coasters and the adrenaline of fearing an immediate and untimely death. I supposed he'd just given me a taste of my own medicine.

He carefully unfolded the napkin that had gone untouched at the setting in front of him, then used it to dab some of the perspiration away from his bald head. It was the kind of bald head that inspired fear, I noticed only now that I'd seen the fangs that went with it.

He was an older gentleman, yes, but by the look of him he'd shaved that head long before he'd needed to. His thick eyebrows still had plenty dark in them, and the shape of the bulk underneath his expensive suit was undeniably the shape of obscene strength. He probably didn't even need the body-guard, a lovely young dark-haired lady who stood at attention in the corner, watching us.

I folded my hands together on the table and sat still, ever smiling, trying not to let my eyes wander towards his wallet. *Why did he have to be a vampire?* I wondered, teeth clenched. I really needed this money. I wouldn't have even dreamed of risking my job and closing the cafe early to take this session, except that he'd promised to pay ten times my normal rate. And if I couldn't come up with a few thousand pounds by the weekend, I would lose what might be a once-in-a-lifetime chance at a good, honest life.

"Is that all?" he said levelly.

"Errm, well . . . that's all I got from the leaves, yes. But—"

He slid something toward me across the table. A small jewelry box. "What about this?"

I raised my eyebrows and reached for the box, trying not to hesitate. Not good to hesitate in front of a vampire for anything. "What about it?" I asked.

"Can you read it for me?"

I cracked open the box, my fingertips sinking slightly in the plush black velvet that coated the outside. A single black feather lay inside, attached to a silver chain.

It looked like a jeweled carving at first—a large pendant. But when I looked closer, I couldn't help but think it might be real. So intricate . . . I almost wanted to run my finger along the edge and see if it would bend, if the barbs of the vanes would unzip with that leathery, soft snap I remembered from my childhood collecting the fallen feathers of pigeons in the park.

But I looked up instead, back at the vampire, whose expression said his question had not really been a question at all.

"Mm hmm." I bobbed my head, then closed my eyes and reached forward to let my fingertip brush the feather.

It was hard, as I'd suspected. Sharp, almost. But when I slid the tip of my finger over the top, I couldn't feel it anymore. It wasn't just the sharp edge that was gone—it was everything. My fingertip was numb.

My brows drew together as I opened my eyes. Poison? Was it so sharp it had made a cut in my skin?

I brought my finger up to inspect it and found no damage, which was confirmed when the numb feeling vanished as quickly as I'd taken it away from the feather. Not poison, then. Magic.

"A void," I said, looking up at the man across from me.

He gave me an almost imperceptible smirk. "So, nothing?"

"Yes, exactly. Very powerful nothing." That feather was acting like a tiny, weak black hole. It would suck the life out of anything it touched, albeit slowly.

I frowned. There was something sinister about it, such pure evil dressed up as fine jewelry.

He laughed, and I bit my cheek in confusion.

"It's a good thing I didn't really come to you for a reading," he said, and I didn't know whether to be offended or frightened.

If he wasn't here for a reading, then what?

"I'm looking for someone to take it off my hands," he said, and I froze.

That was not something we advertised with a sign outside the cafe. It wasn't something I'd done in a long time.

I pressed my lips together and snapped the box shut, then slid it back across the table towards him. If he was looking for a buyer and he'd come to me, that meant it was hot. And I wanted even less to do with it than I had a moment ago.

"No need to pretend, Mouse," he said with a smile, not taking his eyes off me.

Bloody hell. Only two people in the world had ever called me Mouse. One of them was dead, and the other had been dead to me long before he'd apparently given this American bloodsucker my name.

"I'll make it easy for you," the vampire continued, ignoring my obvious shock. "You can have eighty percent of what you sell it for."

I had to work hard to keep my jaw from dropping open. Not that it would have mattered. I was sure he could hear how wildly erratic my heartbeat had become.

An American vampire comes from out of nowhere, dangling my very secret criminal past over my head and offering me an obscene cut of his takings if I can only find a buyer for his Evil Necklace of Doom . . . ?

There was, without a doubt, nothing good that could possibly come of this.

"Well?" He eyed me confidently.

He knew. He must. That I needed money desperately enough to make a very bad decision.

I let out a breath. "Fine."

"Excellent." He slid the box back across the table towards me, and I nearly jumped out of my seat. Instead, I leaned forward quickly to push it right back.

Before I could blink, his bodyguard was on me, gloved

fingers circling my wrist as she yanked it behind me and curled a strong arm around my neck. Impressive. Well, now I knew— no sudden movements around this one. Unless I could get her alone, that was . . . She smelled sweet and spicy, under the crisp chemicals of her perfectly pressed suit and the metal of the weapons she must be hiding underneath it.

"Enough, D," the vampire said without breaking his glare away from me.

The bodyguard fell away from me, leaving me cold and vulnerable as the danger of her presence remained directly behind me. She had been warm, I realized now.

Not a vampire, that one. I shivered, not wanting to think about the kind of power a not-vampire must have to be protecting this man.

These were exactly the kind of people I never wanted to mess with ever again. I always seemed to be a hair away from death when supernaturals were involved, and yet they always found a way to make it so I couldn't say no.

"I'll try to find you a buyer," I explained, "but I'm not keeping that in the meantime. A picture will have to be good enough."

He looked like he wanted to press the issue, which only solidified my decision to keep that necklace as far away from me as possible. He wanted to get rid of it and he didn't care about the money, which meant it must be more dangerous than I could imagine.

After a moment of glaring at me, he said, "Understood." Then he got up and adjusted his suit. "But you'll have to work quick. I'm on a plane back to the States in two days."

"No promises," I said, and I meant it. Really, I had no clue if I could do this. I'd had no contact with anyone in the London underworld for at least two years, and before that I'd been an expert in lifting, not fencing. But if this man had come to me, it meant he was even more out of touch than I was. It meant he must know Evan, my old partner, and it meant Evan must have fled across the pond and stayed there since I'd last seen him.

"All I ask is that you try your best," the vampire said, and he looked at me expectantly.

Why wasn't he leaving? I tensed again. Would he try to drink from me to seal our deal?

"Your phone?" he prompted, and I let out a sigh.

"Yes, of course." I fumbled for it in my pockets and then held it out to him in a shaking hand.

He pressed his phone against it for a moment, and I heard a light chime. File transfer. Pictures and specs for the necklace, I hoped.

Then he slid a card across the table and lifted his eyes to me. "So you know where to find me."

The bodyguard brushed against me on her way out, more of a threat than a misstep, and they were gone into the dreary December daylight of early afternoon. If only I lived in a place where the sunlight was strong enough to make vampires burst into flames. Here in London, they could usually get around just fine with nothing more than an umbrella for protection.

I fell back into my seat, not remembering at what point I'd stood up, and picked up his card as I attempted to calm my racing heart.

The card didn't help.

Simeon Drake, United States Senator, it said.

The vampire-with-a-bodyguard thing suddenly made sense. The woman protecting him must be more for show than anything else. No one trusts a vampire politician who seems too confident, but a bodyguard implies vulnerability. Just the right amount of caution. Fear. Humanity.

I knew better than to fall for that act.

I dropped the card and got up to clear the table, and the teacup clattered against the saucer as it shook in my hands.

A part of me I'd buried relished this fear—*actual* human fear, which I hadn't felt in too long. It had been my drug of choice, once upon a time. Now, I could only hope it would get me through the week alive.

Want to know what happens next? Go to www.erinembly.com to get the book!

CPSIA information can be obtained
at www.ICGtesting.com
Printed in the USA
LVHW111351230120
644580LV00001B/22

9 781734 457001